SECOND SIGHT

ALSO BY AOIFE CLIFFORD

All These Perfect Strangers

SECOND SIGHT

AOIFE CLIFFORD

PEGASUS CRIME

NEW YORK LONDON

SECOND SIGHT

Pegasus Crime is an imprint of
Pegasus Books, Ltd.
148 W 37th Street, 13th Floor
New York, NY 10018

Copyright © 2019 by Aoife Clifford

First Pegasus Books cloth edition July 2019

Interior design by Maria Fernandez

Library of Congress Cataloging-in-Publication Data is available.

ISBN: 978-1-64313-076-7

10 9 8 7 6 5 4 3 2 1

Printed in the United States of America
Distributed by W. W. Norton & Company
www.pegasusbooks.us

For my siblings Ciara, Sinead, Aisling and Aidan

for the love and the laughter

"He lies like an eyewitness."

     —Russian proverb

1

Here it begins. Trouble, I think, when I see the two of them slinking out of the pharmacy. There is nothing more dangerous than a bored teenager in a country town. It's when the stupidest ideas start making sense.

Sitting in my car, stuck in Kinsale's traffic, I watch them. He's a walking cliché, his hoodie pulled up over his head, and the girl wears a denim jacket that's too small. She reminds me of someone, her face is familiar—unless what I'm seeing is a glimpse of myself twenty years ago walking out of the same shop.

He slips his hand into hers and weaves through cars, pulling her right in front of me. The girl, hair streaked with salt, leans forward to stare through my windshield. She looks at me with shrewd eyes. The boy yanks her arm and she skips across, escaping to the beach on the other side of the road.

The traffic lights change and cars edge forward. Out of my side window, I glimpse the green ocean behind the enormous Norfolk pines that dot this part of the coastline. Before me is a tidal wave of slowly moving metal, all heading back to the city. The population of Kinsale expands and folds depending on the weather and locals know never to drive near the center of town on summer weekends.

The sun pours through the glass and warms my bones to jelly. I roll down the window to take in the salted scent of my childhood: sea mixed with the crusty tang from the deep fryers in the takeaway shops. It's all sunscreen, tan lines, peeling skin and bad holiday traffic.

I flick on the blinker to turn into the center of town, the windshield wipers go off instead. I'm driving a rental with nothing where it should be. More cars are banked up along the stretch of shops that subsist on tourist dollars. Only the pub, The Royal, is familiar to me.

My phone lights up with a message from the expert witness double-checking my arrival time. Legal cases can be won or lost because of your expert, which is why I've agreed to meet mine in Kinsale, a place best avoided under the circumstances. I shoot a text back explaining the delay and then creep up the hill in fits and starts. I tap my impatience on the steering wheel, a kind of Morse code, reminding me that I escaped this town once and I can do it again.

A woman in a shiny silver SUV scoots up the inside of the cars, pretending there's an extra lane just for her, and then attempts to merge in front of me, trying to jump the queue. She barges her way forward without even a cursory wave of thanks. There is a smug "My Family" sticker set on her back window. The stick-figure mum has one skater dude, a ballerina, a baby and a pet dog. There's a gap where stick-figure daddy should be. Perhaps he has come unstuck.

I follow the SUV until the ocean disappears from view. This part of town is quiet except for all the cars. Locals and tourists alike prefer the beach, the park or the pub. My turn-off is in a couple of blocks and then it's another twenty minutes to the historic mansion, built in the 1870s as a homestead for a large farm, where I am meeting Rob. It's been nicknamed The Castle for as long as I can remember, a joking reference to the pretensions of the landowners who built it in the 1870s. It is almost time for another apologetic text when the sticker family lady decides she's had enough driving and reverses to park.

Without indicating, she starts squeezing her enormous car into a spot that leaves no room for error—except she makes one, backing straight into a Landcruiser parked by the side of the road next to me.

It is more than a nudge but less than a crunch. Her mouth is reflected in her rearview mirror and I read the emotions. The roundness of the initial shock, the downward sag of realization, then the guilty glance over her shoulder, as if trying to assess the damage. Almost as quickly, she faces forward, lips determined, and rejoins the traffic.

Beside me, the Landcruiser's door opens. A man gets out—ripped jeans, a loose T-shirt, mid-brown hair cropped close to his head, a widow's peak—clutching a cell phone. He is so angry it has a cartoonish quality, as if a black cloud hangs above his head. He throws the phone inside his car and slams the door. Not stopping to check for damage, he marches stiff-legged around my bumper. By the time he reaches her, he is shouting.

"You stupid fucking bitch!" he yells. "You were going to drive away."

He smacks his hands against her window so hard that the momentum pushes him back and he launches again.

Shocked faces surround me, frozen like mannequins, all of us waiting to see which of us will do something.

His voice sounds familiar.

Putting up the window as a precaution, my brain whirs through the index of faces that is my own personal identity parade. "Luke Tyrell" pops into my head and when a mop of curly hair is added to the angry profile it's confirmed, even though I haven't seen him since we were bored stupid teenagers. Part of me is amazed that he has aged twenty years all at once but the rest of me is more concerned that he seems to have turned psychotic.

If the woman in front of me had any brains she would do a U-turn and drive off but the car, too clean, too new, suggests she isn't local. Maybe she's desperately checking her phone for an alternative route back to the city. Maybe she's just frozen.

Now Luke is pulling on her door handle but it's locked so he kicks the door instead, a nasty, vicious kick designed to dent. The woman is getting out of her seat, scrambling onto the passenger side. Luke launches himself onto the hood, slamming his hands against her windshield, his face distorted. He is hitting so hard that the car is actually rocking. The sticker family cheerfully wobbles, as if they're waving goodbye.

Do I call the police? The station is only a couple of streets away, within running distance, but it might be shut with those on shift out along the coast. The public expects the police to be genies, magically summoned with a phone call. Still, there is a chance they could be nearby, up on the highway in a booze bus or raising revenue by issuing speeding tickets. I hunt around the car for my discarded phone which has somehow managed to slip between the seats and fall into the footwell behind me out of reach.

How long has all this taken? A minute, two? Luke is on fast-forward when everyone else is caught on pause. My clumsy hands open the door and I stumble onto the road. I don't even know what my plan is. Call out to him and say, "Hi, it's me, Eliza, remember when?" In the Mini behind me is a teenage girl, a learner's permit stuck to her windshield. Her mother is in the passenger seat. The same look of horror is clear on both generations. The girl has her phone out, videoing, while the mother has another phone up to her ear. She mouths "police" to me.

A man jogs up the hill toward us. He's dressed in jeans and a dark polo shirt, with a ridiculous green hat on top of his head. A cheap, novelty plush one, like he's celebrating St. Patrick's Day at an office do a couple of weeks early. He approaches Luke, calling out as if he's trying to calm down a horse.

"Whoa there," he says. "C'mon big fella."

He reminds me of my father, calm in a crisis. As he passes by he winks at me, like he's a superhero in his spare time. Then he walks straight up to Luke and asks him what he is doing. His accent is Irish, or maybe that's just the hat talking. It's the way he sounds conversational that impresses me most. No judgment, just genuine interest, like they know each other, that they might be friends.

"You're frightening her," he says, pointing at the car. Luke turns his head and there's a pause in the yelling as he gets off the hood, but only for a moment and then it starts again. All about the damage to his car and how she was going to drive off.

Other people start to appear, like rabbits being pulled out of the green plush hat. Everyone is brave now. When Luke realizes the situation has shifted, he pushes through the onlookers, yelling still, and disappears.

Attention turns to the almost hysterical woman who climbs out of the passenger side of the SUV. People swarm, sitting her down on the footpath. Another man gets the keys and parks her car, right in front of the Landcruiser, which doesn't seem ideal but it was blocking traffic and suddenly the road is clear. We are all in a terrible rush to get away, including me, because I'm running so late for my meeting.

I turn at the next intersection, testing out my old local knowledge. It is a shabbier strip, not as tourist-friendly. A few of the shops are empty, and CLOSING DOWN signs in a couple more give the place an apocalyptic feel, as if everyone is hightailing it out of here. Posters saying BAYLESS—BEST FOR BUSINESS appear in windows. Beneath the slogan, a blonde woman in her sixties with hair fixed into a hard halo wears a plastic politician's smile. There must be a local election coming up.

Bobbing up and down along the street, past Hooked-On-U Bait & Tackle, Surf City and the thrift store, is a green hat. I could ask the Good Samaritan where he is headed and offer him a lift. But I don't usually offer lifts to strangers, and on closer inspection he does look a little strange. Maybe you have to be mad to calm down a crazy person. Mad or a cop.

Driving past, I see there is a confident swing to his arms, as if he knows where he is headed and can take his time getting there. So I accelerate past him, heading up the street, but as I do there is a sudden blur in my mirror: a gust of rage like a squall out at sea, voices yelling.

In the time it takes to stop the car and turn around in my seat, Luke and the Hat Man are in the middle of the road, wrestling like two drowning swimmers clinging to each other. The hat is knocked clean off. They move so fast they merge into one.

A raised fist. A punch. A fall.

Before I can scream, Luke is gone and the Hat Man is lying on the ground.

My hand slams on the car horn before I burst out of my car and run toward him. Rolling him into the recovery position, I hook my finger into his mouth to clear his airway. Bloodied teeth fall to the ground like chips of stone. A cut bisects his eyebrow. A woman appears and starts shouting for help but he doesn't make a sound. Sitting next to him, squeezing his fingers with my hand, I ask his name, where he feels pain. His mouth doesn't move and mine doesn't stop, telling him he did the right thing, helping that woman.

It feels like years pass before the wail of an ambulance floats toward us. After the Hat Man has been examined and then parceled up, I grab an EMT wanting to know the prognosis. He gives me the professional blank look they use when there is bad news you don't need to hear.

"We've called a chopper to take him to the city. You kept him alive." He gives me a comrade-like pat on the shoulder. "We'll try and do the same."

The policeman who talks to me is a young constable, probationary at a guess. He had been assigned to traffic for the weekend, he tells me. A serious assault seems an exciting alternative.

"Name?" he asks. When I tell him Eliza Carmody, he doesn't seem to recognize the surname so he can't be local.

"What do you remember, Eliza?" He's one of those people who use your first name a lot to demonstrate he's on top of the situation. Before I answer he is already distracted.

"Your eyes," he says. "They're not the same color."

It amazes me how people always assume they're the first one to notice. I answer his question.

"He just ran up and punched him, it was a king hit," I say. "Luke Tyrell did it."

"You're an 'eye' witness?" he asks, smirking slightly. I can tell I'm becoming the punchline of his day but I don't react.

"Yes. I saw it all."

He takes down my details in his notebook and then heads back to his car, conferring with the second cop inside, who's been radioing in.

The passenger door is flung open.

"Are you all right?"

This cop is older, taller with a slight stomach bulge over his belt. He has a ridiculous moustache that looks like a Muppet has died. It wasn't there the last time I saw him. Senior Sergeant Gavin Pawley, my brother-in-law, comes over. He grabs both my arms and guides me to the police car, putting his enormous hand onto my head so I don't bang myself as he firmly places me onto the backseat.

"Eliza, what on earth are you doing here?"

My teeth are beginning to chatter and the words come out bite-sized. "Visiting a friend," I lie.

'What friend?' he asks.

A momentary pause, "Amy," I tell him. "Amy Liu."

Kneeling down, he holds me upright.

"Are you hurt?"

I shake my head, fixated on the clumps of blood on my fingers.

"You can't drive," he says. "I'll take you to your dad's house to have a shower. You can borrow Tess's clothes."

Looking down, I realize that my top is splattered in a stranger's blood.

"No," I say. This day has been bad enough without having to deal with my sister as well.

"I'll take you to Amy's then. She can check you out." Scooping my legs into the car, he pushes me back until I'm resting on the seat. He has a quick chat with the constable who agrees to follow in my rental car.

"Can you get my bag?"

"Sure," says the constable. He jogs over to where it lies, the contents spilled onto the road in my haste to get to my phone to call for help.

The green hat lies beside it as though they belong together.

2

Surprise," I say.

We are at the front of an old-style bluestone home. Parched-looking geraniums swing from hanging baskets either side of the open doorway. Amy stands inside, an enormous stomach on tiny legs. She doesn't flinch at the sight of me, but then, she is a doctor.

"Tell me this isn't related to your case, Eliza."

"None of the blood's mine." I throw a warning look in Gavin's direction but he's on the phone and not listening.

"Maybe I should be checking out someone else then," she says when he glances up. He directs Amy away for a quick whispered conversation. The blood is starting to harden on my shirt, clinging to me. Amy returns quickly and starts assessing the damage.

"Look at you," I say. "How much longer?"

"With a bit of luck, four weeks," she answers. "Now let's see if you have any cuts before we start panicking about hepatitis."

Later, I'm clean, my skin intact, wearing a T-shirt that belongs to Amy's husband, Gus, and a cardigan of hers. I sit on the couch with a glass of inky merlot at my elbow, strictly medicinal. The green hat sits next to me.

"This is great," I say, raising the glass.

"Friends of ours made it. They're using a new French clone of merlot in their vineyard," she says, stirring spaghetti marinara on the stove. "I've had it waiting here especially for you."

"How did you know I was coming?"

"You had to return sometime to visit Mick."

I look away because there are no plans to see my father. I have already said my goodbyes but that will be hard to explain to Amy, who has been my best friend ever since I tried sucking on her licorice black plaits in kindergarten. For years she's been visiting me in the city and I've done my best to avoid return trips to Kinsale.

"Where's Gus?" I ask to divert her.

"The Royal's trivia night. It's a fund-raiser for Janey's election campaign."

I reach out for the security blanket of my phone to check if there are any messages from Rob in response to my garbled one canceling our meeting. There's nothing and my fingers swipe-swipe-click on the internet instead. The news sites have already posted about the attack, which seems far too quick but then this is the third king hit resulting in a death this summer and all other stories seem to have gone on holidays. The Hat Man is Paul Keenan, a twenty-nine-year-old tourist from Ireland. People who don't know him are #prayingforPaul because apparently God regularly checks his Twitter feed. I want to see that his attacker is in custody "assisting the police with their enquiries," but he is "yet to be apprehended."

"Are you sure it was Luke?" she asks. "Luke hit him?"

I see a raised fist and then the punch.

"Definitely," I say. "Remember the fights he used to get in at school? I thought he'd have grown out of that."

Amy sighs. "It isn't only Luke. This whole town's on edge ever since . . ."

"The bushfire was almost two years ago," I interrupt. "You can't use that as an excuse to go crazy."

"Tell that to my waiting room," she answers. "It was his girlfriend who got trapped in her car. He lost his property and I hear he was underinsured. Luke's been working odd jobs on other people's farms trying to earn money to start rebuilding. He's part of your class action."

"It's not my class action," I correct her. "It's Colcart's class action."

"You're their lawyer," she says. Her tone is gentle but it stings a little. Amy is the only person in Kinsale I have told. Not even my family know.

"You really had to take this case?" she asks. "There wasn't a choice?"

Amy is looking for reasons to defend my decision because she always has.

"It would have been really hard to say no, career-wise," I explain. "I'm a partner at the firm, I need to bring work in. Most solicitors would think this case was a gift."

"Most solicitors didn't grow up in the town that Colcart almost burnt down."

"I think you're missing an 'allegedly' there," I say. "If the evidence shows that Colcart caused the fire, they'll be found responsible but if they didn't, they shouldn't have to pay. That's how the justice system works. It's not right to target them just because they have the deepest pockets."

"People here won't understand," Amy says.

"I thought people here blamed Tony Bayless for the fire," I reply. Amy opens her mouth to argue but I keep speaking. "The reason I'm in Kinsale is to meet with our expert. It's his job to work out what happened. He calls it 'reading the ashes.'"

"Very poetic."

"If he says the fire was Colcart's fault, then I'll be the first to suggest that they should settle, and do it quickly, but if he doesn't, the case goes on. That's how the system works."

"It's not a 'case' to these people," Amy says quietly. "It's their lives and the deaths of those they loved. Luke's girlfriend and all the others."

An image of a burnt-out car comes into my mind. The smoke had been so thick she'd driven it off the road and lurched into a ditch, unable to move, like a boat stuck on a reef. The fire had done the rest. The first day I started working on the case, I looked at the list of the dead, eight of them. I read their names and traced my one degree of separation from each of them—school, family friends, vaguely remembered faces from the beach or shops—and then put the paper in my filing cabinet. Sometimes the only way to cope is to separate out bits of your life and keep them in solitary confinement.

I try to remember her name. "Alison?"

"Alice, Alice Newbury. She was the year behind us at school." The name conjures up braided hair, a wide mouth and freckles but not much more.

Amy pats my arm and then heads to the fridge. "So, how's the love life?"

Swapping one quagmire for another.

"I've been too busy."

"What happened to the architect guy?" she asks.

"That finished over a year ago."

"He was cute. I liked him."

"You like all of them," I say. "Face it, Amy, not all of us are lucky enough to marry our childhood sweethearts."

"You just need more wine and then we can update your profile after dinner." She comes back to the table brandishing cheese.

I laugh. "So, when are you finishing work?"

"Replacement starts in three weeks," she says, grating curls of Parmesan onto the pasta. "A tired, overworked city GP looking for a relaxing sea change." A cynical half-smile accompanies this because we both know that country doctors work even longer hours than litigation lawyers.

"Promise me they'll last long enough that you get a few days with the baby."

"I'm telling the sick of Kinsale to have a holiday for at least a month, so as not to scare him. Even Dad promises to go easy—if my replacement likes it in Kinsale then perhaps Dad can think about retiring from the practice when I come back from maternity leave."

I can't imagine Kinsale without Amy's dad, the original Dr. Liu, hard at work.

Amy brings the plates to the table, steam snaking upward. I put down my phone and twirl a fork into the pasta.

"Jesus, it's hot," I say, stirring the sauce.

"Have to nuke everything to avoid listeria," she says, sitting down next to me. Her belly is even bigger up close. "Every time I stop moving, the little rascal starts. Feel this." She grabs my reluctant hand and presses it firmly against her.

At first there's nothing and then thump. "Did you . . . ?" she asks, but I'm already saying, "Yes, yes," as another watery punch pushes upward.

There's the sound of keys jingling and then a creak as the front door opens. "Amy, you here?" The voice comes down the hall toward us.

"Kitchen," calls Amy.

Gus appears in the doorway and I stand up to greet him. He was a perpetually smiling boy who has grown into the type of man I never meet when internet dating. I'm enveloped in a giant hug and then he pulls back to assess me, scanning for damage. Amy must have sent a message.

"I'm OK."

He gives another quick hug before swooping down on Amy. She arches her head back and he kisses her softly with upside-down lips.

"How's the bump?" he asks.

"Active," she answers.

Gus kicks off his boots and pads into the kitchen in footy socks. "Trivia night canceled," he calls out. "Janey Bayless was very upset about Paul."

Amy explains that Paul worked behind the bar at The Royal.

As I check my phone for messages, the news site I have open refreshes and video footage begins playing. There are shaky images of Luke's pure rage, kicking the SUV door and then throwing himself onto the hood. Then it cuts to black-and-white footage of Paul walking down the street and Luke running after him. They move out of the frame until suddenly Paul is back, falling. In a blink, he is lying there. A shadowy pixelated figure comes running toward him. It's me but only because I recognize the shirt. Kneeling next to Paul, my mouth is stretched open but no sound. There's a momentary flicker and then the video starts again. It has been looped, programmed to play over and over.

I can't look away.

One moment Paul is walking along the street and then he's down, but in the next second, magically, he is up again and if only I could turn the video off now, perhaps he could keep on walking.

Amy grabs it from me.

"Enough of that," she says. "Doctor's orders."

I touch the back of my hand to my cheek to dash away the tears that have appeared from nowhere.

"Since when did Kinsale have security cameras?"

"Couple of ice addicts rampaged through the bait shop a while back, so they've got some," answers Gus. He retreats into the kitchen. I hear the clatter of bowls.

"Can you find out if Paul is going to be OK?" I ask Amy.

"He's probably been taken to Southern Cross in the city like your dad was," she says, picking up her phone. "Anything Kinsale Community Hospital can't handle usually ends up there. I'll start with Tristan." There are quite a few cousins on the Liu side and they all studied medicine. Tristan is an intensive care specialist and Amy's least favorite relative but he promises to find out the prognosis and ring back. The lawyer in me has a momentary quibble about patient confidentiality, but I appreciate the gesture enough to shut up and be grateful.

"The stuff you find online," sighs Amy. She flips the phone over to me, showing me the Hat Man's Facebook page.

"You're going to have to get it back to him," she says, pointing at the hat on the couch. There are pictures of him wearing it in front of the Eiffel Tower and at Machu Picchu. There's even one of him grinning in front of the Opera House in torrential rain, a smart-ass comment about sunny Australia beneath it. The last picture wasn't of him but a sturdy looking toddler frowning at the camera.

Amy stands up and starts clearing plates.

"I can do that," I begin.

"Leave it," says Gus. "It's my turn."

"Back's sore. I've got to walk about anyway."

Gus reaches out to her, a worried expression on his face but Amy pushes his hand away. "Don't fuss."

There's an unexpected sharpness to her words, followed by a spiky silence. Finally, Gus turns and picks up the bottle of wine and pours himself a glass.

"Enjoying it?" His voice is overly hearty.

"Yes," but I shake my head when he waves the bottle in my direction.

"First vintage from a friend's vineyard," he says, and begins explaining how good merlot grapes are harvested earlier, giving it a balance of savory and a suggestion of sweetness, but I'm watching Amy. There is tension in the way she moves as if everything is at right angles.

"So what else has been happening?" I ask her, when Gus finally pauses.

"Demolition order has come through for The Castle," she says, leaning over the open dishwasher.

"Oh, no."

"I guess it was inevitable once Janey sold to developers," continues Amy. "But all that history being destroyed."

"It was badly damaged," says Gus. "Would have cost a fortune to restore. Janey's been looking for any excuse to get rid of it."

Janey is the lead complainant for the class action as the bushfire started near The Castle and almost gutted it. There has been plenty of public speculation and a long investigation into whether the fire was deliberately lit. Tony Bayless, Janey's son, was interviewed by the police several times, something that will have to be explored in the case.

"Remember when we waitressed there?" I ask Amy. "Just after Janey and Wes bought it."

"Only the once," laughs Amy, "because you spent the night flirting with Tony instead of working."

"I did not." But we both know this is a lie.

"And you spilt dessert all down the back of Jim Keaveney's tux," she continues.

"You smashed a full dinner plate on the kitchen floor," I protest.

"And then Wes refused to pay us, saying after all the breakages we probably owed him." She is helpless with laughter now, holding her sides as if she might burst. Gus warns her not to laugh too hard which only makes Amy double up even further. It's a seismic event and takes a while to settle.

"Time for bed, I think," says Gus. "C'mon, Eliza, I'll sort you out."

He leads me down the hall to a small room.

"This is going to be the baby's," he says. The walls are bare, there's clutter on the mantelpiece, and the queen-sized bed in the corner is camouflaged by cardboard boxes. There's not one fluffy bunny or oversized teddy bear anywhere.

"Minimalist approach to nursery decorating," I say. "Industrial. I like it."

"Amy's banned decorating until the baby arrives."

"Everything's OK, isn't it?"

Gus doesn't quite say yes but he doesn't say no either.

"Gus!"

"Her blood pressure's high so there is extra monitoring," he says. "I'm sure it will be all right, just there's some increased risks. She should really have finished up work early but you know what she's like."

Amy comes in with sheets, a towel and some spare pajamas. She gives us a narrowed look, as if guessing what we've been talking about. Gus shifts the boxes to the floor and then, seeing his chance to escape further interrogation, slips out.

"When are you meeting your expert?" Amy asks me, after we finish making up the bed.

I check my phone. Finally there is a reply from Rob. He can't reschedule. He promises to send his draft report to me as soon as possible and we can arrange another site meeting if I think it's necessary after that. It won't be. I've had enough of Kinsale to last me a lifetime.

"Canceled. An eight-hour round trip for nothing."

"Not for nothing," Amy says. "I'm on morning rounds at the nursing home. I'll give you a lift to see your father."

"Please no, Amy."

"Eliza, you owe it to him."

"He won't even know I'm there," I say.

My mother died when I was four and is only the haziest of memories now. Dad brought up my sister and me by himself. It seemed to work until I was sixteen but after that not so much.

Amy can sense vulnerability and presses, "You can't be certain of that."

I pick up some photos from the bedside table to avoid giving her an answer. To my surprise, there's one of us when we were kids, dressed as angels for a nativity concert, not the lead role but better than being sheep. A tiny Amy is looking straight at the camera, tinsel braided through her hair, eyes squinting. I'm at the end of the row staring at the lens, my right eye almost covered by my bangs. That's deliberate. I have been self-conscious about my eyes for as long as I can remember. Before digital cameras and Photoshop, most of my childhood snaps feature me with one eye glowing red from the flash. I still spend a fortune on sunglasses.

Standing between the two of us is Grace Hedland, half-smiling, half-biting her bottom lip, so she looks a little like a chipmunk. Turning away from the camera, her black eyes gaze beyond it.

Amy rests her head on my shoulder, looking at the photo with me.

"Remember the wings," she says.

They were yellowed with age, scratchy and molting. Each year they were pulled out of storage with more feathery gaps but we loved them, flitting around our classroom in them.

"Grace kept squawking like a cockatoo," I say.

"Drove the teacher crazy," Amy agrees. "She was always a bird nut."

A hazy memory is coming back to me. "Her file was in Dad's car."

Amy straightens up.

"When he had the accident, that first night at hospital someone told me. Gavin, I think. There were a couple of files in the car and Grace's was one of them. Weird."

Flicking through the rest of the photos, I see the three of us are in every one, growing older until we reach sixteen and then Grace is gone, a runaway who never came back.

"Gus likes the name 'Grace.' It was his grandma's," Amy says. "I'm still trying to work out if I would be OK with that."

I breathe out slowly.

"That night on the beach," I say. "Luke Tyrell was there as well."

Amy raises a slender eyebrow. "I'm not likely to forget that."

"I was such an idiot but I didn't know she liked him."

"Back then we were all idiots," says Amy. "We probably still are."

"I never asked what you and Gus got up to that night."

"What, after you left with Luke?"

I nod.

"We looked for Grace for ages and eventually decided she had walked home and then afterward . . ." There is the smallest of smiles on her face.

"You didn't," I say, in mock disbelief.

"It was cold and he did deserve some attention after the night had been such a disaster. Of course, I felt incredibly guilty afterward."

"At least something good came of it," I say.

Amy reaches her arms and tries to give me a hug, but it's mostly belly.

"Is everything OK?" I ask. "With the both of you?"

"All good," she says, in a flat voice that puts a stop to that line of questioning. "Trust me."

"Good," I echo. Amy is the person I trust most.

"You need to see your dad," she says. "You'll regret it if you don't."

"OK," because I don't want to argue with a very pregnant woman.

"Get some sleep," she says. "It's been quite a day. Don't worry if you hear noises in the night. Just me and my squashed bladder."

She closes the door behind her.

I sit on the bed. There's something special about your childhood friends that can't be replicated later in life. Looking at these photos, being back with Amy in Kinsale, it feels like part of me never left.

My father used to drum the words "every contact leaves a trace" into all the junior cops he trained. Mostly he meant don't screw up a crime scene but it could also be taken as a philosophical statement. With the exception of Amy, I thought I'd put everything in Kinsale behind me twenty years ago. Watching the bushfire on television, I saw black snowflakes falling from a red sky and flames creeping across roads, turning telephone poles into burning crosses, and felt sorry for my old town. I worried about my father, who was caught up in it, but I thought I was insulated. Pretended I could switch off the footage and walk away.

Perhaps that was a mistake and the wind is changing direction.

3

New Year's Eve 1996

Amy

A my lay on her back nestled beside Eliza. Grace sat staring at the teepee of sticks.

"There," said Grace. "Your seagull is back, Eliza."

Lifting her head, Amy saw the bird watching them, its mismatched eyes looking hopeful.

Eliza chucked a cold chip towards it. In a flash it darted forward, pecked the sand greedily and the chip vanished.

"No more," said Grace. "Chips aren't good for gulls."

"Chips aren't particularly good for anyone," said Amy.

"My gull loves them," said Eliza, but she stopped all the same.

The seagull turned its beak skyward, gave a quick wing-shake, hopped and then flew away, its wings a steady metronome flap until it got high enough to glide into the darkening sky. The day had disappeared into dusk.

"Poor thing is probably trying to find somewhere to go to sleep," said Grace.

"Wait until the fireworks," said Eliza. "Dad will spend most of tomorrow rounding up lost pets." She hitched up her sundress to scratch a mosquito bite. The rain had left stagnant pools, excellent breeding grounds.

"Quick girls, the light's almost gone." Janey Bayless came bustling up clutching a camera, bossily insisting they all get into the photo. Eliza was the first to agree. "Thanks, Mrs. Bayless, that would be great," and she pulled Amy to standing before dragging the sunglasses perched on top of her head over her eyes in case the flash went off. Grace draped her arms around the others, grabbing them close. Amy smiled her no-teeth smile that she had perfected after two years of wearing braces. Behind them, Jim Keaveney poured more gas on the wood.

"Lovely," said Mrs. Bayless in her baby-doll voice.

"Can we get a copy?" asked Eliza.

"I'll give one to your dad when I get them developed," Mrs. Bayless promised. "Now you lot keep an eye on my Tony tonight. Make sure he behaves himself," and she turned to walk back the way she had come. Grace stifled a giggle.

Amy looked up and saw Sergeant Mick Carmody in front of the first-aid tent on the foreshore. Two country fire trucks were parked next to him, the occupants bored.

"Your dad's still watching," she said.

"He's not waving again?" asked Eliza. "So embarrassing."

Amy shook her head. "He's standing there, looking at us."

"Just wait," replied Eliza.

Within minutes, a crying child clutching a bent arm headed into the tent. After taking a quick look around to check that everything was under control, Mick Carmody followed him in.

"Now," said Eliza, "while he's distracted."

The three girls hurried down the beach, winding their way through territory-marking picnic blankets, unruly gangs of kids, frustrated mothers with tired toddlers and fathers clutching beers, oblivious to it all. Amy saw Tess Carmody, lying on a beach towel next to the lifeguard from the surf club, sit up and watch as they went past.

"Your sister," Amy hissed.

"She won't say anything. Not when I know she's sneaking off to the paddock party tonight."

An impatient Gus, tortoise-like with his enormous school backpack, was waiting for them down at the south end of the beach. The last light had left the sky and behind them the bonfire roared into life. Amy turned back for a quick glimpse of it.

"Hurry up, the tide's already coming in." Gus handed Grace a flashlight and all four of them quickly clambered up onto the slippery stones and began walking single file.

Out on the rocks, the waves seemed more ferocious, crashing close enough that a fine mist flecked Amy's face. Her head filled with images of the sea racing in and dragging her back out with it—yet another reason why tonight was a bad idea.

Grace, athletic and with the longest legs, went first, moving carefully to avoid the knee-deep rock pools that they had spent summers exploring, though never at night. Amy tried not to think about bluebottle jellyfish, knife-sharp shells or broken glass. They made their way forward under the shadow of the headland, leaving the lights and people from Main Beach behind them. It was darker than Amy expected, much darker, and she began to move more slowly, checking and rechecking every step. Eliza muttered about the lack of progress until suddenly she slipped and had to grab onto the back of Amy's T-shirt. The girls wobbled violently, just managing to stay upright.

"Are you still wearing your sunglasses?" asked Amy furiously. "It's night time."

"I'm not, promise," answered Eliza.

"Then it's those ridiculous shoes."

Eliza had insisted on wearing brand-new strappy sandals that had no grip.

"I'll take them off," Eliza said. Amy could hear the anxiety in her voice. Eliza wanted this night to be perfect.

The flashlight shone in their direction. "Next bit's easier," said Grace, trying to be encouraging.

As Eliza took off her shoes, Amy put a hand out to Grace, who hauled her up onto the next rock. Rounding the point, Amy could see two flickering figures standing around a tiny campfire up above the high-tide watermark.

"There, Amy," said Gus, proudly. "Didn't want you to feel like you were missing out."

Amy looked at the almost nonexistent fire, which was giving off more smoke than heat. This would be one of those nights where the retelling was going to be about a million times more exciting than the actual event, she thought. Sneaking off from the community celebrations for their own private New Year's Eve party at Cromwell's Beach had been Eliza's idea. Nicknamed "Crummies," the beach was overlooked by tourists and ignored by locals, both put off by the temperamental rips and lethal tides, the large jagged rocks scattered along it and the long walk from the road. Eliza had been inspired by the fact that her older sister was going to the paddock party. It was the latest skirmish in the Carmody sisters' ongoing war.

Clambering down crevices, they waded through the cold shallow water, until they reached the sand, fine, white, under their feet. Tony Bayless and Luke Tyrell had already set up camp around the fire, along with their beer bottles.

Eliza and Grace ran up the beach as Amy trudged slowly behind them.

"Hi, Tony," said Eliza.

"Took your time," Luke said, grinning up at them, his curly hair slicked back against his head. "Waited until all the work was done."

Tony glanced up as well and looked like he might say hello but then didn't.

"What do you mean 'work'?" demanded Gus, who was pulling towels, lollies, chips and more beers out of his schoolbag. "You've nearly let it go out." He grabbed a large stick that was lying in the sand and began stoking it. Luke opened his mouth to argue and Amy shot Gus a warning look because Luke had a temper.

"You're useless, Tyrell," Gus said in a way that defused the situation and then shot Amy a grin. "Right, we need more kindling."

Eliza flopped onto the sand next to Tony and gave Amy an imploring look.

"I'll go," volunteered Amy dutifully.

"Me too," said Grace, who still had the flashlight.

Together they walked slowly up the beach toward the tangle of wind-swept shrubs and gum trees.

"Does Tony ever talk?" asked Amy, once they were out of earshot.

"Maybe he's the strong silent type," Grace said. "Besides, Eliza does enough talking for two.'"

"Eliza says he can drive us home later."

"If they're drinking, I'm not getting into a car with them." Grace's mother was a nurse at the local hospital and regularly told stories of horrific car crashes by drunk drivers.

"What will we do?" asked Amy.

"Could hitch."

"Hmm," said Amy. It was a long way home but Amy didn't like the sound of hitching any more than a drunken Tony. She started hunting through the undergrowth for twigs.

"Snakes," reminded Grace. Amy quickly took a step backward. The boys could get their own damn kindling. Grace shone the flashlight and carefully began to forage.

"My New Year's resolution is to stop listening to Eliza," Amy told Grace. "Her and her crazy schemes."

"I don't know," said Grace. "Tonight could be fun."

"With a certain Luke Tyrell, perhaps?" said Amy, trying to give Grace a push but missing completely as her friend saw it coming and dodged.

"I don't know what you're talking about," said Grace, but Amy knew she had been shyly edging toward Luke ever since the beginning of summer.

"Don't worry, I haven't said anything to anyone. Your secret is safe."

"Well then, just a bit," admitted Grace.

Amy ran her fingers along the top of the dried marram grass, feeling the sticky rasp of it against her skin. Grace had one of those kind hearts and overactive imaginations that made her see the best in people. If there was going to be a general pairing off, then that left her with Gus and she wasn't sure how she felt about that.

Grace needed to pee so they moved further into the shadowy scrub where the trees stripped the moonlight into pieces like the bark peeling off the trunks. She chose the biggest gum they could find, stomping around the base of it to scare away snakes. Grace handed Amy the flashlight and disappeared around the side. As she held it, Amy felt that somehow the small circle of light only served to make the rest of the darkness so dense she could feel it pressing against her skin. That made her shiver. She switched it off to see if her eyes could adjust properly.

"Grace," said Amy.

There was only the sound of her own breath, loud in her ears, an empty sound like the wind in a shell.

A faint rustling.

"Grace," she repeated a whisper as her heart began to quicken. She had a sudden feeling of loss in her bones.

A loud mournful scream from overhead made her jump.

A shape moved from behind the tree. Two eyes peered and then blinked.

"That's a black cockatoo flying over from Main Beach," came Grace's voice. "Another one bothered by the bonfire and the crowd."

Amy switched the flashlight back on.

"If there's a flock of them it means that rain's coming," said Grace.

That's all Kinsale needed, thought Amy. Luckily, her family was heading north tomorrow for a couple of weeks' holiday where, hopefully, the weather would be better.

They took so long getting back to the campfire, trying to give Eliza plenty of time to work her charms on Tony, that Gus came looking for them. When they finally returned, their arms full of sticks, Amy could see quite a few empties next to Eliza.

"Look, Tony brought us drinks," said Eliza. She handed her one, and Amy could smell the cordial pinkness of alcohol on Eliza's breath.

"Great." Amy decided to pour it on the sand when no one was looking. Gus grabbed the sticks and began throwing them on the fire, which was looking healthier.

Tony stood up. The only son of Janey and Wes Bayless, who owned the local pub, he was tall, much taller than the others, a man-shape with a boyish face standing there with his hands awkwardly thrust into his jeans. Maybe that was part of the attraction, Amy thought, because it wasn't his conversation.

"So anyway," he said, not really looking at anyone and certainly not at Eliza, "I should head back. I promised Dad I'd make a delivery to the paddock party."

"Where are they holding that this year?" asked Gus.

The venue changed every time to outfox the police.

"On Ophir Road, at the far end of our property, well away from the house."

There was more than a touch of brag to this, Amy thought. It wasn't like the Bayless family actually lived in The Castle, they just ran a function business out of it that wasn't making any money, according to town gossip.

"You can't go yet," said Eliza, standing up as well. "You'll miss the fireworks." She pulled on his arm and checked his watch. "It's almost midnight."

"I'm already late."

"Maybe we could go with you," she said.

"Sorry," he said. "There isn't room in my truck for everyone."

Amy could see disappointment ripple across Eliza's face. She'd been planning this New Year's Eve for weeks. This wasn't how it was supposed to end.

"Besides, it's not for kids," he went on. "You are all underage, right?"

"But you don't have to go right away. Let's go for a swim first," Eliza wheedled. She was standing close enough to the fire for it to warm her to a red-hot glow. There was a boozy shimmer to her.

Tony stood there, looking uncomfortable, watching as Eliza slipped out of her sundress, revealing a bikini underneath.

"Didn't bring anything to swim in," he muttered, starting to hunt around for his jacket.

"We can go skinny dipping," said Eliza and before anyone could argue she was reaching around and unhooking her bikini top. Amy wanted to stop her, but instead, she watched as Eliza, aware that all eyes were on her, started to wriggle out of her bottoms.

Amy had spent most of the last year worrying if her boobs would ever grow, and trying not to get caught peeking at anyone else's chest in the school locker rooms. Here, for the first time, someone was actually standing there, daring her to look. The fact that it was her best friend complicated matters, so she watched the others instead. Tony was frozen to the spot, Grace had her hand over her mouth and Luke's eyes were hanging out his head, blood rushing away from his brain at high speed. She couldn't bring herself to look at Gus, to see him staring at another girl.

Eliza stood there, a beautiful brazen bronze, then raised her hand and even twirled the bikini around before flinging it on the sand. It was Tony who dropped his gaze first. Eliza's chin stuck out defiantly. Amy knew she'd never back out now.

"Last one in," she said, then turned and started running toward the sea.

All her hard work hit a target but it was the wrong one. Luke threw his head back and gave a kind of strangled coyote howl, before going after her. He stripped at the water's edge then tumbled into the sea, puppy-dog eager, a sleek seal head in the waves before Amy lost sight of him.

Amy glanced at Grace to see if she was going to join them but Grace just stood there. The look on her face made Amy decide she did need a drink after all, and she scrabbled in the sand to find the bottle. This was what boys like Tony and Luke always did, they hurt girls' feelings and were too stupid to realize it. Sometimes she wondered if boys had any empathy at all or if they were just a mix of testosterone and muscle. She had been especially wrong about Luke and felt terrible that she had said anything encouraging to Grace. Gus caught her eye and shrugged his shoulders as if he was confused about what had just happened. Tony still hadn't left and

Amy felt like shoving him hard. Couldn't he have waited until midnight? Shown Eliza some attention?

There was a loud whistle, a bang and fireworks exploded above them from Main Beach. The four heads turned as one to watch the papercuts of gold and silver against the blackness. If only, Amy thought, her eyes blurred with the cold beauty of them, if only they had started a few minutes earlier. Eliza would have launched herself at Tony whether he liked it or not and Luke might have kissed Grace.

"Happy New Year," said Gus to no one in particular, but slowly his hand crept out towards Amy's until he touched her fingers. She didn't move away.

The sky quickly emptied of all but moon and smoke.

"There were hardly any fireworks this year," Amy complained to Gus. "Blink and you'd miss them." She spoke to try and cover up her heart beating a little faster, in anticipation that he might come closer but he stayed where he was. Then Tony coughed, and Amy wished he was at the bottom of the ocean. Couldn't he just hurry up and go before Eliza came back.

"Let's nick Luke's clothes," said Gus. Amy thought this was inspired. It could turn the whole thing into a joke, maybe even cheer up Grace a little. She picked up the limp bundle of Eliza's clothes from near the fire, determined that these should be hidden as well, and then grabbed Grace's arm to drag her to the water's edge. Grace was like a dead weight, but she didn't resist. Gus darted the flashlight this way and that, trying to find what Luke had discarded.

"Where are they?" asked Grace. The words came out clotted, as if she had a cold. Gus shone the light out into the ocean, small and rippling on the vast stretch of water. Amy realized she couldn't hear splashing or talking or anything above the monotonous crash of waves. No blue-lipped naked bodies running up to warm themselves by the fire. Her skin prickled like sunburn and the start of a hot rush of dread began sloshing inside her. Surely it was too quick for anything bad to have happened.

Gus ran along the beach shouting out their names. Amy tried as well, but the sea seemed so loud and her voice was so small and all she could do was follow the flashlight's strange tunnel vision as though it was a stage spotlight waiting for a grand entrance that didn't come. She ran through the tangled seaweed at the water's edge, panic eating holes in her as she tried to work out what to do next. Tony had his car but it would take far too long.

It was Grace who wordlessly grabbed the flashlight out of Gus's hands and shone it sideways, away from the water and further along the beach. They were on the sand, lying down, naked Luke on top of naked Eliza, both of them very much alive.

The flashlight fell from Grace's hand and she immediately ran back toward the fire. Amy saw her swoop down to grab her sandals before running up the beach so fast that there was no hope of catching her.

"Grace," Amy shouted, her voice strong and loud now. "Wait."

But she was already vanishing into the dark and Amy could only make out the flicker of her legs, the backs of her feet, as she kept running.

4

My phone dings.

"You," says Amy. "Again!" She turns the car into the driveway of Emerald Coast Homes. There have been three work calls, two meetings postponed and a long conversation with my personal assistant about what I need her to email me ASAP and what can wait for my return. The text turns out to be from Gavin, reminding me to drop by the police station to make a statement. I reply: "Caught Tyrell yet?"

A waiting cloud and then a sad emoji.

I already regret agreeing to see my father so any other family catch-up is out of the question today. I'll visit Dad, and then drive four hours back to the city.

"Heard from Tristan?" I ask Amy.

"Apparently he's too busy for us mere mortals," she says, "but I'll keep trying."

She parks in the dedicated doctor's spot next to disabled parking. The lot is almost empty which makes the surroundings look even more antiseptic. The building is made of anemic cream bricks with two squares of lawn on both sides of a large electric door. A couple of small trees have been pruned to within an inch of their lives. The gravel is swept, the footpath white and smooth. The building is all nursing and no home.

"A little soulless," I venture to Amy.

"I've seen worse," she replies. "Much worse."

An old lady, weathered as driftwood, sits on a bench in front of the Emerald Coast Home sign, looking at us. Although the day is already swimming weather, she's wearing a slightly too large overcoat that might actually be a dressing gown. There's a suitcase an arm's length away.

"Who's that?"

"Mary Young," answers Amy. "She's always there."

Reversing the name in my head, I try picturing a younger Mary but it's almost impossible.

"Shouldn't she be inside?"

"It isn't a prison," Amy says.

"What if she wanders off?"

"She hasn't yet. Just sits there patiently, waiting for her grandson to come."

"Does he visit often?"

There's a pause before she answers, "Died years ago."

My smile disappears. "That's awful, the poor thing."

Other visitors walk past Mary. One woman stops to chat to her but Mary just shakes her head, her mouth a firm refusal.

"Let me take that," and I grab Amy's large square doctor's bag from the back seat before she can.

"My own personal porter," she says. "I could get used to this."

Mary watches us as we walk up the path. The skin around her eyes has a reddish tinge, which, combined with her lack of eyelashes gives a tortoise-like quality to her gaze.

"Morning, Mary," calls Amy.

I nod, trying to look friendly.

"Travis will be here soon," Mary tells me. Her teeth are coffee-brown, her gums dark, but there are remnants of a beautiful smile.

"That's nice," I say, but I keep on walking.

A notice by the door has a code printed on it. Amy punches it into a keypad on the wall. The first automatic door slides open. Another code is punched in and then the next door opens. Warm air comes rushing out, smelling of disinfectant.

Amy takes her bag. "Sign in the visitor's book and Laurelle will give you directions to your dad's room." She points out the lady sitting behind the counter, middle-aged with frizzy hair pulled back into a ponytail. Laurelle is already gesturing to me with a pen.

"You'll be fine," Amy says. "I know it isn't easy but you'll be glad you've done it."

"As long as you're sure," I grumble half-heartedly at her back as she moves down the corridor, in full doctor mode. She calls out cheerfully to some inhabitants shuffling past and is gone.

My father's asleep in his chair when I walk in. Pale hair, slumped body, sitting by a floor-to-ceiling window, a pillow behind his head. I stand in the doorway and for one fleeting moment it could be twenty years ago with him asleep in his favorite brown leatherette chair, his work files around him. The image disappears so quickly it's like I passed a reflection in a car window. He is tilted back and the streaming sun from the large window catches him full in the face. Nothing moves, except for his blinking eyes. His hair has gone completely white.

I drag his wheelchair backward into the shade.

There is a hospital bed, a small table with tissues and a vinyl visitor's chair with a slightly ripped seat that is pushed up against the wall next to a small television. I pull out the chair and sit down. Its legs leave indents in the linoleum. The room is stuffy and completely impersonal, as though my father won't be here long enough to bother making it cozy. It was Gavin's idea to move him home to Kinsale. I had tried to argue for him to stay in the city, nearer to me, but he and Tess were already preparing to transfer back to town to look after him, so I was outvoted. The night before he was moved I said goodbye for what I thought would be forever. Tess had made it clear my help wasn't required.

"Hello, Dad, it's me, Eliza." I tell him.

His eyes, no longer moving, have an unfocused quality as if he's day-dreaming. I think of stories where people communicate only with their eyelids.

"Dad, blink if you can hear me."

Nothing.

My gaze travels over his body, taking in the pajamas, a mismatched button, a smear of something on his collar, until I slowly return to his face. It is so recognizable and yet he is a gentle ruin of his former self. Always a quiet man, now he is silent. His face has healed in a strange way so he seems less fragile, but more collapsed as well. He is both thinner and flabbier since the accident, as though what has disappeared was internal, the structure that made him an upright man. When I was a child I thought my father was the most important man in Kinsale, the boss cop who took care of the town. Part of me still wants to think that, even though our adult relationship has been remote, reduced to obligations and contact on birthdays and Christmas.

His tongue comes out, slow and sluggish, and wets his lips. There is dried spittle at the corner of his mouth.

"Do you want some water?"

A metal jug has some dusty glasses next to it. I wipe them out with some tissues from my handbag, pour the water and then hold a glass to his mouth. He swallows, a rivulet running down the side of his chin. Another tissue mops it up. One of his hands starts to shake but then stops. My father was always clean-shaven, never even dabbling in the typical policeman's moustache. Now his jaw is covered in moth-eaten silver bristles.

I try to find some words to say, to talk to the parts of him that remain, but they sound forced, like I'm talking to a small child.

"Hi there." There is a baby-faced man in the doorway, tall, with shaggy blonde hair and thick eyebrows, wearing a short-sleeved shirt and dark trousers. He has an official badge above his shirt pocket and a white trolley full of supplies.

"Amy said you were here. Thought I'd say g'day. I'm Ryan, the clinical nurse on this morning."

"My father was left in the sun. He was thirsty and blinking." It is my best law partner's voice, the one designed to make junior solicitors tremble.

He seems unperturbed and comes into the room, bending down next to Dad.

"It's been crazy. Cadee called in sick, probably to be expected under the circumstances. We tried calling in extras but no one was available until after lunch."

He starts examining Dad, checking his arms and feet.

"How are you, Mick? Comfortable?"

No response.

"Can he hear us?" I ask.

"Research suggests hearing and touch are the last senses to disappear, so I always assume that they can."

His gentle movements and professional manner, much more natural than I had been, puts me in my place.

"He needs shaving."

"Electric razor will be in one of the drawers by his bedside," he says, standing up. "You can take him to the garden after that. It's supposed to rain this afternoon so he might not get out otherwise."

He heads off after saying goodbye to my father and passing on a message from Amy to meet her by the car in an hour.

There is hardly anything in the drawers. I take out a comb from the top one. The razor is next to a bible in the second. My father has never expressed an interest in God as far as I know, so it seems unlikely that the bible belongs to him. His eyelids are closed. I might disturb him. Perhaps he needs to sleep—but I can't leave those bristles alone.

"I'm going to shave you."

The words are swallowed by the room as if no one else is in it. When I turn the razor on it makes an angry buzz, like a blowfly trapped against glass, vibrating in my hand. Standing over him, the jitteriness is transferred from the razor to me. This feels all wrong. I gingerly put my fingers up to his face, barely touching as if he might give me an electric shock. His eyelids flicker.

"Don't worry. This won't hurt, I promise."

His skin is elephant-baggy and I hold it taut with one hand, pushing the razor against him, slowly moving it upward from jaw to cheek. I try to catch each bristle, explaining to him all the time what I am doing, telling him to keep still, as if he can feel it and knows what is happening.

He doesn't move a muscle.

It's a relief to switch the razor off. I've done a bad job but it gives me enough confidence to pick up the comb. His hair needs cutting, it falls well past his collar, but that can wait for another day.

There is still time to fill before Amy finishes, so I decide to wheel him out to the garden. Although the chair moves easily across the floor, what remains of him is surprisingly heavy. The vanished part, the bit that made him my father, weighed so little.

"Make sure you return him to his room when you're done," a passing care attendant says, like he's a piece of equipment that needs to be put away. The implication annoys me.

The garden is a sunny courtyard with more bricks than plants. I push the wheelchair along the ramp toward the tiled path, past flowerbeds with pruned-back rosebushes and irises and a large herb garden buzzing with bees. A sun-faded timber outdoor setting sits in the middle with a torn green garden umbrella in the center. High-pitched chirps travel from the furthest corner, where there is an aviary, sheet metal for a wall on one side, wire mesh on the others. Birds sit on cut-off branches trussed to the walls. Inside it, an old man, stooped and white-haired, is putting down some pine chips. I push my father closer. A slight breeze picks up and his eyes open, a baby responding to the world.

"Look at the birds." It is like I'm the parent now.

At the sound of my voice, the man in the cage turns. It's Jim Keaveney, the person who ended up with dessert all over him courtesy of my waitressing. When I was growing up he used to run the town pet shop specializing in aviaries.

The birds don't seem bothered by his presence, flapping, preening, pecking, flying back and forth so fast they are blurs. Jim reaches up and as quick as a snake, he has hold of one. There is a little feathery head poking out the top of his large bricklayer's fist, the quivering tip of a tail protruding from the bottom.

"See her," and he holds it out toward us. His voice is deep and gruff. "A little beauty this one, just like her mother." The bird lies there terrified, struggling to move her wings. He holds so tightly that I want to tell him to stop, that he's hurting her, but then he opens his hand and she shoots out of reach.

He shuffles to the side of the enclosure and unlocks an internal wire-screen door, walks through, then opens up the next door and comes through that.

"So they can't escape."

It reminds me of the entrance out the front.

"Do the residents look after the birds?"

"The finches. Not the bigger ones. Only I take care of those." He points to a smaller cage that I hadn't noticed. A bedraggled galah is inside, its white and pink head tucked under a dove-gray wing. "Minimize human contact so once it's strong enough I can take it back to the bush."

The bird's head emerges as though it knows we are talking about it.

"Worth a fortune that bird is," he says. "Treat them like kings in Asia and the Middle East."

"Do you still have your shop?"

He shakes his head. "Retired now but I still do a bit of maintenance here, gardening as well."

"And all these birds are yours?"

I'm only trying to make conversation, but Jim stares beakily at me, an uncanny echo of the galah behind him. It's the combination of a sharp long nose and a flap of hair that falls forward onto his face.

"Got a license." He raises his voice. "It's all legal."

"You might not remember me, Mr. Keaveney, but I'm . . ."

"Mick Carmody's youngest," and he gestures at Dad. "Ruined my best suit once."

I try to remember who paid for the dry-cleaning.

He shakes his grizzled head at me before leaving.

When Dad is safely back in his room, I kneel by his wheelchair and look at his face. "I've got a meeting to go to. I'm really busy at work." A stab of guilt hits me for abandoning him when he's so helpless but he should understand. He was always too busy to come and see me at boarding school and then university. Maybe that's why I chose a career that meant I would be too busy to see him.

He doesn't open his eyes.

"Bye, Dad."

I almost want to tell I love him but they are words we have never spoken.

We are not that sort of family.

5

A couple of days later, I tell my secretary that I'm working from home in the morning and catch a taxi to Southern Cross Hospital. I have to steel myself before walking through its doors. I'm only heading to the café on the ground floor but it brings back the recent memory of racing here one night to see my father after his accident. It has taken all Amy's efforts to arm-wrestle Tristan into meeting me. The time and location were given on a take-it-or-leave-it basis. I sit down, order a coffee and wait for over half an hour—a fortune in missed fees, but Tristan saves lives so there is no comparison. He arrives doing the busy walk of important people and immediately gets the attention of the guy at the coffee machine who has been ignoring my I'd-like-a-refill glances for the last ten minutes. Tristan doesn't even need to order, he just nods, and the guy knows what he wants.

Tristan is high-metabolism skinny. His usual includes two donuts and neither is for me. He checks for messages while he waits for the coffee and doesn't even say hello. I'm tempted to go into cardiac arrest to get his attention.

"You not having anything?" he asks as a flat white is delivered to the table.

"How's Paul?"

Tristan tells me he's spoken to the trauma surgeon and the neurosurgeon and then launches into fluent medico-jargon speak. My legal career started in personal injury cases so I understand enough to translate it into "he isn't good." There have been brain bleeds, CT scans and chest drains, as well as other procedures.

"He's going to get better, right?" I ask.

Tristan sighs as though I haven't been listening. A spray of rainbow sprinkles drops from the donut onto the table. Fussy and precise about the rest of his life, he is a surprisingly messy eater.

Could Paul actually die?

Suddenly I'm possessed with the idea that if he gets his hat back, everything will be fine.

"Here." I scrabble under the table. "You've got to give this to him now." The green hat looks even sorrier and stranger than before. Tristan ignores it.

"Anisocoria," he says. "I always thought heterochromia but it's anisocoria."

He's talking about my eyes. What Tristan is trying to say is that I don't have different colored eyes. They just look like that because I've unequal sized pupils. My left eye appears darker because my pupil is permanently dilated.

"Interesting," he says. "How did it happen?"

"Can you take the hat to him?"

"I'm not doing that."

"Please."

Tristan stands, gulping down his coffee, grabbing the remaining donut and checking his phone because people could have died without him.

"Have they found the guy who hit him yet?" he asks.

I shake my head. "Only the car he stole, abandoned in a national park, up the coast. Look, please, Paul needs it back."

Tristan frowns at me and then the hat. "His brother is here," he says, taking pity. "I'll see if he wants it."

This is delivered with the finality of a man who is always listened to. I give him my phone number and mumble "thanks" at his disappearing back.

A waitress wearing Mickey Mouse ears asks if I want another coffee in that passive-aggressive way that implies she doesn't care but her boss insists on her asking. She forgets my flat white almost immediately because the girl from the flower shop, wearing a set of devil's horns, comes in and they spend the next few minutes taking selfies. That's when the text from Tristan arrives telling me to come up to ICU.

A nurse waits for me at the lifts. She looks straight at my eyes, a useful identifier, then says, "They're in the family room."

We walk down corridors with fluorescent lights that turn everything a skeletal white, until she opens a door into what looks like a budget hotel room minus the bed. The curtain material and chairs are a hideous patchwork fabric that was probably chosen to hide stains. There are two men inside. One has his back to me and is staring out the window. The view is one of the city's most famous parks with ornate flowerbeds and European trees. The second man is sitting down, arms folded.

"Excuse me, I'm looking for . . ." Tristan didn't tell me the brother's name, but the seated man starts speaking.

"Eliza?" he asks. "Eliza Carmody?"

He springs from his seat and comes over to me. Much larger than when I saw him last, with a bushy beard, thick neck and broad shoulders, Tony Bayless stands in front of me. The boy has become a bear.

"God, I can't believe it," he says, in a rush. "The nurse didn't tell us who was coming. So you saw Paul being attacked?"

All I can do is stare. Here is the dasher of teenage dreams who until very recently was believed responsible for the Kinsale bushfire.

Tony takes my inability to speak as confusion. "Sorry, you probably don't remember me."

I recover enough to say, "Of course, Tony. It's been a while."

"You haven't changed at all," he says. "I mean, this has changed," and he spreads out his arms to take in my suit and heels, the silk shirt, my perfectly straightened corporate hair. "You look really great but I'd recognize you anywhere . . ." by which he means my eyes. His enthusiasm momentarily peters out and I take the opportunity to turn to the other person and say hello.

"Sorry," Tony says. "Eliza Carmody meet Donal Keenan. Eliza is from Kinsale as well but escaped."

Donal is a couple of inches taller than me, about five ten, my age, brownish hair, though if we were outside in the sun, it might be a rusty red. His skin is pale. There is a resemblance to the Hat Man, but Donal is slighter and more attractive.

"You found the place all right?" Donal asks. It isn't one of those movie Irish accents, all soft and melodic; it's kind of spikier and jagged. The North, perhaps. I spent three days in Belfast as a backpacker. It didn't rain once.

I nod my head and smile.

"Take a seat," he says.

Tony hovers. "You probably want to talk. I'll leave you to it."

"Appreciate that," says Donal.

"It was good seeing you, Eliza."

"You too."

"Maybe we should catch up sometime," he says, and when I nod he asks for my phone number. We hug awkwardly and then he leaves, shutting the door behind him.

"He's a good man," says Donal. "Picked me up from the airport, found me a place to stay."

I sit down, with my bag at my feet.

In the chair across from me, Donal's back slumps as he rests elbows on legs and rubs his hands over his face. The smudges under hazel eyes are so dark they have a deep blue tinge to them. His eyebrows are two strong lines but his lips have a lovely curve to them. There is a five o'clock shadow, redder than his hair, which gives his otherwise ashen skin a little color. There is something of the fox about him.

"Smoke?" he asks, pulling out a pack of cigarettes.

I shake my head.

"Haven't had one in five years but waiting for my flight in duty-free, I thought, fuck it. Could be hit by a bus tomorrow."

He gives the sort of pixie-ish smile that makes me think he could be fun if circumstances were different.

"Are you allowed to smoke in here?"

"Probably not," he says, "but I'll risk it."

There is a metallic click, click, click of the lighter. He smokes with his first finger hooked around the cigarette, clamping it in place as if he's expecting someone to try and wrestle it off him. He grabs the lid of a takeaway coffee cup to use as an ashtray.

"So, Carmody," he says, leaning back. "An Irish name."

It is hard to work out if this is a statement or a question. There is an upward inflection at the end of all his sentences, a moment of optimism that gets dragged back down at the start of the next.

"Maybe once, a long time ago."

"Well, I'm Paul's older brother. Pleased to meet you, Eliza Carmody."

He takes another drag on the cigarette. In the gloom, the smoke starts to curl round his head and up into the air like a question mark.

"You were the one who helped Paul," he says.

A half nod. I tried to help but it wasn't enough.

"You saw what happened?"

I want to tell him that I saw enough to wake up sweating every night, but the words catch in my throat and there are tears behind them that will start if my mouth opens. Donal waits as if he has all the time in the world and when I still don't talk, he prompts, "The doctor fella said there was something you had to give to me?"

Coughing down the lump, "That's Tristan." Rummaging in the bag, I let the tears that have already escaped drip down my cheeks before putting the green hat on the coffee table in front of us.

Donal gives an upside smile at the sight of it.

"I thought Paul would want it back or . . ."

He puts his cigarette down on the coffee lid and picks up the hat.

"I gave this to him at his going-away drinks. Bet him a fiver he wouldn't wear it. Stubborn bastard wouldn't take it off. Kept sending me all these pictures from around the world, saying I owed him a fortune. Do anything for a dare. Mad."

"It's how I recognized him. Turning down the street, I saw that hat walking along." For the first time I realize that might be how Luke recognized him as well. Donal says nothing but from the look on his face he's thinking the same thing. He puts the hat back on the table.

"Your brother is a hero. The way he helped that woman. What the papers are saying is right."

There has been article after article calling Paul a modern-day Good Samaritan. Some breakfast TV show is even running a campaign that involves wearing novelty hats to #saynotostreetviolence. My Facebook feed is filled with profile pictures of people wearing Viking helmets, witches' hats and green hats like the one in front of us.

Donal hunches over and picks up the cigarette.

"I'm not sure I recognize my brother in those articles," he says, "but then I'm hard pressed recognizing the beaten-up version in the hospital room." He almost spits out the words in a sudden flare of anger.

"How is he?" I ask.

Donal sighs. "All right, I think. Smacking your skull into the road is never a good idea but he's a tough fucker. Trying to get a straight word out of the doctors is like pulling teeth. The operation for the brain bleed went OK. He came round in the ambulance. Talked even. Did you know that?"

I shake my head.

Donal pulls off his leather jacket. There are sweat marks on the armpits of his T-shirt.

"Have you siblings?" he asks.

"An older sister, Tess. We don't really get on."

"Gave you a hard time?"

"Stuck a stick in my eye once."

"Is that what led to . . . ?" He points to my left eye. "Sure she did you a favor there. Makes you look mysterious. Like David Bowie."

Not a week goes by without some guy mentioning David Bowie as if it's a compliment. He asks for the whole story so I tell him about us fighting, me climbing a tree to escape and refusing to get down until Dad got home, annoying Tess so much she threw a stick at me, which struck me in the face. Donal tells me he often threw sticks at Paul so his sympathies are with my sister. I confess that it wasn't entirely bad because I used to pretend it gave me special powers and I could read people's minds.

"What, like second sight?" he says.

We both laugh. Donal is the kind of person who makes you feel like you are in cahoots with him. He finishes his cigarette and puts the butt and the temporary ashtray in the bin just as the door opens. A doctor looks in, sniffs the air and frowns before telling Donal he'll see him tomorrow. Donal says "cheers" and "thanks" and the doctor nods and closes the door quietly.

He returns his gaze to me. "So," he says. "Tell me about Kinsale."

"I grew up there but I've lived in the city since I was sixteen. I was sent away to boarding school and never went back."

"So just visiting," says Donal. "Not the prodigal daughter returning."

I smile. "Just driving through."

"And you were in the wrong place at the wrong time," he says.

"Yeah," I say, "like Paul."

His face tightens, forehead creases and he looks away.

It's time I left. The hat has been delivered and there are ring-binders in a skyscraper on the other side of the city calling my name.

Before I get a chance to say goodbye, Donal jumps in.

"Could you do us a favor?" he says. "Will you go for a walk in the park across the way with me? I hear this city's coffee is supposed to be good but I've had nothing but hospital muck since I got here."

I look at his tired face, his jet-lagged eyes. He needs to escape this world, if only for a few minutes.

"Sure."

6

Donal attempts to buy me lunch but he has no Australian money and we've gone somewhere that makes a virtue out of being cash-only. He promises he'll pay next time but they're only words. We have collided for today only. It is that magical lunch hour that on a sunny autumn day starts at midday and stretches until after 2 pm. People are everywhere. Suit jackets and ties are off, skirts have been hitched up and heels abandoned.

He stretches out perfectly lean on a patch of grass and when he lights another cigarette, I sneak a look at his hands. No wedding ring but that means nothing. A ball rolls toward us and Donal gets up and kicks it back to its toddler owner.

"Have you got kids?" I ask.

He shakes his head. "You?"

I shake mine.

"Paul has. Lovely little fella, Harry." He pulls his phone out of his pocket, scrolls and passes it to me with a proud uncle face. Shading the screen with my hand, I see the child from Paul's Facebook posts. He's got bright red curly hair and a smile so large that his face dimples from the pressure of it.

"Gorgeous. His mum?"

Donal shrugs. "Their relationship wasn't great, broke up when he was a baby."

There's a story behind that, but it's none of my business. We sit and eat in contented silence.

"They haven't caught the fella who did this to Paul yet," he says.

"I'm sure they will soon."

"Are the police looking after you?" he asks. "Being the main witness and all."

"I don't think that's necessary," I say. "They've got security footage." Gavin left another message this morning asking me to get in touch about making a full statement. I make a mental note to return his call.

Donal props himself up on his elbow. His hair is all mussed up from lying down and it stands in twists and tufts. Left to its own devices, his hair would have the same curls as his nephew's.

"I've seen a bit of that footage. It shows before and after but not what actually happens. He could try and argue self-defense or that it was an accident."

"It wasn't an accident," I say. "There was nothing accidental about it."

Donal sighs and asks me exactly what happened. Grabbing my bag, I use it for a pillow and lie down beside him in the shade of a large pin oak. I start with being stuck in traffic. When I get to the part about turning the corner and seeing Paul's green hat, he stretches out and grabs my hand. His grip gets tighter as I tell him about hearing the sound, seeing the movement, stopping the car, turning to look, and then, worst of all, Paul stagger and fall. By the time the ambulance has driven away, Donal's hand has relaxed but still he doesn't let go.

"Do you believe in karma?" he asks the sky above us.

I've run too many court cases to think that karma exists—the world is more random and unfair than that—but I don't say this aloud. Instead I remind Donal that Paul saved that woman, which surely cancels out whatever he had owing. Donal doesn't look convinced and I wonder how large Paul's debts are.

He stops talking and we both lie there, staring at the blue sky. A white cockatoo tumbles high above us and Donal falls asleep. He looks so peaceful that I frown at the office workers, even the ones wearing novelty hats, who walk near us as they reluctantly head back to their salt mines in the sky.

Watching him sleep, I think about karma. The problem is that this punishment doesn't just affect Paul. It has hurt his son, brother, family and friends. Even though I only have a walk-on part in the drama, it has left its mark.

Every contact leaves a trace, especially Donal Keenan's lovely warm hands. I gently slip my hand away, guiding his next to his side.

The bag vibrates under my head. My phone has been on silent and there are a million calls from work. A garbled text message comes up on the screen. It is from Tony and includes the word "immediately."

Tony and I sit across from each other in the room with patchwork curtains. Doctors and nurses are rushing about and Donal has been whisked away. I've tried to find out exactly what is happening but because we're not relatives the nurses stonewall us. All, we know is that Paul is in surgery. I try to imagine what it must like for Donal. What if it was Tess being operated on? Perhaps blood ties are like invisible ink. When the situation heats up, suddenly they appear.

"It's been ages," says Tony. My memory of him is of someone strong and silent, but this middle-aged version is much more talkative. He keeps looking at me with anxious gray eyes until I pull out my phone as a shield and text my assistant that I've been delayed.

I ask Tony if he thinks I should leave but the visibly pale look on his face insists the opposite.

"Do you know Paul well?" I ask.

"Years," he answers, eager to talk. "Through Donal actually. I met him travelling in Ireland. Kept in touch on and off. He rang to let me know Paul was coming to Australia, I told him to visit us in Kinsale and Mum offered him a job." His face falls. "God, I've got to ring her and tell her what's happening."

"Maybe wait until we know more."

"I can't believe Luke would do this," he says. "I had just got him some work. Things were looking up."

"What work?"

"Caretaker at The Castle for the developer, to make sure there weren't any squatters while they got their plan through council. His property isn't too far away so it made sense for him to keep an eye on it."

"Isn't your mum running for council now? I saw posters of her."

"She's desperate to be mayor. Been wanting to do it for years, but Dad thought pubs and politics don't mix. But after he died last year, she can do what she wants. Sold The Castle too. You must have heard about that?"

"Sad it's being knocked down."

"Had been running quite a good functions business out of it for a few years but it got ruined in the fire." His hands start to shake, and he notices me noticing, and pushes them hard onto his knees. "There was substantial structural damage."

It seems to me that the fire and the police investigation might have done similar damage to Tony.

"It's for the best then."

"Yeah, I think so. She's using the money to bankroll the town's legal action against the electricity company," he says.

"All by herself?" My conscience takes a direct hit. I have tried hard not to think about how much this action is costing the other side.

"I don't know how she manages it but she does." He hesitates and then to my surprise, he says, "Eliza, you know that New Year's Eve on the beach when we were kids?"

In an instant, old embarrassments are dredged up and my cheeks begin to warm.

"I didn't want to leave, you know. Just I'd promised my dad . . ."

"Forget it," I say. "I was out of line. Too many drinks, I guess."

"No, really." He leans forward, earnestly apologetic, but we are saved by the door opening and then Donal comes in and our words disappear. There are men who cry easily but I don't think they're Irish. I can't even look at his face—the pain is too naked. Instead, my gaze hovers somewhere between his Adam's apple and sternum. He asks me if I want to see Paul.

Forcing air into my vacuum-packed lungs, I walk into the hospital room. It's all too easy to remember the panic of seeing my dad for the first time after his accident but I force myself to concentrate on what's happening now. Paul is lying on the bed. He is still hooked up to beeping machines because most of him is still alive. Apparently he had a seizure, or so I gather from the little Donal says. In time they will know exactly what went wrong but his brain is dead and there is no getting around that. I think of my father in the nursing home who lay in a hospital bed just like this one and whose brain is damaged but still functions just enough. Part of me had wanted the ability to turn him off, to end his suffering. Now I am being forced to see exactly what that means.

Maybe karma does exist, just never in the way you expect it.

A doctor comes in and stands next to Donal, one eye on us, one eye on the machines.

"My mother's not home," Donal says. "They're trying to find her now."

"Take all the time you need," the doctor says. She nods in a kind but professionally detached sort of way and then heads off, leaving us with Paul who is not fully dead but is definitely not alive either.

"They want to know if we will donate his organs," Donal tells me.

There is something so coldly pragmatic about this. It's one thing to tick a box on your license when it's all hypothetical and never going to happen to you. It's quite another when someone is lying in front of you, all ready to be divided along dotted lines like the posters at the butcher.

"I haven't a clue what Paul would want so Mam can decide. She's probably still thinking he's going to be OK, thanking God for sparing him." His voice is bitter. "They asked me if I wanted a priest but I knew he wouldn't. Paul was never a hypocrite."

Donal tells me about the doctors' shopping list: both lungs, two kidneys, and a liver. He makes a small, sad joke about that last one being sub-par because Paul likes a drink, an activity Donal is thinking about in the present tense. The body snatching extends to his pancreas, his heart and an eye. Only one, because they suspect the cornea of the other was damaged in the attack.

This is the moment when my world begins to dissolve.

"Don't start," he says, "or I'll be crying as well and we don't want that."

"He saved her. That woman. He saved her when none of us were brave enough to try. It means something."

"It does," he answers quietly. "It does."

I look back at Paul and imagine the news reports and headlines. They'll call him a saint or an angel, something his brother seems reluctant to do. When I think of Luke Tyrell I turn to ice. He's a murderer now.

Donal gives me his hand to shake as I leave but it reminds me too much of sitting in the park so I hug him instead and his body quivers with a contained sadness. We are interrupted by a nurse, who brings in the green hat and tries to give it back to him.

"I'm afraid we need to clear the family room for someone else," she explains, an apologetic look on her face. "A bad car accident."

Donal holds the hat by the rim and stares at it, then thrusts it at me and asks if I can look after it for a bit. "I can't deal with it right now."

And I think of all the decisions he has made and the ones that he still needs to make and take it.

7

New Year's Eve 1996

Tony

S ay hello to your aunty," Janey called out from the kitchen. Tony stuck his head through the door. His mother was in a better mood now. He had heard her on the phone yelling at someone about a delayed pick-up. Pat Fulton wasn't his real aunty and he didn't know why his mother thought that just because she was best friends with someone, he had to pretend they were family.

"Aunty" Pat sat in the kitchen, having a cup of tea while Janey ironed.

"Here you are," Janey said, pulling a shirt off the board and handing it to him. Tony put it on over his tank top. It rubbed hot against his skin.

"Look at my baby." His mother put a hand up to his cheek, the bangles on her wrist tinkling. She didn't even reach his shoulder now and that was with heels on. "Shaved and everything." He rubbed his face where she had patted him. There was the bump of a pimple on his chin and he hoped it wouldn't erupt tonight.

"Give us a kiss, then," said Pat, beckoning to him from the table. It was the only kiss she was likely to get, thought Tony. Everyone in town knew that Pat was in love with Mick Carmody and that Mick wouldn't know she existed except for the fact she answered his phone and made him cups of tea.

"Anthony's heading to the beach with Mick's youngest tonight," Janey said, as if reading his mind.

"It's not just her," he said quickly. "Plenty of others." Eliza had told him about it when they'd been working at a function out at The Castle and somehow Janey had found out. His mother always found out.

"She was making eyes at him instead of doing her waitressing," she told Pat. "And he's been smiling ever since."

"Boss know?" asked Pat. Pat Fulton was an unsworn civilian—"a bloody filing clerk," his father said, but Tony thought she behaved more like the police than the police themselves, telling everyone what to do all the time, acting like she was the one who kept the station running.

"Better watch yourself," she said, scrutinizing Tony. "Mick would arrest anyone who looked sideways at those girls, especially Tess."

"Spitting image of her mother," said Janey. "I look at Tess and all I can see is Helen. No wonder Mick wants to keep her under lock and key."

Everyone knew Tess was beautiful. She was way out of Tony's league, but he'd heard plenty of boys say what they'd like to do to Tess Carmody and they didn't seem bothered about her father.

"Poor Helen," said Janey. "Breast cancer's a terrible disease."

"I know. Twelve years last March she died," Pat said, like she had been counting the days.

"About time Mick got married again," said Janey, nodding at her friend. "Help him with those girls."

"Poor Eliza," sighed Pat. "Didn't inherit Helen's looks, and then there's her eyes as well."

Eliza might not be as pretty as Tess but Tony thought she was a good laugh and had guts as well, standing up to his father that night when he'd refused to pay her.

"She might not look like Helen but she got her brains," said Janey. "She'll go places that Eliza."

Tony knew that was directed at him. Janey didn't think he was smart enough to inherit the business and was already looking to match him up with someone that could. "Still, don't mention her to your father." She waggled the iron in his direction. "He's still furious about the breakages."

Janey had his life planned out for him as though he had no say in it. He stood there silent, waiting to be dismissed. Talking about it only made the whole thing drag out longer.

"Both lovely girls. Not the type that end up passed out drunk on New Year's Eve," said Pat.

Janey nodded. "You know I had young Dave Deasey from the footy club in here asking for us to donate the drinks for that paddock party. Not even offering to pay for it at cost. I sent him away with a flea in his ear."

"Mick would ban it outright if he could," said Pat.

"You heard anything about it?" Janey asked Tony. Her mouth wrinkled as her arm pushed the iron back and forth. He shook his head slowly just like his father had told him to if his mother started prying. Wes was letting them hold it on their property out of town but his mother still didn't know. When she found out there would be fireworks to rival the ones going off tonight.

"Maybe it's been canceled," his mother said doubtfully. "Anyway, don't worry about checking The Castle tonight. You take the night off and enjoy yourself. Won't be anyone out that way."

Being unofficial night watchman had been his summer job because Wes was worried about all the equipment getting nicked. He'd even given Tony a shotgun to keep up there. "Just shoot it over their heads if there's trouble. That'll scare them off."

"All the money that's been sunk into it," continued his mother. "Pub mortgaged to the hilt and we couldn't even manage a booking for a New Year's Eve party."

"It's those landslides. Coast road was closed this afternoon as well," says Pat.

"Can't blame the weather," said Janey. "It's too far out of town. Everyone knows it other than Wes. He's nearly sent us broke wanting to play Lord of the Manor."

Pat clucked her tongue. "Something will turn up."

"Actually," said Janey, giving her friend a conspiratorial look. "Got a call from the real estate agent before Christmas." The iron started beeping and she deposited it at the end of the board. "Developer's expressing interest."

"What, to knock it down?" asks Pat. "Council will never allow that."

"Word is they want to make a golf course. It could be club headquarters," said Janey. "Trying to tap the Japanese market. Even the council would have to say yes to that."

"Dad wouldn't though," said Tony.

This annoyed Janey who grabbed the next shirt with more force than necessary. "Haven't you got something better to do than eavesdropping on conversations."

Tony bristled. It was hardly eavesdropping when you were told to come into the room. He slouched toward the door.

"And not a word about it to your father," Janey called after him.

When Tony headed out to the truck he found his father loading it up with several large coolers.

"You're taking this out to the paddock party," said Wes. "You'll get a pretty good welcome arriving with this lot. Keg's already there but that won't be enough."

"But I've got other plans," Tony protested.

"That shitty little bonfire your mother's going to? This is the paddock party. It's a rite of passage. I'd still go if I didn't have to be at the pub."

"Some friends are getting together at Crummie's."

His father looked suspiciously at him. "The thing that Carmody girl was talking about when she was supposed to be working." Wes had overheard more than Tony had realized.

"There are other people going," Tony began but Wes wasn't listening.

"Haven't had another booking since that night, thanks to her spilling desserts on paying customers, smashing full dinners on the floor. She's nothing but trouble."

Eliza hadn't been solely responsible for the mess but Wes still liked to blame her.

"Besides you don't want to be hanging with kids. Drive these out and make sure you get them back at the end of the night. Free booze was the arrangement. They're not getting my coolers as well. There's mixers in here." He rapped a knuckle on a lid. "For the *ladies*," and Tony could tell by the emphasis that his father meant the opposite. "Take one of them back to Bayless Manor for the night."

Wes liked to call The Castle this as a joke, except Tony knew it wasn't really one—more a reminder that Wes Bayless was playing Monopoly with the fanciest estate in the Kinsale area. His mother had started referring to him sarcastically as "King Wes" in the pub.

Tony nodded and Wes slapped him on the back and then, with a wink, pulled out a packet of condoms and shoved it into his son's hand. "Don't do anything I wouldn't do," and laughed. Tony tried to laugh in reply.

"And whatever you do, say nothing to your mother. She's a good woman but . . ."

Tony hopped into the truck and started up the engine. When it came to his parents, sometimes it was safer not to open his mouth at all and just let them live his life for him.

Tony put his beer down as fireworks shot up into the air. It was midnight already and he was still here. The night had been a disaster. The girls had got there later than he'd thought they would, Eliza had practically chugged her drinks and when he'd tried to leave, she'd stripped naked. He hadn't known where to look—she was just a kid after all. Before he knew it she was swimming with Luke anyway. Maybe she hadn't been that interested in him.

"Happy New Year," said Gus, but he didn't sound that happy.

Angling his watch toward the fire to read the hands, he could see it was five past midnight. It was at least a thirty-minute drive to The Castle and then up the track to where the party was. It was at the southernmost point of the property, as far away from any building as possible. It would be almost one A.M. by the time he arrived. Hopefully they'd all be too drunk to notice how late he was. He wanted to wait until Eliza and Luke came back out of the water so say goodbye to them, friendly-like, and make sure she was OK. She seemed a nice person, just a bit mixed up. Maybe it was because she didn't have a mother.

That other girl, Amy, kept shooting him dirty looks until Gus said something about nicking Luke's clothes and she darted over to grab Eliza's discarded dress and bikini, before dragging Grace down to the sea. Grace was upset, though Tony wasn't sure why. He stood up, brushing the sand off his jeans, and noticed the light bobbing about. Then the shouting began. All he could see were figures running around in the darkness. Just when he decided he should go see what was happening, Grace suddenly appeared—almost ran into him, in fact—picked up her shoes and then headed off before he could ask what was going on.

Amy came running up. "Why didn't you stop her?"

"What?"

"She can't run off like that by herself." Amy stood there, hands on her hips.

"She already has." Tony picked up his jacket, deciding it really was time to go. These girls were crazy.

"Where are you going?" Amy demanded. "You've got to help look for her."

"This has nothing to do with me," said Tony. "Besides, I'm already late."

"Are you a complete moron?" spluttered Amy. "This has everything to do with you."

"See you," he said to Gus, who had put his arm on Amy's shoulder. She furiously shook it off.

Tony started trudging back along the sand. It was cold away from the fire. The water would be freezing. Behind him, he could hear Gus saying soothing words to Amy, but before he reached the bush, he could hear them shouting out Grace's name again.

As Tony jogged along the track back toward his truck, the packet of condoms rustled in his pocket and he put a hand in to quieten the noise. Seeing Eliza naked had sent out sparks. He'd had sex before but it sort of didn't count. Wes had taken him to the city and told the woman to make a man of his son. It had been messier and wetter than he'd imagined, no kissing involved, because that was the way she did it. He had got dressed quickly afterward, not really knowing what to say. Maybe he should be the son his father expected and take a girl back to The Castle and lie next to her all night long, get to look at her body properly, spend a long time kissing her on the lips, maybe try to do it more than once.

The truck was alone in the parking lot. Turning on the engine, Tony felt hot-wired in a good, confused kind of way. He swung the car around and bounced up the dirt road, taking it carefully because it had been slicked up from all the rain and he didn't want to get bogged. He was halfway along when he glimpsed a girl in the headlights, turning at the sound of the car.

Grace took a step back into the grass to let him pass, shading her eyes to minimize the dazzle. Tony was tempted to keep driving but he couldn't leave her by the side of the road, alone at night. He pulled up and leaned across to open the passenger door because the window was stuck. Grace took a tentative step forward and he could see her thick lashes, slight ski-jump nose, full lips and the cleft in her chin. Little spider webs of fuzz had escaped from the bun on the top of her head. He hadn't paid attention to her before but now he noticed she was pretty.

"Your friends are looking for you," he said. "You should head back."

"No," said Grace, and she leaned into the car, her arms above her head holding onto the frame. Tony noticed a necklace swinging above the high ripe breasts swelling up under her tank top. "I'll hitch up on the highway," she continued.

"Might not get many cars coming through. They've all been diverted because of the landslide."

"Can you give me a lift into town then?"

"I'm heading in the opposite direction."

The necklace was coiled around itself, twisted like the top of old farm fences. He found himself starting at it to counteract the magnetic pull of what lay directly below.

"You're going to the paddock party," Grace said. "How much have you had to drink?"

He blinked and the spell was broken. "I'm OK to drive."

She thought for a moment. "I'll go with you."

Tony wasn't convinced this was a good idea but then the thought of that bossy Amy wasting the night searching for Grace appealed to him.

"You're Aaron's sister, aren't you?" he asked, as Grace clicked on her seat belt. "Will he be there tonight?" Aaron was the local footy legend, the type of son Wes would have loved.

She shook her head. "He's away. I'll know other people there."

The car bumped up the trail, finally reaching the road. Grace wasn't much of a talker so the silence was thick as honey. Tony kept flicking his eyes over at her. She was lovely really, with long legs and smooth skin contrasting with the frayed ends on her denim cut-offs. Seeing Eliza naked was like dominos falling. Now he couldn't help but wonder what Grace would look like without her clothes. He could tell she was nervous around him, sitting as close to the door as she could get, holding onto the door handle. Maybe she was wondering what he would expect in payment for the lift. He'd heard stories like that in the pub. Truck drivers who got hand jobs from hitchhikers. How did they engineer that sort of situation? Flattery, he guessed, but then maybe they just took without asking.

Part of him wanted to ask her if she was all right because she seemed miserable, but he couldn't think of a way to say it without sounding like an idiot, so he asked her if she was doing anything for the summer.

"I'm going to catch a train to the city," she said. "Spend the summer there rather than in this place." Her tone was bitter, caught up with the night's events.

The trees lit up along Old Castle Road, tangled branches overhead, skeletal in the headlights. Ghostly mobs of kangaroos skittered away in the distance. As Grace got out to open the gate Tony looked up at The Castle, dark and black against the sky, outbuildings dotted around it. He drove through the gates then stopped, idling, and watched her lock up the gate in the rearview mirror. He followed the shape of her curves. Her clothes seemed molded to them.

"Does everyone come this way?" she asked, climbing back into the car.

"No," said Tony. "They're coming in from Ophir Road. Dad didn't want anyone near The Castle."

"No offense, but it looks haunted."

"Maybe it's the Nazi ghosts," said Tony.

"Nazis?"

"Yeah. It was a prison camp during World War II for German sailors."

"That can't be right," said Grace.

"No, really. Dad got these old pictures when he bought the place. They fenced it all off and had guards and everything."

"Did the sailors die here?"

"Nope. Went back home after the war."

"Then how would their ghosts be here?"

"They were supposed to have buried treasure and were coming back after the war to get it."

"That's ridiculous," said Grace. "If they were prisoners they would have been searched. Any treasure would be confiscated."

Tony had never thought of that.

"It's just what they say at the pub," he told her. "I don't believe it."

"The whole thing sounds made up," said Grace. She went back to looking out the window as he edged slowly around the back of The Castle to the dirt parking lot. As he turned the corner, he saw two circles of light ahead in the distance, then they vanished.

"What was that?" he said.

"What?"

He pulled the car up. "There were lights."

"Maybe it's the ghosts," said Grace.

But Tony had definitely seen something. He thought of the shotgun at The Castle and what his father had told him to do.

"No, someone's there," and he opened up his door.

8

"ou seem to be visiting Kinsale pretty regularly these days," my sister
says, giving me a cool stare.

Tess inherited my mother's luminous cornflower blue eyes, along
with long lashes, a narrow face, a kissable mouth and dark curls. She looks
like one of those old-style matinee heroines—looks that make me want
to tie her to the railway tracks and make men, like her husband, want to
rescue her.

She pours the tea and passes me a cup.

"I'm only here for the memorial," I say. "I'll head back tomorrow."

After Tony Bayless texted me the details I had caught the coastal train in
the dark that morning. The draft expert report had finally arrived late the
night before and I spent my time reading about Aeolian vibrations, ignition
temperatures, low voltage conductors and aging electricity assets. By the
time I arrived in Kinsale it was clear that Colcart's lack of maintenance of
its power poles was a significant factor in starting the fire and the smart
thing would be to settle the case.

Gavin had insisted I visit him at home so he could take my witness statement without the entire town knowing, but only Tess was home when I arrived.

"I'm staying with Amy," I reassure her.

"You could have slept here," she says, her tone indifferent. "This is still your home."

But we both know that isn't true and hasn't been for years. I was the one my father sent away, Tess was the one he kept. A memory suddenly appears of homesick me, crying on the boarding school pay phone, begging him to let me come back to Kinsale. Dad had listened until my words ran out and then told me that I needed to make the best of it, that I didn't know how lucky I was. I still find it hard to forgive him.

"Where's Gavin?' I ask.

"He's at The Castle," Tess says. "They were searching up there for Luke Tyrell."

"Tony told me he'd been the caretaker. Have the police got him?"

"No, but apparently they found some bones."

"What sort of bones?"

"It will be an animal. Easy to mistake sheep ribs for human. Happens at least a couple of times a year."

I nod and sip the tea.

"I thought you would be too busy with work to be taking days off," says Tess. She folds her arms. There is an undercurrent of hostility to her words but that isn't new. Our conversations are always littered with landmines. "The rumor is you're defending the heartless bastards who just about burned this town to the ground."

The words carve the air between us, dividing Tess, the perfect sister who always does the right thing, from me, who is always in the wrong.

I take a breath before responding. "Is that public knowledge?"

"I haven't told anyone." She watches me as she brings the cup to her lips.

"How did you find out?"

"Gavin heard it from a police prosecutor in the city. How could you work for them?"

There are responses to this: that our entire justice system, the same system that employed Gavin, Dad and the gossiping police prosecutor, is based on everyone being entitled to legal representation; would she prefer to have a lawyer working for them who cares nothing about Kinsale and plays to win at all cost? But it doesn't matter, Tess never listens to me, so I just bottle it up and look around the room.

The living room is less cluttered then I remember from my sporadic visits over the years. Dad's old chair, where he used to sit at night and work, is missing. The golf clubs that he kept in the corner for years but never used are gone.

"I've put them in his study," she says, when I ask. "Everything needed a proper cleaning." She wrinkles her nose. "I doubt that had really happened since I left town."

Gavin was a constable when Tess married him and they had stayed for a few years in Kinsale before traveling out west to one-man police stations, Gavin searching for promotions. Smaller towns were traded for larger ones until eventually the circle was complete and he inherited the job of Senior Sergeant of Kinsale after Dad's accident, the Brotherhood paying their respects to my family.

"I got rid of a dumpster's worth of garbage from the shed alone," Tess continues. "And," a dramatic pause, like she's gearing up for a big reveal, "I've put the Mustang up for sale."

"You can't!"

"It's just rusting away in the garage," she says. "Dad would want it to be driven."

This is a complete lie and we both know it. My father would prefer to be buried in that car than sell it.

"But you could drive it," I say. "Or Gavin. It would only need a run every fortnight or so."

"I'm not getting in that *thing*." Tess practically spits out the words.

"What's the problem? Is it because you hit that kangaroo?"

The teacup almost slips from her hands, spilling tea in the process.

"You smashed that headlight and did panel damage. Remember?"

Red blotches of anger crawl up her neck, a warning sign.

"You always get things wrong," she says. "I never hit a kangaroo in my life."

I change tack. "But Dad loves that Mustang. You know he does."

"It's time for a change," she says, getting up and walking away.

Stung, I say, "Have you changed your bedroom yet? Or is it still a shrine to Tess Carmody's teenage years?"

I can tell by her face that it remains perfectly preserved.

The minute I was packed off to boarding school, my bedroom was converted to a study for Dad, the one where Tess is piling up all his belongings like it's a junk room. I came home those first holidays to find everything I owned in cardboard boxes shoved in the wardrobe, a not-so-subtle reminder that I wasn't welcome back. Tess's room is still exactly the same. The furniture, the pink walls, the rock star posters and frilly valances, all unchanged while she takes a wrecking ball to my father's belongings in his own house. It is so typical of Tess, finally having to look after someone other than herself and resenting it, despite a lifetime of being cosseted by my father.

"That's completely hypocritical," I tell her.

Her face is bright red now. Three steps toward me and then slap. I hear the whoosh of her hand, the crack on my cheek. It's not particularly hard, mistimed in fact, due to her impatience. She stands there, her arm still raised, as though she's in two minds about whether to give it another shot.

White-hot anger surges up in me.

"Why stop at a hand," I say. "Get a stick so you can damage the other eye."

Clenching my teeth so that more words don't come out, I mechanically take my handbag off the back of the chair and stand up. The chair makes a rasping squeak of protest against the floorboards. The room is so quiet that I can almost hear the thoughts whirring around my sister's head, and not one of them sounds like an apology, because in her mind she is always the injured person. She has never had to say sorry to anyone.

Unsure what to do, I go to the bathroom. Looking at my reflection, there is no great big accusatory welt on my cheek, only a slight pinkish blush to my ear. Somehow that feels even more humiliating, as though I'm getting upset over nothing. She probably expects me to leave, so I decide to stay and wait for Gavin. Part of me wants to tell on her, as if Gavin is proxy for my father.

When I come out of the bathroom my sister is making an implausible amount of noise in the kitchen to telegraph where she is, the smell of bacon in the air. I push open the back door with force and it bounces off the weatherboards, just like it always does. Sitting down on the lower back step, the concrete is lukewarm from an indifferent sun. Autumn has arrived.

This was my favorite spot when I lived here: not quite the garden, not quite the house, the doorway between two different worlds. I was the odd-eyed queen of the step, sitting there, sometimes trying to patch together faded memories of my mother (the feel of her holding my hand, the smell of her) while I watched my father tinker with his car in the driveway in front of the shed. Occasionally at night he would sit with me until mosquitoes forced us inside. The garden is overgrown now, but then Dad was never much of a gardener. Apparently, that was more Mum. He preferred to spend his spare time in the shed. You needed a personal invitation to enter, partly because that's where he kept the ammunition for his service pistol but mostly because he just needed a space for himself and his Mustang, the car that Tess now denies crashing.

That's the thing about being the youngest member of the family: you are always being told you've got things wrong, it didn't happen that way, you were at boarding school, you weren't there. It's the eldest's version of events that is believed. Stubbornly, I push at my memory of the accident like it's a wobbly tooth to see if I can remember something Tess can't deny.

There was a smashed headlight and ripples in the front panel, all surface damage, but Dad looked at it like it was fatal. He had yelled at me to get out, which was a shock because he was such a quiet man.

The younger version of me idolized my father and followed him everywhere. He told me he would lock up all the bad guys, keep us safe and I believed him. I loved him more than anyone else in the world. It was easier to then.

The door swings open and Gavin, in dark blue uniform, all brass and sharp edges, comes out with a plate of eggs and bacon in his hands. He sits down on the step behind me. A large man, he takes up most of the available space.

"How are the sheep bones?" I ask him.

"You a forensic expert now?" he says.

"What, human?"

"I can't tell you," he says, and the fact he's not saying means they probably are. I know how cops work.

"Tess mentioned . . ." he begins.

"It wasn't my fault," I interrupt. "She was the one doing the hitting."

There are deep shadows under Gavin's eyes, inherited from my father, along with the job.

"She shouldn't have done that," he says. "But can you give her a break? Being back in Kinsale has been more difficult than I thought it would be."

"What's so hard about being back here?"

He pauses before answering, wolfing down his breakfast with the practiced ease of someone who has most meals interrupted by work. "I guess it's because nothing is quite the same and yet everything is."

Somehow this captures exactly how I'm feeling but I'm still too angry at Tess to be sympathetic.

"So, what's with the . . . ?" I point to the moustache, which has only become furrier.

"Trying to get into Pat's good books," he says. "She hasn't forgiven me for not being Mick. It's a fund-raiser for our domestic violence initiative. The idea is to raise money growing it, and then raise even more when you look so ridiculous that your family sponsors you to get rid of it."

"It's like your upper lip has gone moldy."

"Put your money where your mouth is then."

"Twenty dollars."

He waves it away. "Anyway, your statement. The charges will be upgraded now Paul's died, and there's a lot of political pressure being brought. We need to do this by the book."

"Have you found Luke yet?"

"A couple of possible sightings yesterday. We're bringing in the dogs again tomorrow."

"How dangerous is he?" I ask. "Should I be worried?"

Gavin shrugs. "Look, Luke's got a temper but that Paul Keenan was no choirboy. Hadn't been here long but he was already attracting our interest. Luke was knocked around by the bushfires, of course, and now he'll be desperate. All this media attention isn't helping."

That doesn't sound exactly like a no. I sit there feeling queasy at the thought of giving evidence. Part of the attraction of being a lawyer is you get to be the one asking questions, not the person being badgered to answer.

"You'll be all right," says Gavin. "We've kept your name confidential. That's why I'm keeping you away from the station. Just a precaution, you understand. You've got more to worry about if the town hears what you're currently working on. There would be some who'd string you up."

Feeling worse, I stare out at the garden. Discarded lemons rot in the long grass under the shade of the large tree. Possums, whose interest is only skin-deep, like the tangy acid of the peel and gnaw them off the branches.

"Garden needs a bit of work," I say, just to change the subject.

"Well, Mick was never much of a gardener," he says. "Remember Alan Sharp?"

"Red-haired cop who worked with Dad?"

"Less hair on top these days. Started a mowing business after he left the force. Mick used to get him in every month or so, but he charged well over the odds. One of the first things Tess did was sack him."

"Dad was probably helping him out."

"Mick was always an old softie," Gavin agrees. "Some ties he just wouldn't let go of."

"You know you're talking about Dad in the past tense."

Gavin blinks like he's surprised and then looks down, a sad half-smile on his face. "Well, it shouldn't be long."

"Is that what the doctors say?"

"They've been predicting his death ever since the accident. Stubborn bugger, he's still holding on. He was always like that at work too. Never gave up until he was satisfied everything had been done."

That reminds me about Grace's file being in Dad's car. "At the hospital the night of his accident," I say. "You said he had two files in the car, Grace Hedland's and another."

Gavin gives me a long hard look and then shakes his head slowly. "I shouldn't have said anything. Must have been the shock talking."

He turns away, picks up his plate.

"What was the other file?"

"Those files are confidential, just like the names of witnesses," he says, mopping up the remaining egg yolk with his bread. "Let's head inside to get this statement done and then I can drive you to the memorial."

Standing up, I look at the shed and something clicks. "No need," I tell him. "I'm going to take the Mustang." It is as much a surprise to myself as it is Gavin.

"It will cost you a fortune and it's not suited to city traffic."

I had only meant to drive to the memorial but why not. I haven't owned a car in years—with public transport and Uber there seemed little point. But my apartment has a designated car spot and it will definitely annoy Tess, which is an added bonus.

"I'll drive it home."

"Hope it makes it," says Gavin.

He stands up, balancing his plate in one hand.

"A hundred bucks," I tell him, "if you shave it off now."

"Done," he says.

9

Slamming both feet on the brake, my hands are white-knuckled around the steering wheel. There is a deep growl of protest from the engine as I lurch into the church parking lot, picking the easiest spot I can find.

"Well, look who's here," says a loud voice, as I step out of the car.

Janey Bayless stands there. With her red-lipsticked mouth and diamante earrings there's nothing drab about her, despite being dressed head to toe in black. The platinum hair is the same shade as twenty years ago. Her curves are now more globe than hourglass but otherwise she's the same.

"Eliza Carmody, as I live and breathe," she exclaims, her perfume enveloping me like a hug. Tony stands behind her.

"So good to see you. If only it was for a happier occasion," Janey says, and then turns to her son, "Tony love, I left my sunglasses in the car. Could you grab them?" She hands over a set of keys. "I always cry at funerals," she tells me. "Can't think a memorial will be different."

Tony, grim faced, immediately sets off through the lot but stops only a couple of cars away to shake hands with another arrival.

"This has knocked us all about," Janey says, "especially Tony. He told me you were a comfort in the hospital." She pats my arm, her rings rubbing against my skin. "Last thing Kinsale needs as well. We'll be lucky if we see another tourist this side of Christmas."

"But you must be busy. I saw your posters in town."

She gives me a mischievous grin. "Got a banner as well, the type you tow around on the back of a trailer. My face is six foot tall on it. Mayor Janey Bayless. I reckon it's got a nice ring to it. If I get in I'll be the first woman mayor."

"Good for you."

"I knew a professional lady like yourself would be supportive. Did Tony tell you that we're involved in a legal case as well?"

My heart begins to hummingbird flutter.

"One of the biggest class actions in the state and there's me being the public face of it. At the start I wasn't sure, but you've got to stand up for what's right, don't you? I mean the way Tony got treated by those Arson Squad Detectives, dragging him in for interview after interview. Still, what's done is done. Kinsale has got to pull itself up because no one's going to do that for us."

Tony returns and hands his mother her glasses.

"Have you seen how many reporters are here?" he says. "They shouldn't be at a memorial." He nods in the direction of a tight knot of people standing near the porch of the church.

"Journalists?" I turn my head in that direction.

"Have they no respect for people's privacy?" asks Tony.

Janey pulls out her phone and then turns on the camera, flipping the view to check her makeup. She wipes away excess lipstick with her pinky finger. People around us begin to move herd-like toward the entrance.

"Time to go in," Janey says.

A journalist calls out something to her as we pass. I hear the word "bones."

"Where are your manners?" Janey calls back. "It's a memorial, for goodness' sake."

Janey and Tony go up the front as they are family friends. I find Amy and Gus sitting about a third of the way from the back and slip in beside them.

I've always loved the simplicity of this building. Anonymous from the outside, the wooden interior is peaceful and the crowd hushes automatically as they enter. Sun streams in through long windows and makes what would otherwise look plain and sparse beautiful. This is the church I was baptized in, where my sister was married, and where my mother's funeral was held, not that I can remember it. When the time comes, this is the place we will say goodbye to my father.

A row of girls from my old school stand at the back next to the electric organ, dressed in my old uniform, thick rough woolen blazers with pinafores of maroon and blue squares that at a distance blend into sullen gray. A girl with two long plaits stands at the front of the group. It's the girl who walked out of the pharmacy with the boy in a hoodie, the day Luke attacked Paul.

I nudge Amy. "Who's that?"

Amy cranes her neck. "Kayla Deasey. Dave's daughter."

"Not Crazy Dave we went to school with?"

Dave Deasey was a few years older than us and spent so much time sitting outside the principal's office, I'm a bit surprised he's not still there.

Amy nudges me. "There he is." Dave stands up the back, tall and lanky, dressed in clean slacks and an open collared shirt—formal wear for farmers. I look from him to his daughter and see the same thin face and long nose. Dave catches my eye and raises his hand. Amy notices. "He's single, if you're interested." I roll my eyes at her.

My sister and Gavin, now minus his moustache, walk past me and, after a momentary hesitation, sit on the other side a couple of rows from the front. There is only one other occupant and although the church is now packed, people seem reluctant to join her. A large woman, she sits there praying, her head bowed and face hidden.

A priest I don't know begins and the refrains and responses dredge up of their own accord. Automatic *amen*s and *also with you*'s slip into place. The words are so familiar that if I shut my eyes I could be back at school mass, sitting between Amy and Grace, trying to swallow down snorts of teenage laughter. Instead, I keep them open and am comforted by the order after the chaos of the last week. I don't believe in God but being in this church with people who do is reassuring and right now that is enough.

Memories float into my mind like sunlight on water as faces in the crowd slowly come into focus. Family groups with additional members attached and some with gaps where others used to be. It is an exaggeration to say everyone in town is here, but the place is so full, it feels like that. Country towns do funerals best of all, being practiced in tragedy. The farm accidents. The car crashes. The suicides dressed up as farm accidents and car crashes. Businesses shut down, the local school choir turns up, people take the time to pay their respects. Suddenly and perhaps irrationally, I feel something close to love for Kinsale.

The priest starts talking about Paul and his words are greeted with nods of approval. He gestures to the front row when he mentions Paul's family and through the crowd I see Tony's head in profile, half-turning as he places a hand on the person beside him. It is Donal.

Surprised, I almost will him to feel my gaze and turn around, but everyone in this place is probably looking at him; another pair of eyes adds no weight. The priest continues to talk about all those devastated by the attack and this time he stretches out an arm toward where Tess and Gavin are sitting. There is a ripple through the congregation, a gravitational pull of interest as heads turn toward the woman sitting next to them. Amy moves uneasily in her seat and faces around me are rigid with disapproval. The woman is kneeling, her body a tight bundle. She turns slightly and I realize that it's Luke's mother.

There is a pause in the words from the pulpit and from somewhere behind us comes a shout.

"Where is he, Cadee? Where's that bastard son of yours hiding?"

It's a blustering man at the back of the church. Another person comes out of the distant past. Less hair and a beard covers the lower half of his face, but he's an easy pick. Former constable, and now man with a mower, Alan Sharp sways on his feet. He could be drunk.

"Shame," comes another voice, and there are murmurs. As the sound swells, to my surprise it becomes clear they are actually agreeing with what Alan Sharp has said. The sentiment is taken up and amplified. Outrage is contagious. A young woman with thick-framed glasses and mermaid blue hair in the row across from me pulls out her phone and types something into it.

The priest seems at a loss and gapes. Slowly, Gavin gets to his feet, walks along the pew and stands in the aisle, staring down the malcontents. The room shuffles back into silence but Alan doesn't move, his face ablaze.

"What are you going to do?" he snarls at Gavin. "Arrest me?"

"You're in church," Gavin answers, his face stony. "Show some respect."

It's like two gunslingers facing off, a battle of wills, and it's Alan who is first to turn away. The congregation is so quiet that we hear his footsteps clatter on the floor as he walks through the doors. Next to me, Amy audibly breathes out, and Gus drops his arm which he had protectively put around her shoulders. At the front of the church, Donal hasn't moved.

The priest, clearly not used to heckling, tries to regain control but fumbles his words until finally returning to "Let us pray," which seems ambitious given so many in here want to throw stones.

After the service the three of us sit there waiting for the crowds to move. Donal disappears behind a wall of well-wishers so I give up on trying to talk to him.

"What was that about?" I ask.

Amy shakes her head. "Sometimes I think this entire town has PTSD."

"You all right?" I ask.

She sighs. "I'm fine. Better head back to the hospital."

"C'mon, Amy," Gus protests. "Let's go have a drink at The Royal. Most of the town will be heading there anyway."

She shakes her head. "I can't leave Dad to see all the patients."

The three of us walk out and I head back to the Mustang, unsure what I'm going to do. I don't think I want to go to the pub in case the conversation is all about the aftermath of the bushfire, and the court case. Twirling the keys on my fingers, I think about my father all alone in his drab little room and how much he loved this car. Maybe I should do the right thing and go visit him.

Crazy Dave Deasey lopes across to me and for a split second I'm worried that Amy's had a word to him and he wants to ask me out. I quickly turn and unlock the car.

"Hey, Odd Eyes, Odd Eyes Carmody, wait up." It's a reminder of the schoolyard and one that still makes me wish colored contact lenses had been around in my teenage years.

"Oh, Dave, how are you?"

He's tanned, tall and junkie-thin. His hair is pulled back into a ratty ponytail and the shirt he is wearing exposes the paleness of his chest below the T-shirt tan line. The overall effect makes him look vulnerable, like a snail out of its shell.

"Good, good. This your dad's old car?" He raps his knuckles hard on the roof in a way that would make my father want to arrest him.

"Mine now, actually," I say.

"Nice." He runs a finger along one sharp cheekbone. "Saw you in the church before."

"That's right."

Dave shuffles from one foot to the other looking shifty. "Got thinking about your dad and how you're related to Gavin and wondered if you could do us a favor."

I hesitate before answering as old memories of Dave's harebrained schemes at school come rushing back.

"Like what?"

"Believe me, I've got no problem with Gavin, not like Sharpy, but he doesn't understand the town like Mick did. I mean he's only been back here five minutes."

"He's lived here before," I say. Dave looks unconvinced.

"Anyway," he says, "there are these bones up at The Castle."

"The ones the police found?"

"Well, that's the thing." A slow grin creeps over his face. "I kind of found them first."

"What?"

"I was there digging around when I found the skull."

"What sort of skull?"

"A human one." Dave nods. "I didn't think anything of it. Reckoned it was so old it wasn't worth going to the cops about it. Just left it lying there."

"You did what?"

"I mean everyone knows there are bodies up there."

"Whose bodies?"

Dave makes a wide-open gesture with his hands. "Who knows? Just bodies. Old ones. And now the cops have found it and all those journalists back at the church were talking about it. You know someone on the Facebook was saying Luke Tyrell might have killed someone else and buried them up there."

"Luke's a serial killer now, is he?"

Dave's stories were always about as tall as he is.

"That's what people are saying." Dave is starting to get defensive.

"What do you mean by bodies, plural?" I ask. "Was there more than one skull?"

"Could be," he says. "I didn't dig any further, didn't seem right."

"Why were you digging up there anyway?"

Dave drops his head, a slight red glow making its way through his tan. "Just doing a bit of metal detecting." His tone is even more defensive now.

"Metal detecting at The Castle?" Despite the seriousness of what he's said, I almost want to laugh, because old stories are coming back to me. "Tell me you weren't looking for the legendary Nazi buried treasure?"

"No, of course not," he answers too quickly, but he can't look me in the eye and instead gazes out over the cars in the opposite direction.

"What has any of this got to do with me?"

"It's a bit awkward, but before I found that skull, I found something else. I was going to give it to my daughter, Kayla, so I cleaned it up a bit, but now the police are investigating, I don't want any trouble."

"Give it to them then."

"And have Gavin charge me with theft or interfering with police investigations? Besides, I'm bidding to do the demolition work on The Castle. Those developers hear about this, I've got no chance. I was planning on dropping it off anonymously but you can't do anything in this town anonymously. So when I saw you today, I thought—you're a lawyer, I'll just give it to you. Won't be strange you seeing him, he's your brother-in-law. Tell him it's from the site. Just don't say I found it. Say you are working on behalf of a client."

It was this sort of reasoning that saw Dave spend most of high school in detention.

"You aren't my client."

"You don't live here anymore, Eliza. What happens in Kinsale doesn't affect you."

Dave fishes a clear plastic ziplock bag out of his pocket and hands it to me. There's an envelope inside.

"I used gloves so there's no fingerprints."

I'm about to tell him how idiotic he's being when Dave looks behind me, sticks out his hand and says in a loud voice, "Sorry for your loss. Paul was a good bloke."

"Thanks," says Donal.

"Best be going," says Dave.

"Hang on," I say, but he thrusts the plastic bag into my hands and strides back across the parking lot.

"Did I interrupt something?" Donal asks, but the sight of him chases all concerns about Dave from my mind.

"Nothing important." I slip the ziplock bag into my handbag. "I'm really sorry . . ." but he jumps in.

"Please God, no, not sorry. I don't think I could take another sorry."

We stand there looking at each other. Donal is more fragile with hollowed cheeks and a lined face. The impact of the last few days is coming to the surface. I imagine him at The Royal having to eat the neatly cut sandwiches garnished with parsley, listening to the cover band that's spent the morning practicing "Danny Boy" and "When Irish Eyes are Smiling" as he fends off all the well-wishers.

"Would you like to go for a drive?" I say to him.

He looks at the car and then back at me.

"I thought you'd never ask."

10

pop the trunk when we get to the beach, hoping to find a convenient towel, but instead there's a neat bundle of old documents tied up with a piece of string that resembles a brief to counsel. At first I think these could be more of Dad's work files but they turn out to be related to the car. Some service documents, registration and other bits and pieces.

Following Donal toward the waves, I take my shoes off at the bottom of the wooden steps. Further out, the surf is pounding under a washed-out sky and pale autumn sun. The beach isn't at its prettiest with seaweed tracing the high-water mark. Donal collapses onto the sand, damp with coldness, and I sit next to him.

"Paul hated the feeling of sand on his feet," he says. "When we were little he'd wear his socks on the beach. Didn't care that everyone laughed at him."

"How did he end up here?" I ask. "The beach is the best thing about Kinsale."

Donal shrugs. "He said it reminded him of home."

We watch the waves come and go. Seagulls gather at the water's edge, black-tipped wings and button eyes.

"He liked your birds, though," Donal says. "Kept sending pictures of parrots to our mother. You know, the wee red and blue fellas that look like they've been painted by a four-year-old."

"Rosellas."

"Mad about birds, she is. Forever stopping the car because there's an eagle in the sky."

"Did she agree to the transplants?"

He tenses. I can see it in his clenched jaw, the tendons in his neck.

"She decided there on the spot the moment I told her, didn't even hesitate. She told me that there's always a rainbow in a raven's wing. So they went ahead and now I get to take what's left back home to her." Donal doesn't look at me but instead stares straight out to sea.

I wait a long time before asking if they were successful.

"Don't know. Maybe it's too soon to tell."

He presses tight fists into the sand. Words seem inadequate so instead I reach across and press down on the hand nearest, slowly smoothing it out with my fingers, like uncrumpling paper. He turns his palm upward and locks mine in a tight grip.

"What was happening back there in the church?" he asks. "That policeman saved the day—fair play to him."

"It reminded me of what Paul did. Standing up when everyone else stays sitting."

"Paul the same as a cop? Now, that would be funny," but his mouth twists like it's not. "You're getting cold," he says. "Let's walk."

We head down to the water's edge where the sand has a firmer crust and follow the tidal marks, creased like palm lines. The wind starts up and it becomes hard to hear each other so, for the most part, we don't say anything, caught up in our own thoughts as we plod out the length of the beach.

I used to walk here with Amy most days after school and watch Grace train. She was the school champion for middle-distance running. Some days we tried to keep up with her but she was effortless, gliding ahead without a look backwards, leaving us red-faced and gasping in her wake. We'd head off to get hot chips wrapped in white greasy paper and sit up on the picnic table waiting for her to finish. Until that one day when she kept running and never came back.

I shake the thought away and concentrate on Donal in front of me. He's a fast walker, a greyhound of a man. Thin and wiry, there's a race to him. All at once the sun gets stronger, sunlight dances on golden waves and his hair warms red as he marches in long strides to the end. I have to walk-skip to try and keep up with him.

Surfers in wetsuits are paddling, patiently waiting for perfection as Donal picks his way through the first lot of black honeycombed rocks. Looking out to sea, I gauge how much time we've got before the tide comes in. He turns back to me, well before the point. "This . . . good," he shouts, the wind playing catch and fetch with his words. I scramble out toward him.

"Everyone's been so kind but I just want to yell at them to stop," he says.

"You've got every reason to yell," I say. "So do it."

"What?"

"When I was a teenager, I used to come down here with my friends and do just that."

The three of us, arms linked, united, pitting ourselves against the world. Shouting at the sea while we waited for this boring teenage life to end, the eternal twilight between child and adult, and something far more exciting to begin.

"You're kidding," says Donal.

"I'll yell too if that helps."

And so we do. Hand in hand. It isn't even words, just a sound that is swallowed up by the waves and sucked away with the wind. The two of us shout until we can't anymore. Surfers in the distance sit on their boards with amazed faces.

Another gust and my view of the world becomes tangled up in hair. Donal reaches forward and pushes it out of my eyes. There is a pulse of connection, and all of a sudden we are so close that the warmth of his breath mingles with the brine of the breeze. Our foreheads touch. When I finally kiss him, desire floods through me.

We park the car in a deserted picnic spot off Beach Road. Donal's jeans are around his ankles and my skirt is waist height. It's no-frills frenetic fucking sandwiched between the glove box and the gearstick. There are no preliminaries. We start fast and get faster. I bend over him to keep from hitting my head on the roof, bracing myself on the back of his headrest, praying our efforts don't crack the seat frame. His hands try all sorts of ways to liberate my breasts but in the end, defeated, he holds onto my hips instead and grinds. Sand finds its way into all sorts of crevices. We finish open-mouthed, shallow breathing, pulse racing, in disarray.

When Donal opens the passenger door I almost tumble out, suddenly self-conscious among the towering gums. He lounges there a little longer, unabashed, clearly more comfortable with semi-public nudity than me.

I peer into the back seat for my underwear. Eventually Donal finds them wedged down between the seats and hands them to me.

"Damp," he says, grinning broadly, an unnoticed dimple appearing in his right cheek. "Memorials must really do it for you."

"This will be a town scandal if they find out." I'm only partly joking and almost over-balance in my haste to pull my underwear on. He gets back into his trousers leisurely. I think he's enjoying my embarrassment.

"If Paul was here, he'd buy me a drink and ask how I managed to get the best-looking woman in the church," he says, which only means Donal hadn't noticed Tess. He gets out of the car, puts his arms around my waist and pulls me close. With my shoes on, and him barefoot, we are the same height, eyes level.

"We really should be getting to The Royal. They'll be expecting you."

"Fuck the pub," he says. "Let's do it again but in a bed so I can look at you properly."

Donal is staying at the Ocean Breeze Motel, the cheapest one in town. I park the Mustang between the two half-tires stuck in the ground that mark out his allocated parking spot.

"How did you end up here?" I ask, as he fumbles with a key.

"Janey and Tony were insisting I stay with them, which was kind but I just needed somewhere a bit away from it all, so I picked this one. Liked the name as well."

The name is designed to fool the gullible traveler; the motel is nearer the highway out of Kinsale than the beach.

"It's not much," he says, "but sure, I've been in worse." He gives me a wink, and it's the same cheeky kind that his brother gave me that day in traffic.

A double bed with thin sheets and an orange checked blanket takes up most of the space. Next to it is a set of drawers with a laminate top, clock radio, kettle and toaster sitting on top. There are several suitcases on the floor and a large duffel bag.

"This all yours?" I ask.

"Mostly Paul's," he says, and the joking immediately stops. "Tony had locked up Paul's room and wouldn't let anyone in there, not even Janey who was desperate to clean it before I arrived. He thought I'd want to see it as Paul had left it. I cleared everything out yesterday and brought it back here."

His voice is suddenly gruff, a tone I haven't heard before.

"I might take a shower," I say.

"Sure." He stands there, arms folded, staring at his brother's belongings.

The shower gushes cold and hot at unpredictable intervals as I start washing away the sand. I stay under the water for a long time, wanting to give Donal a moment to himself. I'm not sure what happens now. Do I get dressed and leave? Maybe that would be for the best. Perhaps this was just a one-off, funeral-shag kind of thing, a chance to push away his grief for a few physical minutes. He might be regretting the entire thing. I'm about to get out and dry myself, when a blurred version of Donal is suddenly there.

"Not too late?" he asks.

I put my hands out to him and we are kissing before he even finishes stripping. His tongue finds my lips and presses inside, hard and fast, before tracing a path down my neck, stopping to kiss where it meets the curve of my jaw. His hands outline my breasts, cupping them, feeling their weight before reaching further down, while his mouth dances to the edge of my collarbone. He's a person who likes to explore the in-between places. With my arms around his neck, my back against the tiles, I hook a leg around his hip and his fingers slide slickly inside. I begin to jolt against him, gasping as tension builds. When my release comes, his mouth is on mine, breathing in my desire.

"What about you?" I ask, as we remain tangled up with each other.

"To be honest, I've been trying but the angle's murder," he says. "Do you think we could get horizontal for once?"

Dripping, we lie towels down on the bed for the finish. Then, after a sufficient break, we do it again but much more slowly. "For good luck," Donal tells me. Time stretches, hours pass and the sunlight is fading when slowly we break apart.

I roll over onto my front and lie cheek down on the pillow, with Donal beside me. He has hidden away Paul's belongings as though trying to claim the room for just us.

"Do you often go home with strange men from funerals?" he asks.

I pull myself up sphinxlike to get a better look at his face.

"No, but Kinsale brings out the reckless teenager in me."

He gives a crooked smile.

"And what does your father say about that?"

"My father?"

"Tony told me he's a policeman." There's something in his voice that has an edge to it. I've heard that tone before, especially at university, where students from safe middle-class homes would talk about deaths in custody, police violence, harassment and corruption.

"Just so you know, my brother-in-law is as well. That was him in the church today making sure it didn't turn into a fight." I try to say this lightly but want to make a point.

"Sorry," Donal says. "That came out wrong." There is a pulse at his temple and he looks at me with haggard eyes. He's exhausted. Putting out a hand to hold mine, "I'm really sorry," he says again.

"Dad isn't a policeman anymore. There was a car accident last year. He's in a vegetative state."

"Jesus," Donal says. "Tony didn't say anything about that."

I wonder why Tony felt the need to mention it at all.

"Look," he says. "I have to ask, do you know the fella who attacked Paul?"

It is tempting to say that Luke was a complete stranger. As if sensing my reluctance, Donal says, "I'm from a small town as well, Eliza. I understand how they work. You have to know him, right?"

"It was a long time ago."

A soft sigh escapes Donal. "So, what's he like?"

It is too hard to look at his face because I don't know what he wants to hear.

"When I knew him, he was stupid, senseless, reckless, funny and kind, just like the rest of us."

In my peripheral vision Donal shakes his head.

"I could be wrong. Maybe he was always bad, just I never saw it."

"Was he involved with drugs?" It's a simple question, though surprising, and yet it seems that Donal is asking something more complicated.

"I don't know."

Donal lets go of my hand and rubs his face. He takes a deep breath.

"Last year outside our local pub, a lad was beaten up. He'd been selling in the wrong spot, on someone else's turf. No-one saw anything, of course, it's that sort of town, but it was Paul who came home that night with bloodied knuckles."

I lie down with my head at his feet, trying to give him the space to talk.

"I knew and Mam knew, and we said nothing. No thought of going to the police, because you protect your own, right? But we also knew this wouldn't be the end of it, so Mam thought maybe he could take a trip. She remembered Tony was out here and that he could help Paul find work. Give him time to sort himself out, send money home for Harry. Let this blow over because it wasn't his fault, it was the downturn and no work, the crowd he ran with, breaking up with his missus. It was everyone else's fault because he was a nice guy too.

"Paul being Paul turned it into a jaunt around the world, like the whole thing was a bit of a lark. That's when I got angry and there were words. I told him he needed to shape up. He had plenty of words for me as well." He stops and gives a half-chuckle, but it's laced with regret.

"I wasn't even planning to go to his going-away drinks but Mam got upset so I took that stupid hat for him because he always liked to fool about. It was supposed to mean even after all he put us through he was still my brother. That I knew the real him. The one who didn't mean to beat someone half to death.

"Then the whole way over on the plane, I kept thinking that getting punched is his punishment, that he'll end up brain-damaged like that lad he hit. And then, when I go into his room, I find this." Donal leans over and pulls out the duffel bag from under the bed. He unzips it. There are neat bundles of hundreds in there, thousands of dollars.

My voice is more of a gasp than an actual question but I manage to ask how much is in there.

"Over fifteen thousand. Paul spent every penny he had on his round the world tour. He arrived in this country six months ago, completely broke. And I had to stand there today, acting like I was proud of him, like he was a hero, when I know what our town will be thinking: Paul Keenan was trouble and he got what was coming to him."

He sighs, a deep tearing sigh, as though his heart has been ripped in two.

"What if the punch wasn't about that woman in her car? What if it was something else altogether?"

11

Tony pulls up outside early to drive Donal back to the city to catch his plane. As he waits in the car, Donal and I sit on the bed with the bag full of money between us.

"Do you think Tony knows about this?" I ask. "That's why he locked Paul's bedroom up?"

Donal shrugs. "Tony's always seemed a pretty straight person to me."

"What are you going to do with it?"

"Take back the maximum amount I can without too many questions being asked and give that to Paul's ex for his kid."

"And the rest?"

"Donate to the hospital and hope that's enough to wash the dirt off it."

He opens the door and tells Tony he'll just be a minute.

"Well . . ." I begin. I've got a goodbye rehearsed in my head but he gets in first.

"Look, I wouldn't blame you for being glad to see the back of me after what I told you, especially you being a lawyer."

I did stay awake for a lot of the night working out what should be done legally but every time I looked at Donal my concerns melted away.

"Eliza, if there's anything I've learnt from this mess it's life is too fucking short." He passes me a piece of paper. "I don't want to be Facebook friends or any of that kind of thing but if ever you're passing through, here are my details."

"I can return the hat when you're ready."

"You keep it," he says. "I'll just want to see you."

He gives me a fierce red-bristled kiss and I find it hard to let go of him.

I hold tightly to that piece of paper as he gets into Tony's car and it pulls out onto the road, raising my other hand so that he might see it in the rear mirror.

His writing is angular, impatient and quick, a bit like him. I fold the paper and open my handbag, intent on finding somewhere safe to store it. The zip lock bag with the envelope Dave gave me is sitting on top. Flopping onto the unmade bed, I unseal the clear plastic and take out the envelope. Ripping it open I look inside. Something gold is caught in a corner.

There's flat-palm knock. "Housekeeping," comes a chirpy voice.

"Just a minute," and I tuck the envelope back into my handbag before unlocking the door.

A pretty woman stands there, about my age, warm brown skin, large dark eyes, wearing a blue satin blouse with frills along the neckline and snug-fitting jeans.

"Oh, hello," she says, looking me up and down. "I just wanted to chat to Donal."

"Sorry, you missed him. Tony Bayless picked him up."

"Oh," she says, and her mouth puckers as if she's worried about being stiffed on the bill.

"I'm happy to settle up," I tell her.

"There's no charge," she says. "Least we can do seeing he's still got to bury his brother."

"That's very kind. I'll be gone in a few minutes as well."

She goes to leave, the blouse straining across her back in tight wrinkles, then notices the Mustang and turns back, frowning.

"That's Mick Carmody's car." She points a thumb at it.

"I'm his daughter."

"Eliza?" A generous lopsided smile comes out of nowhere. "It's me, Bridget Walker."

Bridie Walker. She was in my sister's class at school. For a while they had been good friends. "Can't believe I didn't recognize you," she says. "Must be the suit."

I look down at the crumpled version of yesterday's clothes, having left my overnight bag at my father's house.

"Hear you're in the city these days," she says. "A fancy lawyer. Mick was so proud of you."

"I'm not sure about the fancy part," I say. "Did you know Tess is back as well?"

"Yeah," she says, but there is a hesitation. "I saw her at the supermarket. Said we should catch up for a cuppa but I haven't heard from her."

Typical Tess, I think. Still, a remnant of family loyalty kicks in. "Probably busy," I say. "She's been looking after Dad, getting his place in order."

Bridie shrugs. "We fell out years ago. I promised to go to a party with her and didn't. She never really forgave me for that."

That sounds like Tess, too.

"Look, have you got a minute?" she asks. "I was going to mention it to Tess but seeing you're here. It's about your dad."

"All right."

"Come with me, then."

I pull the door shut behind me and we walk along the gravel driveway, past the other self-contained fibro bungalows. Bridie keeps up a steady stream of conversation. She's been managing this place for about five years or so, having come back to town after a bad divorce. "It's good," she says. "Owners are sensible and let me be my own boss. Trade has been steadily building up after the fire. Mind you, had a cancellation this morning. Apparently, the media has dubbed us 'Killsale' after Paul

Keenan, and now those bones they've found up at The Castle." She shakes her head.

We have reached the last bungalow, a dense bushland of eucalyptus behind it. Bridie pulls out a key.

"This is the one," she says.

My first impression is that this is nicer than Donal's room but as I step inside my senses become confused. Everything I see belongs to my father. There are copies of *Mustang Monthly* sitting on the table. Family photos are stuck up on the wall by the bed. A teenage Tess is smiling sweetly, unaware that ten-year-old me is doing bunny ears behind her head. Wedding photos of Tess and Gavin are next to me graduating from university. There's even my favorite picture of Mum. She's on the beach with Dad, smiling at the camera while he looks at her as if he can't quite believe how lucky he is. I walk over to the wardrobe and pull it open. His clothes are in here including a striped jumper I bought for him as a Christmas present.

"There's more of his stuff in the drawers," Bridie says.

It feels as if he's just walked out of the room.

"I still come in once a week for a quick dust and airing out. He paid six months in advance. I didn't ask him to," she says. "Just how he wanted to organize it. In arrears now, of course, not that I mind, but I need to know what your family wants to do with it all."

"But what is it doing here?"

"It started with his domestic violence cases. There isn't a refuge within a hundred kilometers. When I first started managing the place, your father came to see me. He wanted somewhere tucked out of the way for the women and children and we suited. Gave him a good rate, because outside summer we need more than just sales reps and truckers. I fed them, organized a room while your Dad would see what they wanted to do, try to convince them to press charges."

"But why are Dad's belongings here?" I ask.

Bridie's face takes on a no-nonsense expression. "He would stay here to keep an eye on things. Wanted to sleep in his car at the start, but in the end we set up this place for him. In the bad times it was like he lived here.

I used to hear the purr of the Mustang and put on some more pasta or extra potatoes. I think Mick was a bit lonely."

"What's happened since Dad's accident?"

"I've tried talking to Gavin about it but he's not interested. I still take those girls in when I can."

"What if there's trouble?"

"My eldest is a bit of a tech freak. He's set up some sort of motion capture thing out the front that's attached to his computer. Also, Jim Keaveney lives up along the ridge ever since he sold his shop."

"Isn't he getting on?"

"A bit deaf perhaps but you wouldn't want to mess with him. He's still a pretty good shot. I'm not bad either. Put up with shit from my husband for years, so I'm not going to take it from anyone else's."

If this stuff goes back to Dad's house, chances are Tess will throw it out.

"Why don't I pay the rent?" I ask. "I'll go through his belongings next time I'm back. I'm not sure when that will be but should be soon. Amy Liu's having a baby."

"You still friends with Amy?"

I nod.

"Can't beat old friends. That's why I wanted to sort things out with your sister."

We walk to her office and I pay the next couple of months' rent and insist on making up the shortfall as well. Bridie is all business and accepts. Her two teenage boys give me sleepy slit-eyed looks over their breakfast and Bridie goes into sergeant-major mode to start getting them ready for school.

The three of them watch as I reverse the Mustang out of the parking spot and head out on the highway. Without even thinking, I turn toward town and the nursing home, as if it is the car choosing the way and not me. Bridie told me about a side of Dad that I knew nothing about. No doubt, Tess rang him every week to check in but my calls were sporadic, conversations running out of steam as our worlds grew increasingly distant. I never knew anything about him helping those women or living in a motel room.

Donal said life was short. Bridie told me no regrets. If she got solace from hearing the Mustang's engine, then perhaps Dad will as well.

Standing in the doorway to my father's room, I see a care attendant's backside jiggling as she bends over to adjust something on Dad's wheelchair. Dad's bed has been stripped and there's the smell of urine and something earthier I'm reluctant to identify.

The attendant, a large woman, works efficiently. She fixes up a button on his shirt and then, humming, grabs a toothbrush and deftly coaxes it into his mouth. She explains everything to my father and her instructions are kind.

I tap lightly on the door, not wanting to startle her and in a split second I realize who she is.

"Hello," I say.

She straightens up, toothbrush and napkin in hand. There's a plastic name badge saying "Cadee" attached to her light blue collared top.

"I'm Mick's daughter, Eliza."

"I know who you are," she replies.

Dad's hair belongs to someone else. It's parted the wrong way and is longer than he wears it but still, it's been combed and his clothes are clean and correctly buttoned.

There's a kind of animal quiver to Cadee as if she might bolt if I wasn't blocking her path. I decide to forgo any polite pretense. "You're Luke's mum."

"I don't want trouble," she says. "I need this job."

I'm not sure what she thinks I'm going to do. Storm out of here and demand the manager sack her or insist that she must never be left alone with my father again. Perhaps other people in the town have already done this.

"That Paul Keenan was no saint," she continues. "I don't care what anyone says." It sounds like this is an argument she's been having with herself.

"Did you know Paul well?" I ask.

Her eyes are wary. "He was just someone down at the pub but he heard Luke was desperate for extra work. The new building codes have made the farm's rebuild almost impossible."

My heart sinks. What sort of work does a recently arrived backpacker have to offer?

She shakes her head. "Now they're talking about some bones as well. People are just blaming him for everything. It isn't fair."

"What about the woman Luke attacked?"

Her chin juts. She becomes more angular with squared shoulders and hard elbows, efficiently stripping the sheets off my father's bed.

"That tourist wasn't hurt. If he's charged with that, then she should be as well. Started the whole thing, she did, hitting his car and then trying to drive away."

Another mother blindly defending her child, just as Paul's mother had defended him.

"You know my Luke's a good boy," she says.

I look at her in surprise. How am I meant to know that? I haven't spoken to him in years. "She did hit his car," I say, "but I saw him terrorize her and then attack Paul."

Cadee pounces on what I've said. "You're the eyewitness. You were there." It's an instant accusation. "The police keep saying in their press conferences that there was one but they never say who."

I've made a terrible mistake. I shouldn't have started talking to her about it.

"You've got it wrong," she tells me. "Luke would never kill someone."

"I know what I saw."

She appraises me, a complicated look, almost greedy, like she wants to argue but then retreats, saying, "I haven't given you a chance to say hello to your father yet."

Sitting there, he's a bystander to what has been going on. But I've got no idea if he's understood a word. His breath rattles as if his heart is a dried pea clattering against his ribs. I put my handbag down on the side table and pull out the car keys, one for the trunk and doors, the other for the ignition. The keyring is pliable leather with the worn image of a galloping horse still visible. Walking over to Dad, I give him a kiss on the cheek. His skin is so papery soft that if I pressed hard against it my finger might go right through.

"Hello, Dad, it's me again."

Today he is wearing a polo shirt with a beige cardigan that looks as if it was bought for someone bigger.

I place the keys into his hand and close his fingers around them, hoping he can feel the familiar shape. "The Mustang's here waiting for you." I turn to Cadee. "We won't be long."

I push Dad through the doors to outside and park him next to Mary's bench. Mary gives me a shifty look, like we're invading and snatches her suitcase, hugging it to her. Problems blossom now we are out here. I can't get him into the car by myself but if I go to get someone else, could he tip out of his wheelchair?

"What are you doing with Mick?" asks Mary, leaning forward to peer at him.

"He's come to see his old car." We both look at him. His eyes are shut.

"Maybe he can hear it, then," I say.

Mary's nose wrinkles as if that's not going to work.

"Could you hold onto the wheelchair while I turn on the engine?" I ask. "Just so he doesn't roll away."

When Mary stands up she is so thin you can see the skeleton under her skin, but she clutches tightly to the frame. Taking the key from my father's hand, I open the car door and turn the ignition. The starter motor whines nasally before the engine kicks into a deep chesty rumble.

Dad's head lolls helplessly on his left shoulder, his neck a noodle.

Frustrated, I put my foot on the accelerator so hard it screams and there is the smell of gas and the start of something burning. Mary takes a hurried step backward, but she doesn't let go of the wheelchair.

Dad doesn't even blink an eye and I try again and again. I want to keep trying until the mechanics seize but eventually I give up and switch it off. All my optimism disappears in a cloud of unleaded gas plus additives.

"You finished?" Mary sticks her head in the window.

I nod, feeling helpless, but manage to say thanks.

"You could take me for a drive in that car," she says.

"We'd have to check if it was all right, get permission."

"Why would they need to know?" she wheedles. "Plenty of people get taken out on day trips." There is cunning in her eyes.

"Where would you want to go?"

"To sit on my grandson in the park," she says, picking up her suitcase. "We can go now.

"Sit on him?" My first thought is that I misheard but then she repeats herself. "I thought he was coming to pick you up," I say, trying to make sense of it. "That's what you told me last time."

"He's not coming." She's getting cross now. "I just say that so people will leave me alone. Pretend you're daft and you can get away with anything."

"What?"

"It's like sharing a house with the living dead. That's why I sit outside—so I can forget I'm stuck in this bloody place."

I am saved by Laurelle from reception, who starts frantically waving at me from the door.

"Time to take Dad back inside," I tell Mary. "Maybe another day?"

She doesn't answer, just sits back down on the bench.

Laurelle presses the door open for me.

"You didn't sign Mick out," she says, frowning.

"You could see us from where you were sitting."

"You didn't sign in either." She points to the notice stating that all visitors must sign in. "It's important."

The look on my face makes it clear that I don't agree.

"Ever had to evacuate elderly residents, staff and visitors during a bushfire?" she asks. "I have. I'm really glad Mick has got family visiting him at last, but please follow the rules."

Her phone rings, and she answers it with a calm, gentle "Emerald Coast Homes, Laurelle speaking," while making fierce impatient jabs with her finger at the visitors' book.

Chastised, I turn to the right page and sign. Gavin's careful print catches my eye from last week and I wonder what Laurelle meant by family visiting Dad "at last." Looking at the list of names, Tess's isn't there. Perhaps Gavin

90

signed both of them in. I leaf backward to see if her name is in the week before. It's not there. Nor the week before that.

Laurelle finishes the phone call.

"Does everyone have to sign in when they arrive?" I ask.

"I get them all," Laurelle says, giving me a squint-eyed look like I'm a bad guy trying to make her day. "No exceptions."

"Has my sister, Tess, been in lately?" But the phone is ringing again and her attention is diverted.

"Mick's tired," she says, before picking up the receiver.

The room is empty when we arrive. Dad's breathing is thick, drool falls from his lips. I grab my handbag from the side table and hunt around for a tissue, dumping things out to find one crumpled at the bottom. Dave's envelope upends and the glint of gold spills out. I try to right it but it's too late—unwinding its coils it slithers onto the floor in slow motion. It's a necklace.

I check the envelope and bag, to make sure that's all that was in there. But there is no pendant or anything else. It's just a plain gold chain. Crouching down next to my Dad's wheelchair, I put my hand in the ziplock bag and use it as a makeshift glove to scoop it up. It could be evidence after all. I lift it to eye level. As the chain drapes and dangles, a memory flutters in my mind but subsides before I can glimpse it properly.

The smell of dirt is mixed with detergent, which must be from Dave's half-hearted attempt to clean the necklace. Grime still outlines the grooves and one section is completely covered with mud, but the chain itself still glints as it catches the light. At first I think the links have warped, that age has kinked it. But as I keep winding, there is uniformity. Every four links there is a twist, like a simplified strand of DNA, and again I feel a sudden pang of familiarity. Feeling the bumps and ridges against my skin, it bunches and tangles, but I manage to hold one end up, trying to work out the length. The links catch on themselves as they spin around.

At a guess the necklace is mid-length. When worn, it would sit well below the collarbone. But no one is going to do that because it's broken, which is perhaps the real reason Dave didn't give it to his daughter. The other end of the necklace doesn't finish with a clasp. Instead, there is a c-shaped link where the chain has snapped.

The moment I realize the chain is broken, an image bubbles up in my mind and this time it becomes fixed. It is of another necklace breaking long ago. A twisted gold chain. I can see the warm contrast of the metal against skin. A flash of school uniforms, mucking around in the classroom waiting for the teacher, leaning back on my chair, balancing it on two legs to tag Amy behind me. Amy, arms flailing, throwing herself sideways, smacking into Grace. A little cry, a clutched throat and there the chain lay in her hands, in two pieces.

In Grace's hands.

I feel a sudden lurch like you sometimes do the moment before you fall asleep.

"This is Grace Hedland's necklace," I say aloud to my father in amazement and then like a button has been pushed, his hand jolts up of its own accord and slaps against the arm of the wheelchair. It's as if a bird hit the window. A moment of startled movement and then nothing.

I press the buzzer hard and keep my finger down, staring at my father all the time, willing him to do it again. A different care attendant arrives. She's all teeth and hair. The name badge says "Diane."

"He moved," I tell her. "My father moved his hand."

"It happens," she says. "Doesn't mean anything. Just automatic. Nerve twitches."

But I know she is wrong.

"Dad," I say, getting down on my knees. "Can you hear me?"

I sit there with him for half an hour, saying Grace's name over and over. His eyes remain closed and his hands don't move again.

12

Tess's car isn't in the driveway and no one answers the doorbell. I go through the side gate into the back garden. The spare key is in the usual spot, under the third flowerpot to the right of the back door—surprisingly lax for a police family, but Dad always assumed that no one would be stupid enough to rob the local cop.

My overnight bag is right by the front door as if Tess wants to keep any visit to pick it up as short as possible. I sit down at the kitchen table and take out the necklace again.

Could this really belong to Grace?

I find a pen and slowly run it underneath the necklace, until it's halfway along, then lift it to eye level. It's unbalanced, threatening to slide back down. I stare at it until the rest of the world goes out of focus.

The memory is insistent now, almost throbbing like a headache.

The spring clasp had snapped. It was Amy who had the idea to use a paper clip, looping both ends onto it, as a temporary fix, apologizing all the while. Grace kept patting it the rest of the afternoon to make sure it hadn't fallen off. That weekend the three of us caught the bus to the next town to get the clasp replaced. She was upset because even with pooling all our money together we could only afford a sterling silver one. Amy and I spent the whole trip home telling her that nobody was ever going to notice but she told us that she would.

I drop it back down on the table. One end of the necklace is all covered in dirt, the clasp well hidden. This should be handed over to Gavin exactly as I was given it and yet I put my hand back into the ziplock bag and carefully pick up the end covered in earth. Chunks of dirt have been dislodged but I need something finer to scrape off the final stubborn layers of compacted mud. Putting the chain down on the table, I rummage through the kitchen drawers for a toothpick and begin chipping at the grime, digging down until the wooden tip clinks against the metal. Then, blowing away the dust, I scrape away a patch to see a dull silver clasp appear.

My heartbeat fills the room.

The front door opens. I am sliding the chain back into the envelope when Tess comes into the kitchen, balancing a grocery bag in the crook of her arm.

"How did you get in?" she demands.

"The spare key. You should change the spot."

"And perhaps the locks," she says.

The "this is your home too" sentiment didn't last long.

"Quite a dramatic exit yesterday, taking the chief mourner away with you." Her tone is one of sarcasm with highlights of small town gossip. "Two people stopped me in the supermarket to mention it and then I had the butcher saying he spotted Dad's Mustang at Ocean Breezes early this morning when he was heading into work. He was assuming it had been sold."

I start praying that the picnic spot was secluded enough.

"It was Donal's decision not to go to the wake," I try to explain.

There's a sharp intake of breath, but she hasn't finished.

"And Gavin's worried you've damaged the prosecution's case. The defense could have a field day. Spending the night with the victim's brother. Hardly an unbiased witness."

That does make me sit up.

"How would they find out?"

Tess snorts with derision, which I probably deserve.

"Fine. I'm just going to grab a few of my old photos and go."

She gives me a look that has a fair degree of sisterly smugness attached. Our arguments are never resolved, they're rounds that are won or lost. She walks into the kitchen to put away her shopping.

I try to think about what pictures I might have of Grace that would include her chain. Dad always kept the photo albums in the bookcase in chronological order, as if they were files at work. There's his wedding album, our baby ones, us as kids, family holidays. There was one for every year except the year I'm looking for. It's missing.

Frowning, my next stop is the old mahogany dresser where loose photos and brown strips of negatives sit in plastic concertina cases. Plenty of our photos never made the albums because my father was a dreadful photographer. Most tended to look like shots of a crime scene, with missing limbs, heads half chopped off and shifty expressions. I grab out handfuls and begin flicking through my family's past. I was given a camera for my fifteenth birthday and all I ever did was take photos of my friends.

Grace doesn't appear.

I take the drawer and dump the contents on the table. There's teenage Amy, braces and glasses, and me with a healthy scattering of acne. Grace probably took that picture. Another has the two of us, standing outside, the sun making us screw our eyes shut. Again, Grace is missing.

It is as if she has disappeared from my photos as successfully as she did in real life.

"I don't understand," I say aloud. "Where is Grace?"

In an instant Tess is standing over me. "What are you doing making all this mess?"

"I'll put it back."

"You can't just come here and start wrecking everything."

There are dozens of pictures of a beautiful Tess smiling up at me from the table and they make me angry. "Not happy with wiping out all traces of Dad, now you've been throwing out my photos."

"I haven't touched your stupid photos and that isn't what I'm doing to Dad."

"Really? When was the last time you visited him? Because I didn't see your name in the visitor's book at all."

"Get out," she says. "Get out of this house."

"Don't worry, I'm going." I'll go the police station and give the necklace to Gavin before driving home.

Walking down the corridor, there's movement behind me. I turn in surprise. Perhaps she's come to apologize, perhaps she's waving a carving knife.

"Why do you want photos of Grace Hedland?" she asks.

13

leave without saying another word to my sister and drive straight into town along the beach. On the car radio the local announcer is almost breathless telling listeners that the mystery of The Castle's bones has gone viral on social media. Kinsale is now "Bonestown."

I turn left at the Surf Club and there, tucked away in a side street, is the police station. It is an uninviting brick building, designed to be locked up and left when all the cops are out on patrol. As I walk toward the familiar blue-and-white checkerboard sign sticking up on a rusty pole out the front, a group of journalists swoop down, beady-eyed. Logos of different city TV stations are stuck on cameras and there is a station wagon rakishly parked right outside, as if the journalist had arrived in a hurry.

"Just getting a stat dec signed," I lie.

They judge me to be unimportant and quickly return to chatting among themselves in a friendly but combative way.

The police noticeboard is full of sun-faded posters advertising victim assistance, counseling programs and giving the contact numbers of the closest twenty-four-hour station, two towns up the coast, for when this one is unattended. In reception, Pat Fulton sits behind a glass partition, talking to a man at the counter who seems to be showing her his new neck tattoo. Pat has been the office manager at Kinsale Police Station my whole life. It feels very strange to be walking in here without Dad being somewhere in the building.

"I hear you're back playing the slots, Tye. Where'd you get the money to do that?"

The tattooed man mumbles something inaudible.

"You don't want to get in trouble again," she says. "Wouldn't want bail revoked."

If most things in Kinsale seem a bit smaller and shabbier, Pat Fulton is the exception. Everything about her is large: the hedgehog spikes in her silver hair, the chunky jewelry on her fingers, and her laugh, which was always loud. She sits there ballooned behind the glass, wearing an expression that always made me feel guilty.

The one-sided conversation with Tye comes to an end and he shuffles past.

"Why, it's little Eliza," Pat calls. "Heard you were in town for the memorial."

"Just wanted a quick word with Gavin," I tell her. "Is he in?"

"Up at The Castle," she says.

"Is this about the skull?"

"They've recovered a complete skeleton now. That's the reason those vultures are out the front. Some bright spark hired a helicopter to get aerial footage and made a nuisance of themselves. I've had three complaints in already." Her mouth curdles at this. "Anyway, can I help you?"

"It might be nothing."

"If I had a dollar for every time I've heard that, I'd be lying on a beach in Bali with a mojito right now."

"Does it usually turn out to be something?"

"Nope, mostly it's a waste of time. Tell you what . . ." She looks up at the clock behind her. "We're not going to get many people coming in with those clowns out the front. I'll just close up and we can grab an early lunch. Do you eat tuna salad?"

I nod.

"Good, you can have Gavin's because he won't get a chance. Give us a minute, I'll divert the phones."

Coming out from behind the glass with a large plastic bag in her hands, she puts a sign on the front door directing people to use the external phone if they need help, and then locks the door behind us. The yells begin the moment we are spotted. Reporters start to swarm.

"Has a decision been taken to dig the entire site?" asks the tallest one, swinging his camera up to his shoulder, a fluffy boom mike attached. "Can you confirm that Luke Tyrell is a suspect in this death as well?" says another, while a third comes forward brandishing his phone. He sticks it right in Pat's face. "Have more bodies been found?"

"Just the filing clerk, fellas," she says, "heading out for my lunch break," and she ploughs through them like an icebreaker. I duck my head, clutch my handbag and follow in her wake. If this is what it's going to be like giving evidence at Luke Tyrell's trial, I don't want to do it.

They fall back again. This time the muttering seems more mutinous. We walk out of hearing distance and Pat slows down, "Now, let's get in my car and we'll eat up at the park, away from busy ears."

"I've got the Mustang," I say. "I can drive."

"Mick's?" she says, delighted. "Begged him for years but he never took me for a spin once."

We're almost at the car when there is the sound of footsteps behind us.

"Excuse me." It's the girl with mermaid blue hair who I saw at the memorial. She's wearing the geek girl uniform of a short-sleeve checked blouse, A-line skirt and silver brogues.

"Could I get a copy?" she asks.

"Of what?" says Pat.

"The police statement about Luke Tyrell being a suspected serial killer."

Behind her the journalists, all men, are clutching coffees and sniggering in our direction. The tallest one cranes his neck to try and see her expression.

"If Luke Tyrell has anything to do with those bones," says Pat, "I'll run through this town naked and they can put that in all their news bulletins."

"So no statement?"

"They're having you on, love," says Pat. "No serial killer, no statement."

The girl's face hardens at the hoots of laughter behind us. She gives a kind of this-day-could-not-get-any-worse sigh. "And they won't pay for their bloody coffees either. They say it's my shout."

"Giving you a hard time?" Pat asks.

"Just new girl shit," her jaw tightening. "Stella Gibson," she adds, sticking out her hand for Pat to shake. "I've just started interning at the *Coastal Times*."

Pat narrows her eyes.

"Interning?" she asks. "Do they pay you?"

"It's good experience for my CV," says Stella. "At least, that's the theory."

"How's the practice?" I ask.

"Got that CCTV footage of Luke Tyrell's attack in record time. That went viral around the world."

"Tell you what," Pat says. "You got business cards and a pen?"

Stella nods.

"Give us one like you're arranging something."

Stella delves into her bag, which is the size of a small child.

"Now put our heads together like we don't want to be overheard. You too, Eliza."

I move nose to nose with Stella, so close I can see mascara clumps on her eyelashes.

"Good," says Pat. Her lipsticked upper lip curls, exposing denture-plate pink gums and slightly snarled teeth.

Behind us the chuckling dies down.

"Nothing's going to happen here for most of the day but try around five P.M. No guarantees but google the name Dr. Pernilla Adler and don't tell those idiots anything."

Stella smiles, beginning to enjoy the ace girl reporter act.

"What's happening at five P.M.?" I ask after Stella leaves.

"Adler is the forensic anthropologist on site. Gavin will be pushing hard for some concrete details to be released to stop all the speculation. If he gets anything, they'll release it then to make the TV news bulletins."

"I'll make sure to watch."

"Really?" Pat asks. "I'm sick to death of the whole thing. That development could bring some good jobs to Kinsale and now it's all up in the air."

We drive through Main Street, which seems empty except for multiple Janey Bayless posters, which range in size from modestly small to narcissistically large.

"How's Janey's campaign going?" I ask Pat.

"Pretty well, I think. This Castle stuff could throw a spanner in the works. Finding a skeleton in a place you once owned will set tongues wagging."

I turn right and drive past the supermarket, two liquor stores and the Chinese restaurant. "You don't think she's involved?"

"Of course not," she says. "If the police didn't find that body, the developers would have. Janey's no dill. She didn't put it there."

Pat nods at the Norfolk pines that keeps this part of the shoreline in constant shade. "When we were all in the water, the day of the bushfire, I kept watching those trees," she says. "Just staring at them, thinking if they go up, it will be the biggest bloody sparkler ever." She directs me to pull over.

"What was that day like?"

It's a question I never asked my father. I suspect he wouldn't have answered even if I had, because he never spoke to us about his work.

"Scary. But the aftermath was worse. The searches, the funerals, the buildings lost. It just wore everyone down." Her face slips slightly. "This place might not look so different to you, everything growing back now, but it's changed Kinsale."

"Amy said it's like the entire town is suffering from PTSD."

"Well, she'd be dealing with it every day, same as us at the station." Pat sighs. "Families that were here for generations just up and left. Assaults and domestic violence all skyrocketed, and don't get me started on the drugs. Still, it's not everyone. Some people just woke up the next morning and got on with life as normal. And then there's some like Janey. That fire was rocket fuel for her, running for mayor, organizing the class action. Now we can look forward to people's settlements being finalized and some money coming back to the town."

"Settlements?"

"Haven't you heard? We're all suing the power company."

The guilt is needle sharp.

"Our lawyers say they're bound to settle. Too much bad publicity otherwise."

So that's what the defense lawyers are saying. Not just telling their clients they will have their day in court but promising an actual settlement.

"Do you want me to grab the bag?" I ask, to change the subject.

"Sure," she says. "We'll sit up on the bench."

We walk through the empty playground where Amy, Grace and I smoked cigarettes for the first time. I think it was Amy who threw up. Pat leads me past the faded blue nautical themed house with anchors, portholes and a smiling cartoon whale slide up to a wooden bench. A tarnished plaque on the back of it reads, In Loving Memory of Travis Young, then, after the dates, Forever Young is written in copperplate script. It's hard to know if the pun was intended. The name rings a bell but it doesn't come with a face attached. I have a vague memory of a big town funeral that my father attended but refused to let me go.

Pat settles herself down.

"When did this get put here?" I ask.

"Must be ten years ago now. His mother couldn't face visiting the cemetery anymore so the family did this instead. His favorite spot in town apparently."

There is broken glass littered throughout the pine needles on the grass, cigarette butts and chip wrappers under the swings.

"The cemetery must be bad."

"Most of the town can't face that place. Too many people ended up there too early, your mum included."

Dad never took us to the cemetery, preferring to go by himself.

"Still, Maggie Young's an idiot," Pat went on. "Babbles on about the importance of family and then when her mother loses her house in the fire, shoves her in the nursing home. Poor old Mary." I start at the name but Pat keeps talking. "And Travis was nothing special. Got drunk and wrapped himself around a tree."

Travis Young was the grandson Mary had spoken to me about.

"So," says Pat. "What did you want to talk about?"

"I was given this yesterday." I pull out the envelope from my bag and open it up to show her the necklace. It doesn't seem real but I'm more convinced than ever that it belonged to Grace.

Pat takes a look, then pulls out a container and fork and hands it to me. "Tuna salad," she says.

"The person said they found it near that skeleton at The Castle."

"Who?"

I shake my head. "They asked me not to say."

"And they found it buried up at The Castle?"

I risk a nod.

"Any chance it was that idiot Dave Deasey?"

My face tries to neither confirm nor deny. "Why him?"

"Someone spun him a line about there being World War II memorabilia buried there. Dave's been mouthing off about it for the last few months, telling anyone who would listen he was going to give the place a once over with his metal detector. I'm guessing this is the extent of his treasure trove."

I had forgotten that Pat knew everything about everyone in town. I give up pretending in the face of her superior deductive skills.

"That and the skull," I tell her. "He's worried the necklace could be evidence and Gavin will be mad at him."

Pat sniffs and then stabs an olive with her fork and pops it into her mouth. "Why didn't he come and tell us about it then? Bones get found all the time, washed up on the beach or dug up in a paddock. Now we've got morons claiming Luke Tyrell is a serial killer only because we found the skeleton during the search for him, and conspiracy theorists from all around the world keep typing nonsense about a place they'd never even heard of."

The wind picks up, tracing its way through the trees.

"The thing is, I think I know who the necklace belongs to."

Pat listens, eating steadily, as I show her the twists and the silver clasp and tell her about Grace. My words run over the top of each other until she takes the envelope from me and looks at the necklace again. "To lie like an eyewitness. That's what your father always used to tell me. It was a saying he picked up." She gives me an almost pitying look.

"I'm not lying."

"The most dangerous eyewitness of all is the one who's overconfident, who knows for sure he is telling the truth, because he'll shape the evidence to match what's in his head and convince himself. You're a lawyer, Eliza. You should always be professionally skeptical. All you've got here is a battered old chain. Where's the evidence it really belongs to the Hedland girl?"

In the distance a wave rolls in with a small black speck of a surfer gliding across it, like skating on ice. Peeling back the container's lid, I begin to eat.

"Let's just say *hypothetically*," Pat stresses the word, "that this is your friend's necklace. What do you think that means? That those bones they found belong to her?"

Is that what I think? My mind has been stuck in gear, refusing to let myself get that far ahead.

"Look, a full skeleton will tell us a lot, whether it's male or female, roughly how old they were when they died. If we get lucky, how they died. Your friend will have dental records. Her family can provide DNA. If it's her, that's how they'll find out. Not some necklace."

"How long will that take?"

"There's pressure on to get this sorted. The sooner the better for the town. Might have some preliminary findings today, but usually the scientists like to get back to the lab before writing their formal report."

"So what about the necklace?"

"I shouldn't be saying this, but if it was me, I'd hold onto it."

"Really?"

"Investigators will wait for forensics before starting. With the manhunt for Luke Tyrell, local resources are stretched to breaking point. Gavin's already pulling out what little hair he has left on the overtime bill. If you give it to him now he'll get that new kid to handle it."

"The one with blonde hair?"

"He's lost three exhibits for a drug case already. Chances are he'll lose this or it will end up forgotten in a box somewhere. You'll be lucky if anyone has looked at it this time next month. Wait until Tyrell's caught. Then you might get Gavin's attention."

Pat passes back the envelope to me. "I can remember that case," she says. "Her mum sat in our waiting room for so long she became part of the furniture, desperate for news. Alan opened the file but your father took it over. Mick worked day and night on it. I don't think I ever saw him so stressed. He stopped sleeping, lost weight. He was desperate to find her."

"He had Grace's file in his car when he had the accident."

Pat's eyes become glassy and she drops her head. "Your father was the best there was. No offense, but Gavin isn't a patch on Mick. With him it's all paperwork, targets and spreadsheets. That's not what being a country cop is all about. You know what his current obsession is? Wildlife trafficking. Here we are up to our necks in ice and assaults and all he talks about is wildlife trafficking. Ridiculous."

She takes a few more mouthfuls of the tuna salad and then taps my arm. "Don't mind me. I'm just a grumpy old woman who doesn't like change."

"Any chance I could have a look at Grace's case file?" I ask.

"Not on your life," Pat says. "More than my job's worth. If you want to know more about it you could chat with Sharpy. You remember Alan, right?"

I nod.

"Still, you'd want to pick the right day," she continues. "Six months after the fires, Karen finally left him. Should have done it a lot sooner. Now he lives by himself, just him and the dog."

"Out on Kilmore Road?"

She nods. "Supposed to be doing gardening or security these days. Can't think he's doing any of it well." She picks around the corners of her container with a fork, cleaning up the remnants.

"What if I found a photo of Grace wearing the necklace?" I ask.

"That would be useful," she agrees. "Save us time. Look, I've got to head back. Don't you get up, I'll walk. Could do with the exercise."

"Sure."

"See you again, Eliza. Come back and visit Mick. He loved you two girls more than anything in the world. I think that's what upset him with the Hedland case. He saw her and thought it could be you or Tess."

She walks down the street, surprisingly nimble for a large woman. I sit there and stare at the massive trees, imagining them ablaze like beacons of a world gone wrong. I have spent the last twenty years assuming Grace was alive somewhere, because when you're sixteen, dying seems impossible.

It doesn't seem so impossible now.

14

The town gives way to complacent cows in fields, which in turn are replaced with pockets of bush. The countryside is green and lush, ferns and undergrowth sprouting up quickly, fed by recent rain and the ash of bushfires. Only the blackened gums and new saplings are a reminder of summers past. Eventually I drive out of the fire's path into landscape I recognize from my childhood.

I have decided to take Pat's advice and drop in on Alan Sharp on my way back to the city. It isn't much of a detour off the highway. Kilmore Road is mostly potholes and patches and I try not to think about stone chips or cracked windshields. Just as I'm about to turn around, believing I must have missed the house, the bush clears and a wire fence with wayward posts appears, followed by a wooden-framed gate that sparks memories of when Dad used to take us here for visits. We'd drink lemonade and run through the sprinklers while he and Alan had a beer on the veranda.

What I remember as a friendly home has become a sagging old weatherboard with a rusted tin roof. The only new addition is the sign stuck to the wire fence saying "Beware of Dog."

I pull up in front of the closed gate and a couple of horses come moseying over from the next paddock. They shake their heads as if warning me off. The gate jangles as I grab the chain to unlatch it and instantly, a deep rumble starts, like machinery coughing into action. A dirty pit bull lumbers around the side of the house, with a broad blunt head and four log legs. Catching sight of me, it starts to lope and then, gathering speed, its snarling mouth opens wide with a red raw tongue poking out. I run back to my car, slamming the door shut, as it hurls like a cannonball and then dances vertically over the fence. It picks itself off the ground to body slam the car, teeth bared. Paws scrabble on the paintwork while a face that's all mouth snaps at the window.

My heart is in my ears so I don't hear the dog being called off, but it drops back, the barking changing to more of a yelp. Alan appears, head bald, face hairy, wearing jeans and a denim jacket with sheepskin around the collar. The dog pants, straining as it is dragged away. Alan clips it to a thick chain attached to a porch post. I am panting as well.

Alan Sharp's beard is as coarse as his dog's fur. There are patches of gray among the faded orange on either side of his chin and hair stretches down his neck. His round face has been widened and lengthened by the thick pelt. I open the car door and get out on trembling legs.

He checks out the car and then squints at me as he walks back to the gate.

"Eliza," he says, surprised. "Eliza Carmody."

I try to regulate my breathing, attempting to get the ragged gasp under control.

"Sorry about the dog. I don't get too many visitors."

"That's quite a welcome."

"She's a lamb once she gets to know you. Grandkids climb all over her and she doesn't even blink."

I try not to think what that powerful jaw could do to a child.

Unlatching the gate, he pulls it open. The nails on his fingers are bitten almost to the quick.

"It's been years since I saw you," he says. "You back visiting Mick?"

"I came for Paul Keenan's memorial."

Alan's face colors at this. "Guess you saw what happened. Lost my temper, I shouldn't have done it. But when I thought about the way Tyrell knocked Paul down, just after he helped that woman, I got so mad. Wanted to apologize to his brother afterward but thought it was best if I left it alone."

"Probably the right decision."

He shakes his head like he still can't believe it. "Anyway, won't invite you in, place is a bit of a shambles. But sit yourself up on the veranda and I'll get you a drink."

I walk across the lawn, dodging dog shit as the pit bull growls and strains on the chain.

"Twinkle, quiet!" barks Alan.

"Twinkle?"

"Last time I let a six-year-old name anything. Pull up a chair."

I climb the wooden steps onto the veranda and sit down on a rickety bamboo seat, brushing cobwebs off the arm of it. Twinkle glares up at me but lies down in the garden. Alan is back with two beers so quickly it makes me think he has a nearby stash. This isn't his first one today.

He clinks bottles with me.

I wait for him to ask why I'm here but he doesn't.

"It's about an old case that you worked on."

There's a flicker of an eyebrow but otherwise he doesn't seem concerned.

"Grace Hedland."

He looks at me for a while before saying, "The one who ran away. A long time ago now. It was a pretty straightforward case."

He has bloodshot eyes and broken capillaries map his face.

"She was never found," I remind him.

He shuffles in his seat as he takes a drink of his beer. "Most common people to go missing are girls aged thirteen to eighteen. Six times more likely than any other age group. And the reasons are," he counts them on his fingers, "problems at home, breaking up with your boyfriend, or because you've had a falling out with a mate."

Only the last one applies to Grace, which doesn't make me feel particularly good given that I was the mate.

"But most of them return?" I ask.

"Enough come back when they're ready, some choose not to."

He stretches a foot out and rests it on the bowed railing.

"She caught a train to the city, which is out of our jurisdiction. I passed her details up the line of course. City cops were supposed to keep an eye out for her but she'd just be one of many to them. Maybe she found out the hard way that the city's a dangerous place. Maybe she moved on from there."

Bellbirds' calls float from the tall eucalyptus on the other side of the road, notes of pure glass. The resonance reverberates around us. I wait until they fade.

"How do you know she caught a train?" I ask.

He lifts his hand and scratches at his beard. "There was a witness. Someone saw her at the station catching the early train into the city."

This was new.

"Who?" I ask.

He stretches out, puts his beer down next to his chair and clasps his hands behind his head. "Couldn't tell you. Your dad took over the case and Mick was never one for chatting. He kept this investigation close to his chest. Took it seriously though. He was sure that the girl went to the city. That's why he spent so much time there. Used to go up on weekends."

I feel a flicker of jealousy deep inside me. This would have been when I was at boarding school, and yet he never came to visit.

"Dad had her file in the car on the day of his accident. Do you know why?"

Alan frowns at this. "No idea. Just a missing girl, pretty standard."

"Pat said he was obsessed by it. That he never stopped looking for her."

A smile flits across his mouth. "Wouldn't take what Pat says too seriously. If Mick sneezed, Pat would be there with the chicken soup and tissues. That old case wasn't what was bothering Mick."

"What do you mean?"

"I've thought a bit about that stretch of road where he crashed. When you're struggling, you see life with suicide goggles on, and I used to think it was a perfect place. Straight road, get up good speed and then smack right into a tree. Go out in a blaze."

"But Dad had an aneurysm. The doctors told us that."

He turns and looks straight at me. "How do they know which came first?" he asks. "The tree or the aneurysm."

I can't believe what he's implying.

"Why would he do that?"

"The same reason that's gnawing at the whole town. The fire." Alan shakes his head. "For some of us it never went out. There was this one property past Fowler Creek. The owners had come into town early, ended up being evacuated to the beach with everyone else. I just wanted to check on the property before they did, to warn them what to expect. When I got there the house and shed were just about gone. There weren't any trees, just a forest of burnt sticks. This had been beautiful farming land for generations. I walked up the hill and it was so quiet. No leaves rustling, no birds singing. Just over the ridge were about twenty sheep, these great black carcasses all on their sides, fleeces reduced to charcoal, little legs all up in the air, twisted like hooks, a couple of kangaroos lying beside them. Died in agony, those poor buggers. Didn't matter who you were, the fire got to you."

In front of us, the dog stirs, lifting her head as if sensing Alan's despair. A chesty wheeze of a growl escapes but she stays where she is.

"Work made me see a shrink who reckoned that when I was looking at those animals, I was thinking about my family. One of the grandkids was missing for a few hours. Ended up he'd caught the bus to the next town with some mates without telling his mum."

When he brings his beer to his lips, some spills out of his mouth and onto his shirt but he makes no move to wipe it away.

"That fire was toxic. It burned through all our defenses. There was no fat left to get through lean times. At least that's what it's like for me and I reckon it was the same for Mick."

I stand up abruptly because I can't take any more. "I've got to head back to the city," I say. He nods his head, his attention focused on his beer more than on me. As I close the gate behind me, I hear him yelling at the dog.

Halfway home it starts to rain. Drops of water collect on the windshield until they join together and start trickling across the window, slowly at first and then faster and faster, becoming a blur. Beads of guilt and memories join together inside me like quicksilver and I have to force myself to concentrate on the road. Part of the window seal has cracked and water pools on the dashboard. This car is coming apart just like my father did. It's too late to fix him but I can fix this.

It's not until I reach the outskirts of the city that the radio picks up a clear enough signal for me to listen to the news. The bones at The Castle are the third item. The announcer tells me that they belong to a young woman, then quickly moves on to sports.

15

New Year's Eve 1996

Jim

The jagged piece of wood was visible under the skin. A splinter, courtesy of the dry wood for the bonfire resting in his bed. Leaning against the truck, Jim pulled out his pocket knife. Best to do it now while the light was still good. He pressed the blade to the spot just as a car lurched up next to him. Starting at the noise, his hand slipped. There was a glimpse of sashimi red flesh then the blood began bubbling up.

Swearing, he pulled out a grubby handkerchief, and wound it round his index finger, glaring in the direction of the car, ready to yell at the driver. When he saw it was Mick Carmody's prized Mustang with Tess at the wheel, he choked down his words.

Her entry was crooked so she put it into reverse and pulled out for another go. This wasn't much better as she overcorrected and nearly scraped his truck.

Jim put the knife back into his pocket, and then gestured for her to stop. Tess wound down her window and he stuck his head in. There was another teenage girl, whose face he knew but name he didn't, sitting in the passenger seat.

"Sorry, Mr. Keaveney," said Tess, her face glowing, a mirror to the setting sun above them. "I didn't think anyone would be up here."

She had driven up the trail that wound its way behind the surf club, out of sight from the beach. Jim liked parking up here, away from prying eyes. He looked at the tight space between his truck and the knot of trees and scrub.

"Like me to park it for you?"

"That's a good idea," her friend butted in, leaning over from her seat.

"No, Bridie," said Tess, her mouth a determined line, "I can do it."

"I'll get out then," said Bridie, and she quickly hopped out of the car, moved a safe distance away and stood there, arms folded, as if she could not be held responsible.

"Maybe better to reverse in," Jim said. "Easier for you to get out later." Tess nodded her acceptance.

There was rev of the engine and then the car jolted back. It took several goes before Tess made the 180-degree turn but Jim guided her in, waving his hands like an air traffic controller, splatters of blood falling from his finger.

Tess took off her seatbelt and clambered out of the car. The skirt of her dress had creased. Leaning forward, she pulled at the material and tried to shake it smooth. From where he was standing, Jim could see right down her dress, her breasts sitting there like two eggs in a nest, a warm creamy white. A wave of lust hit him as though he was a teenager again.

"Thanks, Mr. Keaveney," said Tess. "Dad would kill me if anything happened to his car."

"First time I took my father's car out, misjudged a corner, ended up in a ditch and had to get towed home."

Tess smiled at this, then noticed his hand.

"Have you hurt yourself?" The dirty handkerchief was now dark with large splotches of color. He unwound it. The spurting blood had not yet begun to congeal.

"Splinter," he said. "Cut myself trying to get it out."

"What from?" asked Tess.

"Bringing down some old fence palings to put on top of the bonfire, get it started."

Tess looked in the back of his truck. "Need help carrying them?" Jim could tell she was only being polite.

"No point you getting splinters as well," he said.

Tess gave a relieved smile, which disappeared as she saw the line of red splattering down his hand. "Maybe you should go to the first-aid tent."

"Had worse," he said, but Tess was already turning back toward her friend. He watched the two girls preen each other like his birds did, fanning and fluffing, checking each other's hair, brushing off imagined imperfections. They grabbed their towels from the car. Tess looked back at him, "Have a nice night, Mr. Keaveney."

"You too, Tess," but she was gone already. Bridie's arm hooked around her, pushing her forward down the track back toward the beach.

A throb of pain drew his attention back to the splinter. Jim ran his hand down the finger, now blood-slippery. He felt the warm sting of the cut and hard edge of the wood. Gripping onto it with the nails of his thumb and forefinger, pincer-like, he slowly pulled. There was a tug on the skin as it gave way, sharply painful. It came out bloody and broken. There was more still stuck inside but that would have to wait. He rewrapped the handkerchief and clumsily tied it before carefully grabbing the wood, balancing it over his shoulder and heading down the path. The sun had disappeared behind the town and the bonfire needed his attention.

He could see the two girls in the distance, walking up toward the beach and followed in their footsteps. At the bottom of the hill, they joined the crowd. Families were carrying coolers and collapsible chairs, knots of teenagers with reddened skin having spent all day enjoying the fickle sun. None of them were "summer people," which was how Jim referred to the tourists, the ones with their fancy cars who complained when the country wasn't quite the little city that they had expected.

Wes Bayless was there, but didn't even attempt to help when Jim dropped the planks and started to pull the blue tarps off the enormous stack of wood already there. Hidden pools of water splashed down the sides. Despite the sunny day, the heavy overnight rain had done its work and most of the wood was sodden.

"Watch it," said Wes. "You nearly got me." Wes judged others by the size of their wallet and always liked to let people know that his was the biggest in town. At least, that's how it used to be. Jim had heard the bank owned most of Wes's assets these days, and yet Wes still walked round like he owned the place.

"Make yourself useful and give us a hand then," said Jim.

Wes grabbed the other corners of the nearest tarp. Together they tipped it out, then Jim folded it up and dropped it on the pile with the others.

"You're going to need napalm and a flamethrower to get that started," said Wes.

Jim instinctively felt like contradicting him. He started to strategically place the dry wood on top. "Pour on enough gas, we'll be all right."

"Whose stupid idea was a bonfire anyway?"

"Least it's not raining now," was all Jim said, even though he had been the one who suggested it and he expected Wes knew that.

Wes hawked up some phlegm and spat it out.

"Christ, here comes PC Plod," he said, as Probationary Constable Gavin Pawley started to work his way through the crowd. Jim glanced at Gavin all gangly thin, a good half a head above the rest, still looking as if his uniform might be fancy dress. He had only been in the town a month but already Jim wouldn't piss on him if he were on fire. He'd come into the shop twice, "courtesy" visits, Gavin called them, wanting to check the licenses for the birds, making sure Jim's paperwork was in order and talking about wildlife protection. It was harassment and Jim had thought seriously about making a formal complaint but he'd been told that might look suspicious, so instead he'd been all "yes, sir," "no, sir" to Gavin and made a few rearrangements as a precaution against a possible raid.

"It's the aca-fuckin'-demic," said Wes. "Thinks he knows everything. Hope the bonfire follows all the appropriate regulations, Jim, or he'll throw the book at you."

"He should be more interested in finding out who nicked half the fireworks from the surf club."

Wes pursed his lips. "Many missing?"

"Enough."

"Reckon I could hazard a guess." Wes gestured over to where Travis Young was cock-strutting in the middle of a group of admirers. Jim saw the group included Tess and her friend. "Saw that lot hanging round the club earlier. I'm sure they'd want their own private display tonight at their shindig."

"Where are they holding it this year?" Jim asked. Wes would know. He'd been the president of the Kinsale Footy Club for years.

"Not a word to the missus," said Wes, lowering his voice, "but I said they could use a back paddock of mine. The old woodshed on the Ophir Road."

"Up near The Castle?"

"That's the one. Kinsale tradition, this party. Something Mick Carmody would do well to remember."

Jim felt something wet on his leg. Blood had leaked through the hanky again.

"That looks nasty," Wes said. "Get Janey to check it."

Jim looked up and saw Gavin walking along the embankment toward them. His finger was sore and anything was preferable to being caught between Gavin and Wes. There was still time before it got really dark. He grunted his agreement and headed in the opposite direction past the fire trucks to the first-aid tent.

Janey sat there looking bored.

"Been a quiet night," she told him. "You're my first customer." She held his hand steady. Her skin felt cool against the sandpaper roughness of his.

"I'm going to have to dig deep," she told him. Her red nail polish was slightly chipped and when she bent her head, he could see the darker regrowth running along her scalp. Still, she looked good, thought Jim, and Janey knew it, keeping everything on display in a series of low-cut tops and tight skirts. He didn't understand what she ever saw in Wes Bayless.

"By rights you should get it stitched," she said, as she dabbed away at the blood.

Jim ignored this. "Thought you'd be too busy at the pub tonight to be doing the first aid."

"Once a nurse, always a nurse," Janey answered, pushing back the edge of the skin with the metal tip of the tweezers. "And Wes likes to show his face at these things."

More like show people who's boss, thought Jim.

"Besides," Janey continued, "I love a bonfire, the moment it goes up in flames. I'll wait till it's lit and then I'll head back." She glanced up at him, kohl-rimmed blue eyes in a round face, and smiled.

The metal dug in hard, but Jim didn't mind pain. You couldn't deal with birds if you did—the beaks and claws weren't for show. People assumed it was all colorful feathers and listening to bird calls and forgot all about the work that went into keeping the birds healthy. Janey understood, though, asking questions about the shop and the trade. She had a good head for business. Jim thought about telling her where the paddock party was but decided against it. Wes would probably guess it was him and he was the type of bully who would make you pay.

"Will we see you up at The Royal later?" she asked.

"Naw," he said. "Got stuff to do. Need to check on the birds."

"They'll still be there in the morning," she said, and Jim was sure she going to say something else but Wes stuck his head through the flap and told Janey it was time to go.

"Aren't we staying for the bonfire?" she asked her husband. "I've hardly had the chance to take any photos."

Wes said something about a barmaid calling in sick. "Just didn't want to work tonight," he said. "I'll have to sack her."

Janey shrugged, picking up the tweezers. "You go. I'll finish up and meet you back there."

Wes grumbled and then left.

"Got it." Janey flicked the wooden shard onto the fold-up table. "It was a nasty one." She splashed on the disinfectant, a momentary sting, and then deftly stuck the steri strips in place before bandaging it up.

"You want me to get rid of that for you?" She pointed at the blood-stained hanky lying on the table. Jim shook his head and shoved it into his pocket.

"Anyway, drop by for a sing-a-long," said Janey. "Best tenor in town you are."

"Oh, all right," he replied, because it was impossible to say no to her.

Jim left the roaring bonfire in the charge of the Country Fire Brigade around 11 P.M. Pyromaniacs all, he could see them salivating at the prospect as they sent out the youngest to track down more gas. Back at the car, stinking of smoke, he noticed the Mustang had gone. He checked his truck for any scratches then headed out of Kinsale on Old Castle Road, an open bottle of whiskey next to him. He had drunk enough to get the ash taste out of his mouth and warm his blood.

Janey was right, the shop birds could wait until morning, but if the footy boys had nicked the fireworks and were planning a show near The Castle, he definitely wanted to check on the birds for the shipment. Loud noises set them right off and cockatoos could scream blue murder when they wanted to. Besides, he couldn't afford for any of them to get injured.

He almost missed the turn-off and had to reverse before heading through the gates of The Castle. His earliest memory was of his mother telling him stories about the old mansion, how barbed wire had surrounded it during World War II. His older brother had ridden out to it on the back of a neighbor's horse; there'd been no gas or rubber for bike tires with the war on. All the kids in town had wanted to see a real-life Nazi. Jim couldn't believe he'd missed all the excitement, being born a few years too late. His mother had been sympathetic to the sailors' plight. "Prisoners of war, they were, just like the ones from our side. Needed to keep them locked up where no nutter could shoot them," she had told him.

In a strange way, Jim felt the same way about his birds, wanting to look after them and keep them safe. There wasn't enough respect for native birds. People saw them as pests and shot to kill or maim for sport. It was different overseas. He'd been shown pictures of the aviaries where his birds would be treated like kings. All illegal, of course, but Jim couldn't see that he was doing any harm.

It had started off easy enough. An overseas dealer had got in touch wanting an exchange. He'd sent a rosella and got a pretty, little green Amazon parrot in return, an especially good mimic that he'd been able to sell for good money. Then he started to head into the bush for replacements whenever one of his legal birds died or was sold on the quiet. The police couldn't tell a wild galah from one brought up in captivity. He became known as a supplier for natives and that had brought risks, and some dodgy customers. So when an exclusive arrangement had been proposed, more lucrative one too, he had decided to accept. As long as he kept his logbook looking fine, they told him, the shop would be a convincing front. All he had to do was supply the birds and they'd do the rest.

It was only when Constable Pawley started sniffing around, talking about black markets and wildlife smuggling, that Jim became concerned about raids. That's why he'd moved the pick-up of birds to a new location a couple of days ago. He'd been told the police weren't watching him but he wanted to be careful. The Castle hadn't been his idea but it was a good one, all that way out of town and not far from the highway. Of course, Wes Bayless had no idea about any of it. Jim doubted Wes had been in half of the outbuildings since he bought the place, eyes only on the mansion and the bragging rights. As far as Jim could tell, Wes barely even visited it anymore, preferring to pretend he wasn't bankrupting himself. It had all been perfect except for the weather, which had delayed a pick-up, forcing Jim to visit the site twice a day to make sure the birds were OK.

Turning off the engine, he left the headlights on. He couldn't use a flashlight without sending the birds crazy. The light from outside would be feeble, but enough. He should have covered up the birds hours ago but had been distracted by the night's celebrations.

The music was a distant hum, AC/DC he guessed from the baseline, but all was quiet outside their shed. He'd had a parrot once that would go nuts whenever "Highway to Hell" came on the radio. Slipping the key into the padlock, he pushed open the door. A couple of birds shifted in their cages at the noise but otherwise they slept on. He counted them all: the weiros; two galahs; a Major Mitchell; and then, the most valuable, four black cockatoos. More than a hundred thousand dollars' worth in ten boxes. He'd clear more from this delivery than he'd make in the shop in six months.

A male galah had been worrying him. He hadn't eaten properly for a couple of days and his food was still at the bottom of its container. Jim would have to come again in the morning and check it properly. If it was looking diseased, he'd take it away from the others and the delivery would just have to be one short.

Covering up the last cage, he noticed something white on the floor. His hanky had fallen out of his pocket. He was just about to pick it up when he heard an engine roar. Stopping still, Jim listened carefully. It was hard to work out which direction it was coming. The road or the party? Jim immediately thought of the pick-up. The coastal road must have reopened. He'd been told that they'd come straight away once it did. Jim had never met any of them, preferring to leave that sort of thing to the others. Bird-smuggling was only a sideline for this operation. There'd already been wooden crates in the shed when he brought the birds in. He hadn't looked in any of them. It was better not to know. These were dangerous people. What if they didn't realize who he was and thought that he was trying to steal what was there?

Moving fast, he got out of the door, half-closing it behind him, then went to his car and switched off the headlights. The world turned black and he crouched in the dirt. He couldn't move the car now. It was safer to hide and drive out after they'd gone.

Straining his ears to hear what was going on, he crawled back to the shadows of the shed and then, crouching, he moved along the wall away from the noise.

Jim heard the metal clunk of car doors being opened. He could hear they were talking but not what was being said until the engine switched off.

"Maybe it was just your headlights reflecting on something," said a voice.

She was young, female and sounded uncertain—not what he had expected. Pulling himself upright, he accidentally banged his injured finger on the tin of the shed and had to stifle a groan.

"Maybe," came a second, male this time.

They sounded like kids. More relaxed now, Jim poked his head around the corner. There were only the two of them that he could see.

"We should go," said the girl, but the boy took a step forward, peering into the darkness. Jim recognized Tony Bayless.

"I'm sure I saw something," Tony said.

This posed a different kind of threat. If Tony found the birds, he'd most likely tell his father or phone Mick Carmody and that would wreck everything. This whole operation could be easily traced back to him. His fingerprints would be all over it. Not only would this destroy his business, it could ruin everything. The others would blame him.

The boy hadn't moved.

The girl said, annoyed now, "I'll head over by myself then," but she wasn't moving either.

He hadn't locked the shed. If they came closer they could walk right in.

There was a sudden noise in the air. A whoosh, an explosion and the sky filled with light. Fireworks were exploding. There was a muffled squawk from inside the shed. Jim held his breath but there was nothing more from the birds.

"What's going on? It's way past midnight," said the girl. Jim could hear the excitement and surprise in her voice as another went screeching upward, streaks of silver and gold blurring and dissolving.

The boy's eyes turned skyward as well.

"We should go," she said again, moving toward the car.

She was a pretty girl. Jim could appreciate her shape silhouetted by the headlights. Nice long legs, tight ass and high breasts, she should distract any red-blooded male but Tony still stood there, uncertain.

Jim held his breath.

"We're missing the fun," said the girl.

She had him. Tony turned at the word "fun." The boy fancied her after all.

"All right," Tony said.

Jim watched them drive away and quickly got into his own car.

16

spend the day in client meetings with Colcart. Their in-house counsel is
one of those people who lowers the IQ of every room he enters. He was
furious about the expert report putting the blame on Colcart. Not only
would he not even contemplate settling, he wanted a new expert witness,
despite the fact that he had personally endorsed the current one. Someone
who would be "more aligned with Colcart's commercial reality," he said.

By the time I get home I've got just enough energy to screw the top off
a bottle of wine and pour myself an enormous glass and then as an afterthought microwave an anemic square of frozen lasagna to the texture of soft
plastic. The fridge is empty, the flat is empty and I am empty. My soulless
apartment with furniture someone else chose because work was too busy
feels the same as my father's impersonal room at the nursing home. Lonely.

I pour myself another and try to think of a strategy to convince Colcart
to settle but nothing comes to mind so I search for something else to do.
On the coffee table is the bundle of documents that were in the trunk
of the Mustang. I brought them up to my apartment to find out what

sort of window seals I need to order for the car. At least I can achieve one thing today.

Looking at the papers, it seems Dad kept everything. There's the original owner's manual, every registration document, membership to the "Pony Club," some itineraries from old Mustang events. Leafing through them is like bringing my father into the room. His presence is greater in these papers than when I'm holding his hand in the nursing home. At the very back of the pile is a handwritten receipt for some repair work done years ago. The actual date is faded but January 1997 is legible at the top. It's not Dad's usual repairer, it's an address in the city for a replaced headlight, fixed panel and re-chromed bumper. The car was also resprayed.

Here is the proof of Tess's accident.

Sixteen-year-old me would want to wave it in her face to see if she'd keep arguing about never hitting a kangaroo but thirty-five-year-old me feels a hundred and has had enough of this dismal day, so I go to bed instead.

Hours later, something wakes me up. The alarm clock tells me it is too early for the day to start. I'm alert but I don't know why. Living by yourself, there is a vigilance switch that never really turns off, like a dog that keeps one ear open.

Quiet.

I turn over and nestle back into the dent in my pillow.

There are the usual nighttime sounds of the city with far-off cars and the rumble of trucks and the regular wail of a siren. The local fire station around the corner was one of the reasons I chose this apartment. It might not be my dad in a police car, but it is close enough. Settling again, I hear the gentlest tinkle of glass breaking and I know instantly that's the noise that woke me. Keeping my eyes closed, I begin to drift from that sound. Probably a smashed bottle on the street below. Noise always travels further at night.

There is the rattle of the door. A click as the handle turns, a creak as it opens and the world which was firmly outside a second ago, comes rushing in.

I sit up.

Suddenly the cars are not so far away and then as the door shuts, the sounds muffle as though someone has put their hand over a mouth, but it's not as it was before.

This is my door.

I stop breathing, strain my ears and listen.

My brain whirs and spins so much that I almost miss the next noise. The sound of my door locking again. It has been deadbolted. Then a scrape as the key I keep in the lock is pulled out. I cannot get out of my flat without a key.

Sitting in my bed, wearing only a skimpy nightie, I try to convince myself that I am mistaken.

Footsteps are getting closer. The click of a flashlight and the reflection of its beam creeps under the crack in my bedroom door and begins to crawl across the bed.

This is happening.

Doors in my hallway begin to open. It's like a monstrous game of hide and seek.

The first door opened is my coat closet full of boxes of photocopied work documents that I haven't got around to shredding yet. The paper swishes out onto the floor.

There is a quiet "fuck." The voice is deep, accent broad. Paralyzed with panic, I think about screaming but that will only give away my location with no guarantee of help arriving. And if people do come how will they get in?

My eyes start to hunt around the room.

I have to find my phone and call for help. An image of it in my handbag on the living room table flashes into my head.

Another door opens. This time it's the bathroom. There is the rap of shoes on the tiles.

I need to get dressed. I need to think of a way out of here. I need to get help.

It's all been so quick that I haven't even started shaking, but a sense of dread is taking over, making my fingers clumsy and my feet stumble.

Clothes.

I grab my undies and shove them on. Probably useless, but it feels important.

The feet again.

My bedroom is two doors away.

Perhaps they can be distracted. My jewelry box is in the top drawer. Maybe I should tip it on my bed to make it easy for him. He can grab it all and leave. Solitaire diamond earrings, a jade bracelet, a pearl necklace. There's a few thousand right there. But he will know for certain I am here.

Finally, fear focuses me. I need to hide.

I've too much stored under the bed to get in there quickly and easily. I always meant to clean it out but never could be bothered. Something so unimportant now feels life threatening. I swallow an almost-sob.

Instead, I choose the wardrobe, the most obvious spot but there is nowhere else. The sliding door is already open, a mouth waiting to swallow me up. It is a shelter but also a trap. Once in, there is only one way out.

The hall light is switched on and the room moves from grays to muted yellow. Sliding the door almost completely shut, I push past the clothes, the soft rustle of dry-cleaner's plastic loud as gunshots to me. Turning around, I stand unevenly on shoes and huddle down into the smallest space possible, pulling the clothes back, origami-folding myself into the tightest knot I can. My heart beats hard enough to crack ribs. The wardrobe could shake from the force of it. Questions run through my head like ticker tape. What if he has a gun? A knife? I should have grabbed a wire hanger, something to strike out with, to get at his eyes.

The room has been reduced to the tiniest crack but when he enters I can feel it.

Light comes first as he pushes the door open but he doesn't flick the switch, relying instead on the flashlight. He is a dark featureless shape, a shadow made alive. When he stands in front of the wardrobe the room is swallowed up.

Then he moves and the chink of light returns.

I cannot see his face.

He's at my bed now, placing a hand on the sheet and I realize my first mistake.

It should look like it hasn't been slept in.

He can feel my warmth. He knows I'm here.

The sheets are torn off the bed so viciously the material rips. His breath is short and quick. He's making strips to tie me up. I feel a crazy impulse to shout, as if by yelling I will suddenly jolt awake and all of this will disappear.

Instead, I close my eyes tightly, put my hands over my mouth to stop myself from screaming, and imagine him coming toward the wardrobe, opening the door and dragging me out by my hair.

But when I open my eyes again, he is gone.

His footsteps get farther away, toward the kitchen and living room.

All I can hear is the blood thumping in my ears.

There's the jangle of keys, the door opens and then shuts and there is nothing else for a long time.

Eventually a jagged sob comes out, a sound I have never heard myself make before. I'm sweating pins and needles. My stomach is churning. Falling out of the wardrobe, I crawl on the floor until I get to the bed and haul myself up.

I have to ring the police.

Stumbling out into the hall, squinting in the light, I hear him before I see him. He slams me into the wall, my head bouncing forward and my teeth cutting my tongue. I can feel his body pressing hard against mine. My arms are twisted back, held in place and then bound.

Thrashing my head around to try and see him, I open my mouth to shout, but a piece of sheet is stuffed in and as I gag, another is tied around my mouth to stop me spitting it out.

All the time I want to say *please, please, please* as my knees give way.

I am pulled upward and flipped around until we are face to face and when I see him for the first time, my brain begins to scream.

17

New Year's Eve 1996

Tess

Bridie tied the halter behind Tess's neck and then took a step back to assess.

"Not too much?" Tess asked. The neckline was sitting low and she jiggled up and down to convince herself that it wouldn't slip any further.

"Definitely no bra," agreed Bridie. "The straps will show."

As Tess leant forward her breath fogged up the mirror. Bridie leant over and traced a love heart on the surface but was interrupted before she could add initials.

"What are you doing?" asked Eliza from the doorway. She was standing sideways, her face in profile. Walking into rooms like an Egyptian was her latest attempt to disguise her mismatched eyes, which was ridiculous. Probably designed to make me feel guilty, thought Tess. She did feel a pang whenever she thought about Eliza's eye but there was nothing she could do to make it better now.

"Getting ready for the bonfire," said Bridie.

"Did I ever tell you how nice you are, Tess?" asked Eliza. "How you're the best sister in the world?"

"What do you want?" asked Tess wearily.

"Can I borrow your sandals?"

"I'm wearing them." Tess picked up a lipstick and carefully began to rim her mouth.

"C'mon, you've got lots of shoes to wear. I've outgrown all my good ones."

"Just go away." Tess looked at herself critically in the mirror.

"Are you really wearing that dress to the beach?" Eliza continued. "That looks like something you'd wear to a *party*."

Tess knew by the way Eliza drawled it out that her secret had been exposed.

"How did you find out?" Tess demanded.

Eliza looked at Bridie and Bridie looked at the floor.

"My silence will cost you," said Eliza.

"But they go perfectly with her dress," said Bridie, sitting down on Tess's bed.

Eliza pretended to pick up a phone, "Oh D-a-d," she sang out. "I just found out where the paddock party is being held."

"God, you are so annoying," sighed Tess. "They're under the bed."

"Scoot over then." Eliza plonked herself next to Bridie and immediately started to put them on.

"You're not really going with that lifeguard, are you? He's such an idiot," said Eliza.

"An idiot?" squeaked Bridie. "He's gorgeous."

Tess gave a coral-lipsticked smile. When she heard Travis had been busted for drunk driving she'd offered to borrow the family car and drive him to the paddock party.

"Tony Bayless more your speed?" asked Tess. Eliza got the hint and walked quickly to the door. She had one parting shot though.

"By the way, Dad got a flat tire this afternoon so you won't be able to drive the station wagon," and then ran out before Tess could take back the shoes.

"Shit," said Tess.

"What are you going to do?" asked Bridie. "If you stuff up Travis's night he'll never talk to us again."

Tess stood there, looking at her reflection in the mirror. She had been planning this for days, even catching the bus with Bridie to the next town to buy condoms just in case.

"I'll take the other car," she said.

Bridie looked uncertain. "Are you allowed to drive it?"

"Dad's on shift all night. I'll get it back in time. Eliza's going to leave before us anyway." Even if she got caught, she was prepared to wear the punishment. Anything was better than missing the party.

"Woo hoo," said Bridie. "Going to the party in our own Cadillac."

"It's a Mustang," said Tess.

The sun was setting by the time they drove up the hill behind the surf club. The plan was to park the car where no one would see it but Jim Keaveney was there.

"He's creepy, that Birdman," said Bridie, as they walked down the hill.

"He's just lonely," said Tess.

"Keeping all those birds locked up all the time, it's not right," argued Bridie.

Tess didn't say anything because she'd just caught sight of Travis talking to Dave Deasey, the class clown. Tess had always thought he was a little nuts but harmless. Still, why would Travis want to hang out with him? She looked at Travis again wearing a pair of board shorts, a baggy tank top and wraparound sunglasses and suddenly she felt ridiculously overdressed. This was a terrible idea.

"Promise you'll come to the party with me," said Tess, clutching Bridie's arm, but Bridie was too busy yelling out to Travis to answer. Travis's reflective lenses shone in their direction but then he went back to his conversation with Dave. As the girls approached, Dave was the only one who acknowledged their presence, dipping his head at them. Tess's smile was so rigidly fixed that she couldn't say anything in reply.

The minutes stretched as Travis didn't even look at her. Dave's eyes kept flicking between her and Travis as though there was some kind of game here and she didn't understand the rules. When her pride kicked in and she finally turned away, she heard guffaws of backslapping laughter behind her.

"Let's find a spot for our towels," she said to Bridie.

"Do you think he's getting a lift with someone else?" Bridie asked. "Or was it just a dumb joke in the first place?"

Tess didn't answer, just picked up the pace in last year's summer sandals, until she was almost floundering in the soft sand. Bridie fumed until Tess wanted to tell her to shut up. She kept her eyes straight ahead, fixed on the ocean, weaving through the crowd until she came to a family who hadn't bothered to take their umbrella down yet, so she could hide on the far side of it.

"This is too far back," complained Bridie, and Tess hoped that she might decide to sit somewhere else and leave her alone to shrivel up with embarrassment. Tess unfurled her towel just as a sudden wind gust caught like a sail and she had to wrestle it to the ground. Bridie stood there, her towel slung over her shoulder, and decided she'd go up to the shops to get some fish and chips.

"Want to come?" she asked. Tess shook her head.

"You want anything?"

Tess gave her money, relieved to be left alone. Lying there, she stared into the sky, watching it transition from denim to indigo. As the wind picked up again, she listened to the family next to her complain about sand in their eyes and how long would it be before the bonfire started, and she decided once it was properly dark, she would drive home, go to bed and never get up again.

"There you are," said Travis. Tess quickly flipped herself over. "I've been looking for you," he said and sat down next to her, smelling a mixture of Old Spice and beer.

Tess sat up quickly, a kind of giddiness in her head. Snaking his arms around her shoulders, he pulled her closer and she had to steady her breathing.

"Why did you go?" he asked. "We were just mucking about." Tess opened her mouth to reply, but Travis had already skimmed over the space where her answer belonged and moved on to how boring work had been today. His skin was still warm from a day's worth of sun, and as Tess nestled back into him, she could hardly concentrate on his words because she was so acutely aware of where her skin touched his. Eventually Bridie came back with her share of fish and chips, gave Tess a surprised look, and then in line with their earlier plans, said she had run into some other friends, and left again. Tess, too nervous for food, nibbled on one chip to look as if they were sharing, but Travis had no problem eating the rest.

She noticed Janey Bayless clutching her high-wedged heels in one hand, camera swinging around her neck, sashaying her way through the crowd. She stopped dramatically in front of them.

"I didn't know about this," she said, waving a hand and gesturing for them to move in closer. Tess hoped she wouldn't say anything to her father but when Travis wrapped his tanned arms around her narrow body she stopped worrying. She could feel her entire spine pressed up against his chest.

"Don't know what you see in him, Tess, a good girl like you," said Janey, as she looked at them through the camera's viewfinder.

Travis laughed, and Tess could actually feel the bass of it reverberate through his body.

"Now, don't you put up with any of his rubbish," said Janey.

Travis acted with mock outrage. "I always treat my girls like princesses," and Tess was torn between happiness at being called his girl and concern that it didn't seem like an exclusive position.

Janey pursed her lips. "Well, Happy New Year to you both," and then, wagging a finger at Travis, added, "Behave yourself."

"Have a good night, Mrs. Bayless," said Tess.

"Hmm . . . a good girl," said Travis once Janey was out of earshot. "Hope not too much of one," and when he kissed the side of her neck with hard lips, Tess felt a tingle all the way down to her groin.

Travis's hand was getting cocky now, moving from her knee and stroking upward. When Tess felt calloused fingers reach the pillowy softness of her inner thigh, she quickly shut her legs, blocking the path.

"Not here," she murmured.

He said nothing but hooked a finger through the strap of her dress and lifted it away from her skin. Looking down, she could see her own breasts vulnerably pale against her tan marks, and she felt something stiffen, blunt and heavy, behind her. Tess felt a mixture of curious desire and embarrassment all at once.

Travis removed his hand and put it down the front of his shorts to adjust himself. Tess pretended not to notice, instead watching the men standing around the bonfire with jerry cans.

"Isn't that your sister?" asked Travis, craning his head down the beach. The deep blue of dusk was deepening but she could still make out Eliza, no doubt wearing her new sandals, walking down toward the water with her friends. "Got those sexy odd eyes."

And Tess was surprised by a sudden gush of jealousy that masked something more complex. A feeling of uncertainty, perhaps. Everyone knew that she was the beautiful sister and Eliza was the smart sister. It was just the way things were.

"Not as sexy as you, though," he continued and his arm rubbed suggestively against the underside of her breast. "Who's that with her?"

"Just Amy and Grace," said Tess, trying to sound bored because they were only kids.

The three girls met a boy and clambered up onto the rocks. Tess felt regret about her sandals getting soaked and scratched.

"Took long enough," said Travis as the bonfire roared into life. She watched the sparks leap up and as she sat there she imagined that it was her old life burning up into something much more exciting.

"Time to go," he said eventually, standing up.

She shook out her towel before rolling it up. Looking up and down the beach, she couldn't see Bridie anywhere. "My friend's going to come with us," she said.

Travis looked annoyed. "I'm not waiting for her." He sounded like he wasn't that fussed about waiting for Tess either.

She bit her lip and when Travis held out his hand to her, she took it.

"I'm supposed to be staying at her house tonight."

Travis laughed. "That's all right then. I'll look after you," and he picked Tess up and slung her over his shoulder as if she weighed nothing at all.

He liked the Mustang just as Tess knew he would.

"Your dad's?" he asked, running a finger across the sharp ridge at the edge of the bonnet. "I've got to drive it."

"Dad would kill me if anything happened to it," said Tess, hoping he would understand that was a "no" because hadn't he lost his license? She got out the keys, feeling the hard leather of the keyring in her hand.

"I'll be good," Travis said, and he kissed her full on the lips, hot and open mouthed, their first real kiss and she was so caught up in the moment of it that she didn't even notice he'd taken the keys off her until it was too late.

However, Travis could drive well, much better than Tess in fact, and the houses flew past on fast forward, then the streetlights disappeared and Tess's world narrowed to the cat's eyes reflecting on the white posts by the side of the road.

"Is the party in the pine forest?" she asked, suddenly realizing that she still didn't know their destination.

"Just past The Castle," said Travis. "Dave squared it with Wes Bayless."

There was something about the vibrations of the car, the noise of the engine and his driving that made her pulse between the legs. Turning to smile at his profile, she tried to imagine what sex with him would be like, but he was focused totally on the road and seemed to have forgotten that she was even there.

Tess could see the outline of The Castle far off in the distance until the trees of the estate blocked it from view. She wanted to tell Travis to drive up to it so they could get out and dance on its lawn, just like she was a princess with her own Prince Charming, but Travis accelerated along Ophir Road until they came to an open gate and then drove up the track. Tess could see lights coming from the old woolshed.

"Better stick to the middle," said Travis, slowing down to a crawl, following the grooves made by other tires lit up in the headlights. "Don't want to get bogged."

Tess found it hard not to wince as they bounced along, thinking of what her father would say. Finally, they went through another open gate and parked the Mustang among the other cars on grass. Travis threw her the keys and then immediately found some guys from the footy club to talk to.

There were far fewer people than she had expected. Plenty of girls from school had sworn they were going, and had actually been coming to the party for years, and yet Tess couldn't see a single one. In fact, there weren't many girls here, just a handful dancing on the roughly made floor that had been assembled by laying down large bits of square plywood over the compacted dirt. Travis was slow on the introductions but diligent on drinks, so Tess stood there, not quite able to hear conversations over the music, taking large gulps from her beer in order to have something to do. She had decided that she would nurse the same drink all night but found herself having the one cup instead, over and over again. When it was midnight, Travis kissed her abruptly but immediately moved on to other girls and she found his friends kissing her as well. Dave Deasey slipped in an exploratory tongue before she could pull away, and then they went back to ignoring her again.

It was after the mistimed fireworks and her second trip to the port-a-potty, still clutching her cup like a safety blanket, that she saw Grace walking through the now empty dance floor.

"What are you doing here?" she asked. Grace was the first person she had spoken to in a while and her mouth and tongue seemed to be working independently of each other.

"Looking for you," Grace said. Tess was sure Grace was staring at her suspiciously and made a conscious effort to speak more clearly.

"Is Eliza with you?" she asked, clutching Grace's shoulders to steady herself. She was too close to Grace's face and everything seemed out of focus. The world swayed and her feet hurt. Maybe she could just lie down for a bit and someone could drive her home but she seemed to have lost Travis ages ago.

"Are you all right?" asked Grace.

"Great time," said Tess, because full sentences seemed too much and then her legs decided it was time to sit and she did, knocking a boy's drink over on the way down. He told them to fuck off.

"We can walk back into town," said Grace, but her voice sounded doubtful.

"Car," said Tess. Her eyes felt heavy.

"You can't drive like this," Grace said, her face swimming in and out of focus.

"Don't tell me," began Tess. The words were taking too long to connect so instead she pushed Grace hard in the chest, but the delivery was more of a smack.

"Girl fight," hooted a voice.

Tess's eyes shut and when she opened them up again to say "don't go," time had jumped, Grace had disappeared and the long face of Dave Deasey was there.

"I think you've had enough," he said, but his words didn't quite make sense to Tess. "How are you getting home?" he asked, handing her a cup. "It's only water."

She took a sip but her throat burned and she couldn't tell if it was her or the drink.

"I've got a car," she said.

There was a boy juggling beer bottles on the dance floor but he kept dropping them deliberately, trying to make them smash, and people were cheering him on. Tess put her wrist up to her face to read the time on her watch, but the numbers seemed to be jumping with the music.

"Travis?" she asked him. Her head hurt.

Dave looked embarrassed. "He's just stringing you along. How about I walk you to your car? Maybe lie down first before you drive."

There was something about the way Dave said this, a little too eagerly, with his arm slithering uninvited around her waist, that made Tess say no, she was fine, and she stood up and began to walk.

"You forgot your bag," he said, handing it to her. "Happy New Year."

"You too," Tess said, embarrassed, slinging it over her shoulder.

The night had turned cold and shivery around her. A girl she had seen dancing earlier was in the mud, asleep or unconscious, it was hard to tell. Her skirt was right up around her waist, exposing her underwear. Tess felt like she should check if the girl was OK but feeling far from it herself, simply pulled down her skirt, stepped over her and headed outside into the dark.

She tried to guess the direction of the car but got it wrong, so retraced her steps back to the shed and began again. Her head felt worse. Knots of shapes were sitting round a fire in a 44-gallon drum, and she walked nearer to ask for directions until she saw Travis was there and turned away. She never wanted to talk to him again.

There was a patch of silver up ahead which turned out to be moonlight glinting off cars. She picked up her pace until suddenly she fell to the ground. Bleary eyes looked down at her.

"Can't go," Travis slurred.

"Get off me," and she tried to push him away.

His breath was a wet mist of alcohol. He began fumbling at her neckline and suddenly her breasts were exposed. Tess almost expected him to stop and apologize but instead his hand clawed at them.

"No," she said, or was that only in her head, because this was happening so quickly that Tess couldn't believe it was happening at all. He kept talking, whispering in her ear things she had never been called before and when she tried to move, to push away, her arms were pinned beneath her. The strap of her bag was tangled up as well. Persistent fingers pulled her undies down, forcing her legs apart. She could feel his penis flopping between her thighs. Getting a hand free, she pulled at the arm holding her down. It was more a gesture, a demonstration of the words that were stuck in her throat. The backhander she received in reply was enough to make her teeth rattle. When she opened her mouth to cry, not even sure she could make a sound, he clamped an enormous palm over it.

Tess angled her head, turning so she couldn't see the look on his face, but she couldn't stop herself hearing him grunt. All the warmth leached out of her and she became completely still. She forced herself to stare at a nearby tree, to pretend she was flying up to it, until she was at the top, looking down on the bucking naked ass of Travis Young as he drilled into some poor girl she barely recognized.

Only when Travis got up and walked away, leaving her lying in the mud, did she realize several other boys had been watching and had done nothing to stop him. People she had seen in town all her life had stood there. That was when she began to cry.

"She's had enough," one of the shadows said, as if it had all been her idea. It was Dave. He pulled her to standing and Tess, terrified he was going to do the same as Travis, spun her bag around and smacked it into him.

"Fuck," he said. "You're a psycho."

And she felt psycho. The protective shell that was Tess Carmody the good girl, who thought kindly of others and expected kindness in return, had been cracked open and the inside of her spat out.

She didn't turn on the headlights. She didn't want anyone to notice her going, to chase and pull her from the car and do that all over again. Instead, she pushed too hard in reverse and skidded in the mud.

There were no words for the pain, or if there were Tess didn't know them. She could still feel his fingers digging into her skin as if he'd left a trail of bruises marking out his path. Her arms and legs trembled and didn't seem to obey instruction because she wasn't sure they still belonged to her, but still the car kept moving. Just as she came to the road from the dirt track she thought she heard a noise, a call, someone telling her to stop but the world outside didn't matter. Nothing mattered now. She was going to drive away as fast as she could and she didn't care about anything or anyone else and she never would again.

18

Luke Tyrell stands in the hallway in front of me.

Instinctively, I lash out with my legs, trying to kick him. There's a grunt as my foot connects somewhere above his knee and he bends over. I kick hard again, getting ready to sprint to the door, but he was only fooling and in an instant he grabs my foot and twists. He pulls my leg higher, I overbalance and crash into the floor, my hip and shoulder taking the brunt of the impact. He reaches around, grabs my hands and half carrying, half pulling, drags me into the living room and throws me onto the couch.

The gag works its way further down my throat making me choke. Every time I try to breathe the material seems to expand and all I do is cough more, panic more and breathe less.

Luke crouches down next to me.

Feeling that I am suffocating, my eyes fill with tears.

"I'll take off the gag if you promise not to yell," he says.

Panicking, I nod.

He rips it down and pulls the spit-sodden material from my mouth. The air comes in huge wheezing shudders. He stays next to me, gag at the ready. I stare at the floor trying to stop myself from throwing up.

Slowly, I raise my head to take in his dark jeans, the hoodie over his black T-shirt. There's a little ducktail flick of hair just above the collar and heavy stubble across his face. When I get to his eyes there is fear in them. I quickly look away because nothing is more contagious.

"I'll get you water," he says. "Don't move." He knocks into the coffee table on his way out and the bundle of Dad's documents spills across it and onto the floor. He swears, but doesn't bother to pick any of them up. He heads to the kitchen, which is just off the living room, and turns the tap on. Pain comes rushing in. My head and body throb from the impact of my fall. The handbag is sitting on the dining table about five meters away. Testing the bonds around my wrists, my hands can barely pull apart. I stare at the piece of paper in front of me, trying to keep myself from giving in to full-blown panic. My father's signature is on it and I recall a childhood promise to keep me safe by locking up all the bad guys.

Why aren't you coming to rescue me now, Dad?

Luke comes back with a cup and holds it to my mouth. Water rushes out too quickly. I try to gulp but instead cough and splutter. He swears and rights the cup, waiting for me to stop before managing the flow more gently, like a parent helping a child. The water trickles down, smoothing away the roughness in my throat.

He puts the cup on the table and takes the seat opposite me. He sways a little as he sits down. Is he on drugs? And if he is, does that make this situation better or worse?

Dad always carried a cigarette packet with him because there's nothing like a smoke for instant camaraderie. His voice comes into my head unbidden. *Scared people make stupid decisions. Give him a chance to relax. Become his friend.*

"Sorry." My voice is thick. "You scared me. I shouldn't have tried to run." I can still taste the material in my mouth, the fur of it on my tongue.

"People want to kill me, you know. I could hardly knock on your door." His arm is hitting the side of the chair like some sort of tic.

"How did you find me?" It's not the right question but I can't help it.

"Mum checked your car license at the nursing home. She said I needed to explain to you what happened."

Instantly I hate her but I swallow that down for now. It can wait.

"Cadee wouldn't have said to tie me up."

Tap. Tap. Tap goes the hand.

"You weren't supposed to run," he says. His eyes are feverish red, from drugs or exhaustion it's still too hard to tell. I need to improve my position while everything is fluid.

"I won't run now," I say. "So you can untie me."

There's an instant frown as he tries to size me up, to test the logic of what I am saying.

"I swear I won't." I try to smile but it's too hard.

Make an assessment and then work on anything you have in common, Dad tells me.

Luke stands up and walks behind me. Sitting in the small of his back there is a gun tucked into his belt. My heart contracts. Pulling my arms roughly, he tries to get the binds loose but I don't wince. The last knot is undone and then I am free. Instinctively, I want to rub my wrists but don't because I'm play-acting that there is no gun, that we are friends and that absolutely everything about this is normal, because if I do, then perhaps the demons inside him will go to sleep.

My nightie is bunched up around my waist, my underwear completely exposed. I stand slightly and edge the material back down, hoping he doesn't notice. I don't want him to have a single thought about what's underneath.

Luke sits back down in front of me, arms folded.

He must think you are on his side.

"Do you want something to eat or a cup of tea?" I ask, like he has been invited in as my guest. "Glass of wine?"

"No. I'm good." There is the smell of stale sweat to him but the scent of violence is receding. "You know, we haven't spoken a word to each other since that time on the beach." Leaning forward, he looks me straight in the eye.

His pupils are dark black pools and suddenly I am back there, swimming naked in the ocean, way out of my depth, trying to get as far away from the people on the beach, the witnesses to my humiliation. The temperature melts through my drunken haze until my limbs throb with coldness. Blood becomes slush in my veins. I am past the waves but the swell is rough. Blearily I tread water and turn back toward shore. The fire on the beach seems far away and getting further, until suddenly Luke is beside me, naked too. I launch myself at him like I'm trying to ride a wave. The kiss is inevitable, teeth crashing into each other, designed to show the world that I care nothing for Tony Bayless. Luke hauls me back in, holds me through the breakers and we fall onto the beach, all over each other. A bright light flickers on us and the reality of the situation comes crashing in as I see the look on Amy's face. I push Luke off me and am splutteringly sick.

Blinking hard, back in the present, I can still see the boy from that night in the man in front of me. The boy with a reputation for volatility but who had always been kind to me. How he ran and got my clothes, brought me back to the fire so I could get warm, stood up for me when Amy yelled, walked me back to town, took me to his house so I could sleep off the alcohol in his bed and then woke me at sunrise so I could sneak home without my dad noticing. All that and I never spoke to him again. Not even a phone call to say thank you because I was so ashamed.

I pull myself together because if I go to pieces now, who knows what could happen.

"What did you want to talk about?" I ask.

"People are calling me a murderer. I never meant for him to die."

He pauses, waiting for my reaction.

"Good," I say, because right now I will say anything. "That means you had no *mens rea*."

"See, you're a lawyer. I knew you'd understand." He leans forward, resting his elbows on his knees. "I ran up to talk to him and he punched me, said I'd fucked up because of that woman. If the police got involved that was the end of it. No payment, nothing. I know I was angry but he was on a permanent hair trigger. He once went after a guy in The Royal with a pool cue. Tony pulled him away before he killed the bloke. Why's no one talking about that? I tried to push him off me and he fell. He hit me first."

Jumbled images of the fight come into my head. I saw a fist, a punch and then Paul fell. Have I confused who struck the blow? Had I already taken sides because of what had happened earlier? Pat's words come back unbidden—*to lie like an eyewitness*. Paul might not be quite the hero I thought but still, he's not the one who broke into my house and tied me up.

"You should tell all that to your lawyer," I say. "That's exactly the information they will want."

He leans closer. His face is older than the rest of him, worn down and battle scarred.

"What if I give the police information? Tell them about the whole operation and plead guilty? They'd give me a reduced sentence, right? Maybe even suspended."

"What operation?"

"I'm not going to tell you." The volume of his voice increases like he is playing with the dials on a stereo. "That's valuable. I'll only tell someone who I can make a deal with."

Dad in my head says not to back down, to make Luke see I'm someone he should listen to.

"You'll need to give yourself up," I say. "You've got a good case but only if you give yourself up now."

He starts tapping the chair again.

"What about the bones?" he asks. "They're saying I killed someone and left their bones at The Castle."

"No one believes that." I'm scrambling to reassure him, but it's a problem too far. My calm facade starts to slip and my body begins shaking. It must be delayed shock.

Luke notices. "Are you OK?" he asks. "Do you want a blanket?"

"Would you mind if I put some clothes on?"

He hesitates and then nods.

I stand up quickly before he can change his mind. Heading into the hallway, he is only a step or so behind me because he's still worried that I might run. The door's locked anyway. I'm trapped.

Walking into my room, I see the unmade bed and instantly feel vulnerable.

"Can you turn around and close your eyes?" I ask.

He just stares blankly.

"I'll get dressed in the wardrobe then." Panic is starting to overwhelm me. I just need a few moments without him watching me to pull myself together.

A wash of red across his face. "Jesus, Eliza," he says. "It's OK. I'd never do anything like that."

It's the first time he's used my name. Dad would say that was a good sign.

"I just want to get dressed."

"Promise not to go out the window?"

"We're three stories up."

"Oh yeah, that's right," but he walks over to check it all the same. He's getting twitchy again. "I'll wait for you out in the hallway. Five minutes."

This is better than I hoped for.

"Thanks. I appreciate it."

He shuts the door behind him.

I could barricade myself in here, use the bed to block the door and refuse to come out but it's like I can't move. All my energy is still focused on him. There is a deep sigh, and then a kind of slipping sound like he's sliding down the wall and now sitting on the floor outside my door.

"Eliza," he calls out. There's almost a plaintive quality to his voice, like he wants to be reassured he isn't alone.

"Yes." I force myself to rip off my nightie and put on a bra.

There's a long delay before he speaks again as though there's something about the door between us that is giving him space as well.

"Did you really mean it about the bones? That they won't blame me."

"Yes," I tell him. "The truth is they are Grace Hedland's bones."

There, I've said it aloud.

That surprises him, I can hear it in his voice. "Grace who ran away?"

"Her jewelry was found nearby."

I open up my drawer to get a warm top and find my iPad in there. I hide my tech stuff when I go away for a few days and I hadn't had a chance to take it out again.

"Doesn't mean it's her body," he says, a note of doubt creeping in like he's worried I'm lying to him.

I need to keep him occupied while I work out what to do next.

"It's definitely her necklace. I recognized it. I just don't understand what Grace was doing at The Castle." My voice is detached from the rest of me, which is completely focused on the iPad. I stare like it is a mirage and then carefully pick it up. Please let the battery not be flat.

It's only on sleep mode so quietly I click the button.

2:28 A.M., 10% charge.

"She was at the paddock party," says Luke. "Dave Deasey saw her there, and that's only a ten-to-fifteen minute walk away."

"How did she get all the way to the paddock party from the beach?" The answer is obvious but I'm buying time.

Slide to unlock.

Enter passcode.

My mind is blank. I have absolutely no idea what it is.

"Must have been Tony," says Luke. "He left the beach about the same time and that's where he was going."

It's the four digits of my birthday, terrible as far as security goes, but thankfully obvious enough to remember in a crisis. As I press the numbers, there is the slightest click. The volume is up at maximum and I almost drop the iPad in my haste to turn it down.

"I guess," I say, trying to keep my brain divided in two. "But the police had a witness who said she left Kinsale that night on a train."

"No way," says Luke. His voice is so sure that it distracts me. "The trains were canceled . . ."

I press on the messages icon and the list of recent messages comes up. Gavin's sad-face emoji is down the bottom of the screen. All of a sudden my fingers stop moving and start shaking. I take a deep breath and focus on what Luke is saying.

". . . was out all the next day with the emergency services helping get fallen trees off the tracks. Dad made me do it as punishment."

"Are you sure that was the same year?" I ask.

"Yes." He's even more confident now. "He saw you leaving our house. Wanted to go round and tell your dad but Mum talked him out of it. I was grounded instead. That's why I never got to see you before you left for boarding school."

Any other time that information would have made me feel bad but not tonight. My fingers are clumsy and autocorrect makes me almost cry, but after deleting several times, I have: Luke Tyrell in my flat. Hostage. Has a gun.

Is that what's going on here?

If I say "hostage," then it's going to be a big response. If this was a message from an ordinary member of the public it would be sent to the local station and someone would come by to investigate. But I'm a police witness and a cop's kid. Luke is on the state's most wanted list. It will be the Critical Response Unit, if not Special Operations. You don't fuck around with stuff like this.

My hands feel clammy.

"So you're saying that Grace couldn't have left by train that night." My brain grasps that this is important too and I slowly try to process the implications of what he's saying.

"No," says Luke. "Didn't get the track cleared until late New Year's Day."

Do I press send? I think of all the things that could go wrong. This is an apartment block, which adds to the risk. A stray police bullet could kill a bystander or the person they are meant to be rescuing and the chances of Luke surviving are slim. Even after what's happened tonight I don't want that on my conscience. I wait for Dad's voice to tell me what to do but he stays silent.

"But if she didn't catch a train," I say, stating the obvious, "how do we know she left town?"

If I send this message the situation is out of my hands, which isn't good. Getting control is always the first thing to do with a new case. Then it hits me. I might not have my father's skills but I understand about negotiation and giving people legal advice they don't want to hear.

Hiding the iPad under the bed, I open the door quietly and look at him. Luke is sitting on the floor, his head resting back against the wall.

"They *are* Grace's bones," he says, and it is the curious emphasis on "are" that tells me a piece of the puzzle has suddenly slipped into place for him. He's now more certain of it than I am.

"What?" I ask.

I can see the hunter and the hunted in him.

"That's something valuable, that I can use," he says.

"Luke, you need to turn yourself in," I say, but he is caught up with his own thoughts.

The teenager I knew has been replaced by someone much more damaged and dangerous. His eyes narrow like he's assessing options, planning logistics.

"I know someone who'll want to listen to me now," he says so quietly it could be to himself as if he's forgotten I'm even there. "Someone who will help me if they want to keep that quiet."

A siren wails nearby and we both freeze.

"That's only a fire engine," I say. "There's a station around the corner. Another one will leave in a couple of minutes." But he's spooked and stands up, pulling my keys out of his pocket.

"Open the door and see if the coast is clear."

I unlock it and take a few steps outside, almost expecting spotlights to come on and men with guns telling me to put my hands up. The night is a dirty haze, impossible to tell friend from foe but there's no one out here.

"Give me a head start before you call the cops," he says, an acknowledgment of the limits of our friendship. The truce declared on account of our shared history is now over. He slips past me, blending into the night. I watch as he disappears, noting which direction he is heading and then count to a hundred—I don't know why, before running inside to phone the police.

19

'm going to take a mouth swab." There is a grim smile on an otherwise amiable face.

They've taken me to the main city police station. It is busy for so early in the morning but I've been given priority, or rather, anything to do with Luke Tyrell has.

Her gloved hands hold my chin firmly in place. I try not to flinch at the slithering stickiness of the latex, the clinical scent of disinfectant, but she notices.

"Only take a minute and then we'll get you something to drink."

She presses the swab stick against the inside of my right cheek in a circular motion, then, running across the gums, moves it to the other side.

I have a flash of Cadee brushing my father's teeth but I shove that memory away.

The stick is pulled out and she holds it up. There is a colored strand on the tip, the thinnest of threads. A quick look of satisfaction and she turns away to bag it. A bed sheet has become evidence. Science will verify my story. They don't just want to rely on my word, my memory.

To lie like an eyewitness.

Photos are taken of my wrists and my head where Luke banged it into the wall. I undress and my clothes are put into paper evidence bags, which are sealed with tape. When I explain about wearing something different when he broke in, how my nightie is on the bedroom floor, she tells me not to worry, that there are police at my apartment now. I think about them looking at the broken glass and dusting for fingerprints.

I never want to go back there again.

"All done," she says encouragingly. "You can get dressed." She hands me a T-shirt, sweatshirt and tracksuit pants.

I'm taken to the good interview room. There's one in every station, where they deliver bad news to unsuspecting families and conduct the first round interviews. Dad called them the "you-are-not-about-to-be-arrested" room. This one is nicer than most. The chairs haven't been worn in and there's a coffee machine with pods sitting next to it, which must be a recent addition. When I was a kid, Dad's kettle went missing every few months.

Exhaustion hits and all I want to do is curl up on the couch snail-like and sleep but the door opens and two detectives enter. The woman introduces herself and her male colleague, but I don't quite catch their names. She sits down next to me while he heads over to the machine and turns it on.

"Coffee?" she asks.

I nod.

"Black with one?"

"How did you know?"

"It's the way your dad drinks it," she tells me. "You're Mick Carmody's daughter, right?"

I nod again.

She's about my age with a warm smile, a kind face. Her hair is tied back in a messy kind of ponytail that was probably neat at the start of her shift. Her eyes have dark rings under them and her skin is a little gray. It's the face of a police officer who's been working lots of overtime and not getting paid for it. She must be one of the leads on the Luke Tyrell case.

"I used to work in Family Violence. Met your dad at a conference once and then worked with him on a few cases. I kept asking if he wanted to transfer and come up north to us for a bit. How is Mick these days?"

My brain is slow, still trying to process the last few hours. I stare at her for too long before saying, "Since the accident?"

She's puzzled and when I explain—badly—what happened to him, she shakes her head in disbelief and tells me she's just come back from maternity leave. I don't say anything about what Alan told me.

"I'm really sorry," she says. "He's one of the best." The other cop comes over with my coffee, which I leave untouched on the table.

We start talking about tonight and she tells me they think Luke broke into the apartment next door, whose owners are on holidays, went out onto their balcony and then climbed across to mine. I think back to the noises I heard and wonder if that fits.

"How did he find out where you lived?" she asks.

It's on the tip of my tongue to say "Cadee" but the image of her caring for Dad comes back into my head unbidden, the way she spoke to him gently, how she had combed his hair. If I was her, perhaps I'd have done the same. It's enough that I'm telling them about Luke.

I shrug.

"And Tyrell demanded you change your evidence about his attack?"

I take a while before answering. "No," I say. "He wanted to explain that I had got it wrong. That Paul Keenan had been the aggressor and not the other way around."

The male detective sits up a bit straighter. Neutral face, he's assessing me now, calculating, wondering if this might be a problem.

"It happened so quickly and I was inside my car, turning around in my seat."

It is the start of an excuse, the beginning of a retraction and the female detective throws a sideways glance at her partner and puts on a "don't panic" face. I'm not sure if it's for him or me.

"We'll get him," she says. "There's a full-scale hunt right now. He won't have got far. I'm sorry about what happened to you tonight but we will protect you. There's no reason to feel intimidated into changing your testimony."

I'm feeling a lot of things right now but being scared of Luke Tyrell isn't one of them. He isn't interested in me anymore, he's got a different plan. I try to explain that to her.

"It's OK," she says, shutting me down. "Right now, everything must be very confusing. We can talk again tomorrow."

They don't want to hear that their case against Luke is falling apart.

"No, this is important," I say. "I want to look at my earlier statement. I could have made a mistake. And there's something else, something Luke said."

I start talking about how Luke claimed the train wasn't running that night and I don't know if this is right but it must be easy to check and if it is right then the Kinsale bones must be Grace's which would mean that she never ran away twenty years ago but something terrible happened to her.

I am babbling and their initial confusion soon turns to despair because their main witness, someone who looked so good on paper, professional, just what a judge is looking for, has turned out to be batshit crazy. Then, confirming their worst fears, I start to cry.

"We'll stop there," she tells me more firmly, as I grab my handbag and open it looking for a tissue. "You need to sleep."

The male detective's phone beeps. He shows it to the woman, she nods and he leaves the room.

The envelope with Grace's necklace is still in my handbag. I am about to pull it out, to thrust it at her because I can't cope with anything right now, but she is still talking.

"I understand your brother-in-law has arrived. He's just getting an update on the investigation and then he'll come to see you."

She gives me the gentle smile again to show she's on my side but her eyes tell me I'm nuts. She stands up.

I ask the time and she tells me. The hours have merged together and it's much later than I realized. They must have got in touch with Gavin soon after I rang them. I can give the necklace to him. He will understand how important it is.

She's standing at the door. "Is there anyone else you would like us to call?" she asks. "A friend perhaps?"

When I don't answer, she tells me to think about it and that she'll be back in a few minutes.

The truth is there is no one to call. I can hardly ring Amy, who is about to give birth any day now, and besides, she's hours away in Kinsale. It's bad enough that Gavin has to come here but at least he's got a professional interest in this mess as well as personal. I've spent the last ten years negotiating the treacherous route from articled clerk to solicitor to senior associate to partner like it was one of those TV game shows with oversized obstacle courses. Relationships fell by the wayside ("you're married to your work"), weekends were workdays in casual clothes and friends became acquaintances. I would occasionally run into them crossing the road as I dashed to court or back again and I'd be introduced to spouses or see a new baby in a stroller and we'd hastily make plans that never got kept. There would be time for that later, I told myself, when I had made it over the finish line. Then I would be partner and the world would see, my family especially, that I was a success. But upon being made partner the mists suddenly lifted only to show yet another pinnacle to climb in the distance.

None of that matters now. I shut my eyes and try to work out exactly how it came to this.

To read the ashes.

I go all the way back to that New Year's Eve on the beach. At the start of that night I had two best friends. By the end of it I didn't. It's as simple as that and yet I did nothing about it, a fact I have been running from my whole life. It's as if, in that water, my heart froze and by the time I got to shore it had splintered on its own fault lines. I have tried to pretend it was nothing, when it was everything.

And with that realization there is a hush. The noises of a busy police station coping with the usual detritus of the night and the start of another day don't go away exactly but they do become more distant and I am caught up with Grace, the past and present wrestling with each other.

She is dead, I'm sure of that now. She has rushed from runaway to missing to dead like stations passed on the train she never caught.

Dad's office manager, Pat, told me about people's responses to traumatic events. You can sink or swim.

There's a knock, then the detective sticks her head back in. I imagine they've been outside the door furiously whispering their desperation about their only eyewitness going rogue, trying to work out how I can be contained and redirected.

"Gavin's on his way."

They'll be telling him to sort his sister-in-law out and get her evidence back on track.

"Thanks," I say.

"We'll arrange accommodation for you—your apartment will be off limits for the time being."

"No," I answer. "I'll sort that out myself." I've stopped flailing and am heading back to shore.

She's uncertain about what this implies and tries to assess the nuances of it but it doesn't matter what she thinks, because my decision has been made. I'm taking a week's personal leave from work and returning to Kinsale to follow the path back to my past and find out what's been there all this time.

20

Y ou should have just given it to him," says Amy. Her belly extends almost to the steering wheel but she insisted on driving me here, so she could talk me out of what I plan to do.

"This way is better," I say. "Gavin gets the necklace and will be forced to investigate. Besides, Grace's family has the right to know that it's been found."

We are parked in front of a neat weatherboard bungalow. There's an old Falcon in the driveway, the hood propped open like a hippo's mouth, Aaron Hedland peering into it. Twenty years ago he was a tall rangy boy, all long limbs in constant motion, but now he's muscled up in an intimidating sort of way.

"Show me the necklace again," says Amy.

I hand the plastic bag to her and she studies it the way doctors examine X-rays.

"It's hers," I say, but Amy isn't convinced.

"If the Hedlands take it to the police, Gavin won't be able to dismiss them like he did me."

"You didn't tell him about the necklace," Amy reminds me.

"He didn't give me the chance."

Gavin hadn't been prepared to even talk about the bones and he dismissed out of hand that they had anything to do with Grace. All he could focus on was Luke Tyrell and my witness statement.

"I'm surprised Gavin let you come back to Kinsale," Amy says, "with Luke still on the loose."

"He doesn't control my life. I'm still an adult."

"He just wants you to be safe. We all want that. I wish you'd come and stay with us instead of that poky motel."

I shake my head. I'm gambling that Luke doesn't want to pay me another visit but in case I'm wrong, I'm not risking Amy getting involved.

She hands the necklace back to me. "So, you are going to walk in there, effectively saying that Grace is dead."

"I'll be more sensitive than that."

"Eliza, I have to deliver bad news regularly. There isn't a magical set of words that softens the blow. Have you stopped to consider that they might not want to know? That the slimmest hope she is alive is better than none?"

"Is that what you do?" I ask. "Don't disclose a diagnosis to a patient so they won't lose hope?"

"I don't give them a diagnosis based on a gut feeling. I run tests, analyze their symptoms. I have real evidence."

I stare out through the front windshield trying to choose the right words. Farther up the street, kids are playing a game of kick-to-kick on the road.

"This is her necklace. Those bones are of a young woman. I'm not making any of this up. Aren't you worried about what happened to Grace?"

"Of course I am but I'm also worried about you."

"I can't fix what I did that night, Amy, but I can try and make amends now."

"And somehow manage to do something your dad tried for years and couldn't?" Amy closes her eyes, frustrated with me. "Can you hear yourself?

All you are going to do is upend people's lives for no reason. It's just like when we were growing up, you make rash decisions and get yourself into trouble."

"I have to do this."

The car seems too small for this sort of conversation.

Amy shakes her head. "Well, if I can't change your mind then get out because I need to pee desperately."

"Is everything OK with you?" I ask.

"Don't start," she says. "I'm not the one acting crazy."

She drives off, navigating her way through the neighborhood footy game. I cross the road and walk up the driveway.

I'm not really sure how to start investigating, but returning Grace's necklace to where it belongs this seems an important first step.

Aaron is in the driver's seat, turning the ignition key. The engine isn't catching. My hand gives an involuntary half-wave on the opposite side of the windshield from him. The shoulder length hair from his teenage years has been cut short to his skull. Dark eyes dart toward me, his eyebrows changing from frustrated to surprised.

"Don't suppose you know anything about cars?" he says. His voice is deeper as well. It's a nice voice, mellow, and friendlier than his appearance.

"Only that I need other people to fix them."

He gives a generous grin. Grace's was the same. He clambers out of the car, wearing a ripped T-shirt and shorts with a swipe of grease on them. Geometric patterned black tattoos run down both legs and one arm, a mixture of beauty and menace.

"Wish Mum agreed with you," he says. "I'm out here mucking around until she gives up and lets me take it to the mechanic."

"Want me to turn the ignition while you check out the engine?" I ask.

Leaning back in the front seat, I can feel that it holds the warmth from his body. It seems too intimate somehow, as if I accidentally brushed up next to him. I sit bolt upright and turn the key. There's no sound, only a click.

"The starter motor?" I call out, mostly because my father complained about that all the time.

He frowns at the engine and then shrugs. Holding open the hood with an enormous hand, he unhooks the prop and slams it shut.

I get out and hand the keys back to him.

"I'm Aaron," he says.

"We've met before, a long time ago. I'm Eliza Carmody. I was a friend of your sister's."

"Oh," he says and looks more carefully at me. "I remember you." I wait for the comment about the eyes, but he doesn't say it. "You and Amy Liu."

"Yeah," I say. "Amy just dropped me off."

He nods. "She's treated Mum a few times."

"How is your mum?"

"Have you come to see her?" he asks. "She's not home at the moment."

"Actually, I wanted to talk to you."

The two of us sit at a kitchen table with a worn laminate top, warming our hands with cups of tea we don't drink. We look at a photograph that Aaron has kept in his wallet for twenty years, folded over so often it feels as soft as cloth. The sixteen-year-old versions of us sealed inside its edges, stuck like insects in amber. I'm slightly blurred, moving just as the camera clicked, mouth wide open, half smile, half grimace, exposing too much top gum. My eyes are safely hidden behind sunglasses. Amy is on one side, her head bent down looking at her feet and Grace is in the middle, laughing, face tilted toward the lens, clutching onto me, her right arm thrown around my shoulders. She is wearing a necklace identical to the one that is lying on the table in front of us.

"We found the picture in our letterbox after she went missing."

"It was taken while we were waiting for the bonfire," I say, recognizing the clothes.

"So she was wearing it that night," he says and his fingers trace the necklace in the photo. He reaches out for the real version, but before he touches it, he pulls his hand back and folds his arms. We both sit there thinking through the implications.

Eventually he stirs. "You want to take it to the police?" he asks.

"If you take it, they'll give it more attention."

He keeps staring at it lying there on the table.

"I had started umpiring a few footy games, got a bit of money, bought it for her birthday."

"She loved it."

"And this was up at The Castle near those bones?" he asks.

"That's what I was told."

"I heard on the radio that that they were a teenage girl's but I didn't even think of Grace. The police told us she had left town. Even now, after all this time, the doorbell goes or the phone rings and the smallest part of me still hopes." He looks at me with glistening eyes.

The front door creaks open and, as crazy as it sounds, for a moment I think it is Grace. By the look on Aaron's face he's thinking the same.

"Aaron, you home?"

It sounds just like her, except she's tremulous as if worried no one is there, and for a second I wonder if I'm going crazy, like hearing my father the night Luke broke into my apartment. Aaron is already standing up.

"In the kitchen, Mum. We've got a visitor."

Leaning on a walking stick, Mrs. Hedland comes in.

She has changed.

A tall, angular woman, she is much thinner now. Her body seems to be made up of only hollows and absence. The veins in her neck are as prominent as tree roots. Her face is shrunken, her features larger, especially her eyes.

"You remember Eliza Carmody, Mum. Mick's daughter."

There's instant recognition of my father's name. "Course I do." Hooking her walking stick over the crook of her elbow, she hugs me, a far friendlier gesture than I was expecting.

"What a lovely surprise."

Her eyes glance at the table and she sees the photo and the necklace. In a flash her face switches from curiosity to recognition. She clutches her mouth.

Aaron grabs her arm and gently guides her to a chair, beginning to explain why I am here. She leans forward, her breath becoming increasingly fast and noisy, hands outstretched in front of her, rigid as flippers.

"C'mon, Mum." Aaron crouches beside her. "Try to get the breathing under control. Start to regulate it."

He takes one of her hands, strokes it rhythmically and keeps placating her in a calm voice, but she is almost keening now.

"What can I do?" I ask. "Get a doctor?"

"It's just a panic attack," he says in a voice that suggests he has seen it many times before. "Try breathing through your nose."

"Can't do this." Her voice is high and shrill.

"You'll be right, Mum. Do you want to go to the couch?"

He has to repeat himself several times because she isn't taking it in. She stands suddenly, shaking. "Lie down," she says.

Aaron guides her to the couch in the next room. I see a blanket on a nearby chair and pass it to him, who wraps it around her.

This is what Amy was trying to warn me about. Grace's disappearance wore down to a pebble for me, one that I have had to carry all these years but was able to ignore, but it has crushed her family.

I sit on a seat in the corner of the room, hoping they'll forget I'm even there. After twenty long minutes the attack seems to have passed. Mrs. Hedland remains huddled under the blanket but recovers enough to ask Aaron about the necklace. When he gets to the part about taking it to the police, she looks at me.

"Mick rang me every year on Grace's birthday. Every year except this one. I still expected him to call even though I knew he couldn't."

I try to smile but it's too watery.

"He was always there." Aaron nods in agreement. "He'd drop everything to check whatever information came through. Told us to call him day or night if we heard anything."

Pat and Alan had told me that Dad did everything he could but it's reassuring to hear it from her family.

"We'll have to go to the police, Mum," repeats Aaron. "See what they say about it." A tear runs down his cheek. Old wounds are reopening.

Mrs. Hedland nods absentmindedly.

Aaron dashes a rough hand across his face. Without a word, he peels himself off the chair and heads out of the room. Mrs. Hedland watches him go. A moment later, I hear a basketball bouncing.

"That's the sound of my son thinking," she says. "You've given us a lot to think about."

"I'm very sorry."

"Don't worry about him. Some people have a knack for happiness. No matter what life serves up, they can cope. Aaron's like that."

"And you? Will you be all right?"

The smallest shake of her head is all the answer I get. Her eyes slide away from me.

"You go now," she says. "I'll rest up here for a bit."

Aaron is shooting a ball into an old rusty basketball hoop attached to the garage. He gets every single one of them in cleanly. For someone so big, he moves fluidly, balanced and poised like every action is choreographed. His head turns my way and he misses the next shot.

"You're good," I say.

"Used to be. Dodgy knees these days." His voice is huskier than before.

"I'm really sorry that your mother got so upset."

He comes over and sits down on the doorstep. A simple gesture of his hand invites me to join him, so I do. We stare straight ahead, not looking at each other. In the distance is a row of maples, leaves beginning to turn flame red on their way to falling.

The words come out of the side of his mouth as though this conversation is being dragged out of him. "The police said she left town on a train, that she told people she was going to the city."

"The trains weren't running," I say. "The line was shut down." I'd confirmed what Luke had told me with three different sources, even going through the old notebooks of a local train obsessive who lived across from the station.

Aaron slowly shakes his head as if he can't quite believe what he is hearing. He picks up the basketball in his hands and pushes so hard against it, I'm worried it will burst.

"Why weren't we told that?"

"I don't know."

"I used to imagine," and he's talking in such a low voice that I have to lean toward him so I can hear, "that she was off seeing the world and left me stuck here, looking after Mum. I tried to convince Mum to move. Go back north to her people, or further west to her brother, but she could never leave this house because when Grace came back she wouldn't know where to find us."

He stands and hurls the basketball with such force, a great one-armed throw, that it lands right across the road before rolling into the gutter on the far side. The footy game has migrated to nearer the house and one of the kids runs over to pick it up.

"Want it back, Aaron?" a small toothpick of a boy asks.

Aaron slowly nods and the kid speeds over and then chucks it to him.

"Thanks, Charlie," Aaron calls, and then as an afterthought, "Tell your brother he better be at school tomorrow. No more ditching or he's off the team."

"He's been real sick," Charlie says, but gives a wicked laugh.

"I'll kick him off. Serious," says Aaron.

Charlie flashes a freckled-faced grin and then a thumbs up.

"We trusted Mick," Aaron says, turning back to me.

"Unfortunately, he can't give us an explanation," I say. The fact Dad missed something as big as this bothers me.

"Still unconscious?"

"Just about."

"He did help," Aaron concedes. "I'm not saying he didn't. Got me a job coaching basketball down at the Police Boy's Club and when the club cleaner job came up, he gave it to me. Mum couldn't work much then and the money was good. Afterward, I found out he was topping up my wages out of his own pocket. He didn't have to do any of that."

That makes me pause. How could Dad afford it? There were my boarding school fees as well. Police are never paid enough. I started earning more than my father within a couple of years working as a lawyer.

"Why should we trust the police to find out what happened to her now," Aaron continues, "when they got it wrong twenty years ago?"

"You need to put public pressure on them," I say. "Talk to the media. There's lots of interest in those bones already." Hunting through my handbag, I find the card from Stella. "She works at the local newspaper. You could try her."

Aaron takes the card and studies it. His face is creased with worry lines like I've taken a chisel to him and carved them there myself.

"Was it right that I told you?" I don't even mean to say this aloud but it almost falls out of my mouth.

"I don't know," says Aaron. "I really don't know."

21

An enormous pink Janey Bayless is rakishly parked in front of Emerald Coast Homes, the words "She'll Get It Done" emblazoned underneath. The banner sits on the back of a trailer stretched across the two disabled spots. Even the car attached to it has a smaller Janey stuck to its side. It's forced a mini-bus to pull up farther away from the entrance and a group of unimpressed residents, herded by care attendants, are complaining loudly.

Ryan, the nurse I met on my first day, stops to talk to Mary, who is being eaten alive by an enormous mohair cardigan today. Mary looks disdainful, turning her head in the opposite direction like a giant bird, all eyes and fluff. Ryan smiles at me and then gets on the bus as well.

"Where are they off to?" I ask her.

"New fitness center in the next town. Water aerobics." She punctuates the sentence with a snort at the ridiculousness of it.

I sit down on the bench. "Could be fun."

"They fooled me once. Told me I was going for a swim. Thought they meant the ocean but instead it was idiots making tits of themselves, bobbing up and down in germ-infested water."

"Beach or nothing?"

"Spent my life at the beach and got the skin cancers to prove it." She lifts back her hair to show me a nibbled ear. "Husband was a lifeguard, son and grandson too. Only one who didn't like it was my daughter but she's no good anyway."

"I saw your grandson's bench."

Her head swivels and an owlish eye peers at me. "Travis was a good boy."

"It must have been a terrible accident."

"They said he was drunk driving," Mary says. "But I knew something was wrong."

"Like what?"

A hand slides out and clutches onto my arm. Her skin is so cold I'm tempted to check her pulse. "The bottles were wrong. Bourbon ones were all rattling around in his car. But my Trav didn't drink bourbon. He hated it. Only drank beer or rum. Someone ran him off the road," she whispers. "Made it look like an accident. I said so, even went and told your father, told him to test Trav's blood, but no one took me seriously."

There's the smell of conspiracy theory to this and more than a touch of madness in the way her eyes bulge, which makes me want to pull my hand away, but I feel too sorry for her.

"I could take you to the bench, if you like," I say.

She slowly nods and then releases me, her hand disappearing into her cardigan's furry depths.

"You're a good daughter. First time I saw you, I thought you'd be a one-visit-wonder like my lot."

I haven't been a particularly good daughter. Even now, my agenda for visiting my father is complicated. I'm going to tell him about Grace and the trains and see if there is any reaction.

"Promised the world," continues Mary, "and now I'm lucky if I get an invitation to Christmas dinner. My lot will only turn up when my money comes through but they won't see a cent of it. Never coming to visit me."

"There's a few visitors today," I say, pointing to the trailer.

"She's inside trying to get some early votes," Mary explains.

"Are you going to vote for her?"

"Of course," Mary says. "I've known Janey all her life. Father was a bully and she made the mistake of marrying one but that hasn't stopped her. She's just what this town needs right now. If it wasn't for her there wouldn't be this class action. When I get my settlement, I'm going to leave here."

Mary and I sit there, watching the traffic go by. The area looks less tidy today, food wrappers and dried leaves clogging the gutter.

"Getting a bit messy," I say. "Hasn't Jim Keaveney been in today?"

"Been knocked for six by that boy's death. Missing shifts. Word is they might sack him."

"What boy?"

"The Irish one."

"Paul Keenan?"

"A charmer. Always used to say hello when he came here to visit Jim."

"Did he visit often?"

Mary shrugs. "Enough. The two of them used to go bush. Made Jim feel special showing him around. Now he can barely do anything. If it wasn't for his birds, I reckon he wouldn't get up in the morning."

There's a glimpse of blue and white up the street. It's a police car heading in our direction. It slows, turns its blinker on and pulls into the lot, the face recognizable behind the windshield. My brother-in-law parks the car next to the Mustang.

"He's got a face as red as a slapped bum," says Mary. "Someone's for it."

My heart sinks because I've a good idea who that someone might be.

Gavin slams the car door and walks over to us, stiff-legged and serious.

"Mrs. Young." A curt nod is directed at Mary. "Eliza, a word."

"Don't mind me," says Mary, retreating into her harmless old lady act. She cocks her head to one side. "Just out here waiting for my lift."

Gavin actually puts his hand on my arm and forcibly moves me in the direction of his car, like I'm under arrest.

"What are you doing?" I say, snatching it away.

"Exactly the question I want to ask you," he says, towering over me. "You could start by explaining why a journalist rang this morning asking me to confirm The Castle bones belong to Grace Hedland."

There's a type of righteous anger that cops learn to turn on and off like a tap designed to frighten the gullible or get someone to talk, but this is the real deal. Gavin is red-rag-to-a-bull furious with me, but after ten years in litigation I've been yelled at by bigger bastards than him. The best tactic is to shut up and wait until they run out of puff or blow a gasket, whichever comes first. He hunches over so he can get right in my face, trying to keep his voice low enough so Mary can't catch it but I see her in my peripheral vision shuffling closer.

"Or why I've spent the morning talking to the Hedland family because they thought the same thing. I told you not to interfere, Eliza. I said we were waiting on forensic information which would be released to the public at the appropriate time." His nostrils flare. "And the reason I said that is because I'd already seen Dr. Adler's initial assessment which made it clear there was no way these bones could be Grace Hedland's."

It takes a moment for the full impact of this to hit me.

"A fact I had to explain to her distraught family this morning," he continues. "Mrs. Hedland is an ill woman. How dare you give her false hope."

"But the necklace," I begin. "It's hers. Aaron has the photo."

He points a finger directly at me. "A necklace you never bothered to tell me about and instead told Pat Fulton. Even if that necklace does belong to Grace, which is unlikely, it is certainly not related to the bones. I promised Aaron I would send it off to be analyzed, which I will do, a task you have made considerably more difficult than it needed to be. You have done terrible damage to that family."

I move back toward his car and lean against it, turning so I don't have to see his accusing face.

"I'll also be talking to Dave Deasey about his role in finding the neck-lace and disturbing those bones. If I can think of something to charge him with I will."

"Who do those bones belong to then?" I ask.

This stops him short. "Hopefully we will identify them in time."

"Then how do you know they're not Grace's."

Gavin's face hardens. "Dr. Adler is the top forensic anthropologist in the state. If she says it isn't possible, then it isn't."

"What about the rest of the site?" I ask. "When are you going to start digging? Searching for other bodies?"

"What other bodies?" His voice is loud now, like he doesn't care who hears.

"Dave says there are rumors of other bodies being there," I tell him. "What if Grace Hedland is among them?"

Gavin throws up his hands.

"Jesus, can you hear yourself? Are you honestly saying that the police should chase up drunken pub gossip? Are you insane?"

He thinks I'm mad, just as I thought Mary was mad with her conspiracy theories about her grandson, and that makes me pause. We're not getting anywhere.

"All right," I say. "All right. I'll apologize to the Hedlands. I'll talk to Stella."

The tension breaks a little. He shakes his head. "Don't worry about the paper. I've already spoken to her boss. He understands raking up old stories won't help Kinsale."

"You went to her boss?" This seems over the top. Gavin really doesn't want anyone asking questions.

"I did," he says. "That original investigation was thorough. It's no good revisiting the past."

As I look up at him I have vague memories of Dad bringing the new beanpole of a constable around for dinner at our place and me being forced to answer his questions about my hobbies, which I did in typical teenage sullen style.

"Were you involved in the investigation?" I ask.

"That's none of your business." His voice is tense, but I hear something else as well. Gavin is worried.

"Who was the witness that said Grace got on a train?"

Gavin bristles. "You're not her family, Eliza. You have nothing to do with this case."

"But like I tried to tell you before, the trains weren't running. Whoever said that lied to the police."

It's hard to read whether this is news to Gavin.

"That's a pretty big mistake for Dad to make," I continue. "And he wasn't someone who made those sorts of mistakes."

Gavin immediately jumps on this. "Are you attacking your own father's integrity now?"

"And then yesterday," I say, trying to keep my voice calm, "Aaron told me that Dad was paying his wages down at the Police Boy's Club."

Gavin has now switched to full cop mode. His face is deadpan.

"Pat said Dad was obsessed by this case. He had the file with him when he had his accident. He was regularly paying money to the victim's family. That doesn't seem right to me. Something went wrong with this investigation."

Gavin stands up to his full height. "Your father was the best policeman I've known and what he cared about above all else was keeping you and your sister safe. He did everything for this town and for his family and now you have the gall to question his motives. You should be ashamed."

Just like there are cop skills, there are lawyer skills and one of them is staying focused on the main game. Gavin's words are designed to wound but they don't distract me from the fact that he hasn't challenged what I've said.

"Luke Tyrell knew something about what happened to Grace. When you find him, you need to ask him about it."

Gavin almost trembles with anger. "Let me make this clear, Eliza. If I find out you are in contact with Luke Tyrell, a dangerous fugitive, I'll charge you with being an accessory. If I find out that you are continuing to peddle rumors and theories about Grace Hedland, I'll charge you with withholding evidence and impeding a police investigation."

There's a click-clack of heels on the footpath. Janey Bayless stands there, hair a little flatter than the poster, with a worried look on her face. Behind her is a row of shocked looking people behind the glass doors, all staring at Gavin and me.

"Is everything OK?" she asks.

I manage to say "We're fine," but Gavin can barely bring himself to look at her and turns away.

"Don't leave on my account, Gavin," she calls after him.

He turns back. "You are not to leave trailers like that unattended, especially not in disabled parking spots, Janey. You'll be booked if it happens again." He gets in his car.

Behind his back, Janey gives him a mock salute. "Aye-aye, Captain," she mutters under her breath, and then to me, "What was that all about? Could hear the two of you arguing from inside."

"Nothing important," I say. She gives me a look of disbelief.

"You were talking about that girl who went missing years ago."

I shake my head.

"Eliza, I heard you say her name. What's going on?" Another hard look directed my way. "All right," she says eventually when I still don't answer. "Keep being mysterious. Still, I'm glad I ran into you. A little bird told me you were working on the bushfire case for the power company."

My heart skips a beat. "Who said that?" I ask, bracing for another tirade.

"So it is true," she says. "You should have said."

"It's how the system works, Janey," I begin, wondering how many times I'm going to have this conversation. "Everyone deserves legal representation."

"Hey," she says, putting up two perfectly manicured hands. "You're only doing your job. I get it."

I can't quite believe this. Janey is lead plaintiff, and after what Tony went through, I'd blame me if I were her.

"Sometimes we have to do things we'd prefer not to," she says. "I understand. You've got to do what's right for you and I'll do what's right for me.

What I can't work out is why are you wasting yourself back in Kinsale? You're a city girl with a great career." She gives me an enormous smile. "You know, I reckon I would have been good lawyer, but those opportunities weren't available for the likes of me. Things might have been very different if they had. I sort of figure this whole mayor thing is probably my last roll of the dice, to do something for this town and for myself."

I look at her, this five-foot-nothing human dynamo. "You'll be a great mayor," I tell her.

"You know what," she says, "this town won't know what hit it. Kinsale will be like a phoenix rising from the ashes," and she lets rip a great throaty laugh. "Still, Eliza, you need to take care of yourself. Not everyone else in town will see it the way I do. Wouldn't want it to get nasty. Head back to the city where you belong, love."

Before I have a chance to reply, her phone buzzes and she pulls it out of her bag. "Is that the time? I'm supposed to be at a candidates' lunch in ten minutes," and she dashes off.

I walk over to Mary to say goodbye.

"Not seeing Mick today then," she says. It is couched like a reprimand and I'm tempted to tell her to join the line.

"I better go sort out this mess first."

As I follow the big and small versions of Janey Bayless out of the parking lot, I try to work out what to do next. Gavin would do anything, shut down anyone, if he thought my father's reputation was being threatened but this case is unfinished business. Dad must have been carrying around Grace's file for a reason.

My father needs this case to be solved and I do too.

22

The following morning when I drive past the Hedland house for the third time I notice the car is in the driveway but still no one answers the door when I knock. It's school time so the street is even quieter than when I tried yesterday, straight after my argument with Gavin. A teenage boy slouches past, hands in pockets, a skateboard under his arm. The hoodie looks familiar. It's the boy who ran across the road in front of my car the day of the attack. As if sensing my interest, he turns around and there is a family resemblance to the freckled kid who Aaron spoke to a couple of days earlier. I wonder if this is the brother, who looks to be skipping school again. He drops the skateboard next to his foot, all the while keeping an eye on me.

He's wondering what I'm doing here and to be honest so am I.

"Excuse me," I call out. "Have you seen Aaron?"

He gives the kind of teenage shrug that could mean "yes" or "no" or "depends on who's asking." It's the non-verbal equivalent of "not telling."

"It's urgent."

He bites his lip, brows furrowed.

"He's running."

"Will he be back soon?"

The boy doesn't answer just keeps standing there.

Sighing, I pull out my phone and prepare to wait. There are no messages. I click open my emails but there's nothing important that needs a response. Work had been very understanding about me taking time off after the attack and my personal assistant was doing her best to deal with Colcart's demands. Perhaps my whole crusade about Grace is a diversion from not dealing with what Colcart wants me to do. I suspect that's what Amy thinks.

"I like your car," the boy says.

It's a weapon in my arsenal. A conversation starter. "It was my dad's."

"It's in good condition." There is a note of approval.

"It needs a lot of work still." The standard answer.

A man jogs up the street. It's Aaron. I breathe in because I'm not sure how this is going to go. He sees me, immediately stops, and then slowly starts to walk over. I meet him halfway along the driveway. The boy senses the tension and slinks off.

"What are you doing here?" Aaron asks.

"Gavin came to see me."

"They weren't Grace's bones."

"I know," I say. "I'm very sorry . . ." and I hesitate, ". . . but I still think it needs to be investigated."

Aaron blinks slowly, choosing his words carefully.

"I asked about the train and the witness statement," he tells me. "Gavin said it was Jim Keaveney who picked her up and took her to the station."

At last a name. This is progress.

"He told you that?"

"Said that, given the circumstances, he thought I had a right to know. Jim said Grace had been walking home and she'd been upset, because of something her friend had done. Something about a boy." His gaze pins me to the spot. "A friend called Eliza Carmody."

The guilt knocks me sideways like a freak wave.

Aaron stands there impassive as I explain that night at the beach and how I had ended up with the boy Grace liked. My words peter out quickly enough but Aaron keeps waiting to see if there is more. When it becomes clear that there isn't, he says, "Gavin also told me that you work for the electricity company who caused the fire."

I wonder if that's how Janey found out as well. Gavin is playing dirty.

There is no point trying to massage the truth or explain it away in legal pieties. We are way past that now. "I'm not their employee, but I am their lawyer."

"And you're working on that bushfire case against the town."

"Yes."

Aaron looks at me with disgust. "Gavin was right. You are just here making trouble and then you'll head back to the city and leave us to pick up the pieces. This is just a game for you."

"Grace was my friend," I say. "I need to know what happened to her."

"She's been gone twenty years." Aaron's voice is bitter. "It's a bit late showing concern now."

"There are questions that need to be asked about the investigation."

Aaron exhales angrily. He locks his fingers behind his head and walks away from me, but I follow and keep talking.

"The investigation needs to be formally reopened," I say. "Gavin doesn't want to do this but if we can find more evidence it will force him to."

"He said he'd get the necklace looked at," Aaron says.

That's not enough for me.

"I want to go and see what Dr. Adler says about the bones, what she says about the site. Grace was wearing that necklace the night she went missing. It's the first new piece of evidence in years. There could be more up at The Castle. If we can convince her, she'll convince them."

"When are you doing that?"

"As soon as possible. First thing tomorrow probably."

"I'm going with you," he says.

"You don't have to."

"Yes, I do."

With that he walks away, opens the front door and slams it shut.

I unlock the door to Cabin 20 at the Ocean Breeze Motel. My belongings are still in two suitcases—I'm reluctant to reclaim this space from my father. If I make it my own, I might lose the comfort of his presence. The bed has a generous sag in the middle. There is fruit in the bowl and a cheery cloth on the table courtesy of Bridie. This is a safe place and yet I feel the prickle of watching eyes on my skin. Pushing open the screen door, I move out onto the verandah to watch the comings and goings. There is a clear view of the rest of motel from here, which is probably the reason Dad chose it. I cannot be ambushed.

The sky is a perfect blue, with wisps of feathered clouds. The sun is unexpectedly warm as if the last gasps of summer weather are spilling deep into autumn and yet the motel is quiet today. Many of the other bungalows are unoccupied. It's not the right season for tourists but now even the stragglers are disenchanted, giving Kinsale a wide berth. Bridie has taken the afternoon off and gone into town. The occasional car drives past and keeps going. I look at the track leading up to the ridge. Jim Keaveney lives up there, the name Aaron gave me.

I sit there simmering, feeling restless. There should be something for me to do but I can't think what so I decide to go for a run. It's an attempt to reclaim my old fearless life and a way to avoid the imaginary prying eyes at the same time. I just want to get back to when being alone didn't mean being scared. Jim had initiated our conversation at the nursing home. He could be perfectly happy to talk to me again.

Changing quickly into shorts, T-shirt and sneakers, my muscles protest as I jog past the bungalow onto the gravel. At the top of the incline, I stop and turn back, looking down at the cabins below. I can see no one and yet it feels like I'm a specimen being observed. After a few quick breaths, I run on.

This area was unaffected by the fire so the undergrowth is thick and the trees tall. There is the snap of dried leaves under my feet, and the rustle of animals passing by unseen makes me jump. All could be fuel for a future fire. The idea of this landscape turning to flame and ash pushes adrenaline into my legs and the pace becomes brisker. Within minutes there is a slick of sweat down my spine as I find a rhythm along the dusty track. Birds call to one another overhead. A kookaburra starts to laugh and it feels directed at me. Scars in the bush floor suggest the memories of other paths, long overgrown, but the main one is well used. Tire marks have gouged divots during the wet, and constant use has kept them there in the dry.

I run far enough to start panting and realize that I've forgotten both my phone and water bottle. Am I deliberately being reckless or just not thinking straight?

Perhaps I should turn back.

No.

A cathedral of trees surrounds me. Time slows in this green-gray world until it moves only as fast as leaves grow and I begin to walk. Bubbles of anxiety keep rising whenever I come to a corner, a twist in the track, and I cannot see what lies beyond. Then, around a bend, there is a bent metal sign that has been nailed to a tree. Trespassers will be prosecuted. The sentiment has been punctuated with bullets. Walking up to it, I stick my fingers through the rusting holes.

"You having trouble reading?" comes a voice.

My heart almost explodes with shock, a hand going instinctively to my chest.

Jim Keaveney is standing there, his moon white hair glinting in the light.

"Oh," I say, with a nervous laugh. "You frightened me."

He takes a step closer and Bridie's words about not wanting to mess with him come to mind.

"Nothing to see along here," he says. "Track doesn't lead anywhere except my place."

"I wasn't trying to see anything," I tell him. "Just going for a run."

"Not safe to be out here. You could have an accident."

All alone with Jim Keaveney, without the distractions of the nursing home, I realize there's something animal-like about him with his two small dark marbles for eyes and skin sunburnt to a toughened pink shell.

"Bridie knows where I was heading," I lie. "And besides, you're here by yourself." I try to sound lighthearted. "It's such a lovely day seemed a shame to waste it."

"I know this place," he said. "Every inch of it. You can get wild dogs around here, foxes too. I hunt them."

"Did you do that with Paul Keenan?" I ask.

"Who told you that?" he demands, isolation and loneliness rolling off him in waves.

"I heard you were friends. I know his brother, Donal."

"Showed Paul the bush once or twice but that's all. Just being helpful." His voice is confident as if he's decided that I'm nothing to worry about.

"Actually, you helped a friend of mine once," I say, trying to appear to be more relaxed than I feel. "A long time ago, twenty years ago. Grace Hedland."

He frowns at the name.

"Do you remember her?" I ask.

"I know who you mean."

"You picked her up the night she went missing."

"So?" He stares at me without blinking.

"Can you tell me about it?"

"Why?"

"Because you said she caught a train. I'm not sure that's right."

Jim takes a couple of steps toward me and it takes all my nerve not to edge back. The trees seem to huddle in closer, surrounding me.

"I never touched a hair on that girl's head," he says.

"You know some of her belongings have been found? The police have them."

There is a flicker in his eyes. Shock? Fear? It's hard to tell but there is something.

"It wasn't me," he says. "I never hurt her."

The tone is indignant, but his choice of words betrays him. If he didn't hurt her, then he knows something about who did.

"Tell me what happened then."

His eyes are sly now as if he is sizing me up like I'm a bird to be caught and too late I'm genuinely afraid of him.

"Come on," he says at last, and he turns and walks along the track. "I've got something to show you."

I follow at a distance, wary, because I can't turn back now.

Through the army of green gums a barbed wire fence comes into view. Jim stops with a satisfied look on his face. I put my hands to my mouth. Hanging from it, feet trussed, noses rubbing in the dirt, are dead foxes. A wall of red fur, lean bodies and dirty muzzles. White-tipped bushy tails move with the breeze. Most of them have been shot in the head, some cleanly, some not. Jim stands there proudly, a hand outstretched.

"Right curious, foxes. Clever too," says Jim. "The thing is they don't belong. That's what happens to outsiders around here."

The message isn't subtle but it does the trick. My mind empties of all my questions.

"You head back now," he says. "And next time run along the beach. More people about.'"

Wordlessly, I turn and start walking, aware he is standing there watching me. I wait until I'm around the corner, out of his line of sight, and then I run so fast back to the motel that my feet skid and stumble in the dirt.

23

When I see the buildings at the bottom of the hill, I slow to a jog and then a walk. The sun is hiding behind the trees and the motel is bathed in shadows. There's a truck parked outside my cabin with a surfboard in the back. Trying to get my breath under control, I head toward it. A wet-haired Tony Bayless is sitting on the steps in front of Cabin 20, a black and tan kelpie at his feet. At the sight of me he jumps up and comes running forward.

"Thank God you're all right," he says, and to my surprise he sweeps me up in a crushing hug. I flinch at the contact, momentarily confused at his intentions and as the panic rises, I have to steel myself to remember he is not Luke. When he steps back I see the genuine worry in his face.

"Is everything OK?" I ask. My thoughts spiral toward Dad or even Amy.

"I didn't know what to think," he says, and putting an arm around my shoulders, he shepherds me toward the open door of the bungalow. The dog walks beside him but stops at the doorway as if it doesn't want to come in.

The place has been trashed, belongings dumped out of my suitcases. Dad's magazines and books have been ripped apart. Even his clothes have been taken from the wardrobe and trampled. It is gut wrenching, as though someone has physically attacked my father. Spray painted across the wall in red is LEAVE TOWN BITCH.

"I've already called the police," says Tony, and he leads me away outside again. "It was like that when I arrived. I started to panic when I couldn't find you."

The dog lifts its head, ears alert, a growl from the throat and then sirens echo in the distance.

"Quiet, Rowdy," says Tony, and puts a hand down on the dog's fur, scratching between the ears.

When Gavin gets out, he's all business and avoids looking at me as he checks out the surroundings.

"Did you lock the cabin before you left?" Gavin asks.

I shake my head. It hadn't even occurred to me.

"None of the other bungalows were broken into, so it seems to be targeted at you. Is anything missing?"

I walk with him back into the cabin, leaving Tony waiting outside. I try to remember what I'd brought from the city. While things have been trampled and smashed, everything seems to be there until I find my handbag. The contents have been dumped on the floor. My phone has a cracked screen and money is missing from my wallet, a couple of fifty-dollar bills. Gavin asks me who might have done it.

"No idea," I say.

"You've obviously upset someone," he replies, pointing to the wall. "But then you seem to have a gift for that."

"The fact I'm working on the bushfire case seems to have become public knowledge," I say. "Wonder how that happened?"

He has the decency to look embarrassed.

"I was only away from the cabin for an hour."

"Either they got lucky or they were watching," he says, which isn't reassuring. "I'll talk to Bridie before I leave. Maybe she noticed something. Pack what you need but try to minimize what you touch. We'll get fingerprints done tomorrow. You're staying with us tonight so I can keep an eye on you and then you can go back to the city."

This brings back memories of being shunted off to boarding school and something in me snaps.

"You're not getting rid of me that easily. Amy's about to have her baby and I want to spend more time with Dad."

"Do I need to remind you that you're a police witness in a very high-profile case, Eliza? We can find alternative accommodation but it won't be in Kinsale. The place is too small."

"There's no rational reason for Luke to do this. Why would he return to Kinsale to trash a motel room?"

"Really?" says Gavin, dripping sarcasm. "Tyrell's not the sort to break into a house to get someone to change their testimony?"

"It could be about Grace. Someone wanting to stop me asking questions."

That I am saying this to a person who has only recently demanded that I do exactly that is not lost on me, but Gavin would never ruin anything belonging to my father.

"Any information about Grace's necklace yet?" I ask.

His face is grim. "I spoke to Dave Deasey yesterday, right after I saw you. He denies that he was even at the site or that he gave anything like a necklace to you. He says you're lying."

"And you believe him?"

Gavin doesn't answer my question. Instead he tells me that he'll file a report about the vandalism. "Duly noting that police assistance was offered in relation to accommodation and rejected."

"That's all?"

"I'll be in touch when there's news," he says, and heads back to his car.

Tony is waiting beside his car alone. "You OK?" he asks.

"I guess." But I'm not really. "What were you out here for, anyway?"

"Was coming back from the beach, thought I'd drop in to see you. Mum mentioned that you were still in town." He shuffles his foot through the dust. "I thought you might like to have dinner at the pub. The food's pretty good." There is the start of an embarrassed smile on his face. "I mean not tonight after all this but maybe another time."

I'm not quite sure but I think he's asking me for a date.

There's the sound of footsteps and Bridie comes running down the path toward us.

"Just got back from shopping," she says. "Gavin told me what happened. How are you?"

"I'm fine."

She jumps up the steps and disappears into the room. It's a few minutes before she comes back.

"No real damage," she says. "Nothing that can't be cleaned up. It was due for a coat of paint anyway. It will be kids." Her matter-of-fact manner is comforting. "We've had a few issues over the years."

"Any ideas who?"

She shakes her head. "I'll get my eldest to see if anything was caught on his cameras. No matter what, we'll need to get you moved. Cabin 2 is free. You might get a bit of noise from cars but it's right next to us. Anyone coming round will have me to deal with."

"I could stay over," Tony says. "If you want company?" He blushes. "I mean, I can sit out front in the car. Just to make sure nothing happens."

Behind his back, Bridie makes a surprised face and then gives me the thumbs up.

"You can take Eliza for a nice drive while I get the new cabin ready for her," she says.

Uncertain, he turns toward me, "Actually, I was just going to check The Castle. Now the police have finished with it, I promised the developers I'd keep an eye on the place until work starts on site."

"Perfect," Bridie answers. "By the time you get back, I'll have everything organized."

I'm caught in a pincer movement and don't have the energy to argue.

"Is that all right?" I ask Tony.

"Of course," he says. He whistles for the dog before unlocking the truck.

Shooting a frown back at a smiling Bridie, I follow him over and get in. Tony starts the engine as the dog comes bounding out of the bush and springs into the bed of the truck.

We head west on the road but in less than a kilometer Tony wrenches the steering wheel and turns abruptly onto a dirt fire trail.

"Short cut," he tells me. "Can go straight through to Old Castle Road."

The track narrows until it is only as wide as the truck, dusty dry with the edges eroding away. It's bumpy and I grab the handle above the door to brace myself. Tony slows down, glancing periodically back at the dog in the rearview mirror.

"This has gotten a lot worse than the last time I used it," Tony says. "Council will have to fix it up before the next fire season."

He concentrates on driving and I try to work out who wants to run me out of town and why. I still don't have a single name by the time we hit the tar of Old Castle Road and the landscape changes from bush to farmland.

The road is empty of traffic but full of potholes. When we finally pass another car, the occupant nods a greeting to Tony and in return he lifts his fingers off his steering wheel just like my dad used to do.

Around us, the black destruction from the fire has been replaced by a vast ocean of yellow grass. Late autumn rains should turn it green again. Everywhere I look, there are the missing landmarks of my childhood. Cypresses and hedges, planted as windbreaks by long-dead farmers, are gone. Animals and buildings are few. It is a beautiful but eerie landscape.

We pull up in front of The Castle's locked gate. I stare up at the telegraph poles. Several of them are honey-colored new, not yet weathered from the elements. According to the expert report, which Colcart wants buried, it was the conductor on one of the old telegraph poles that broke in the high winds and started the fire. The wire came into contact with the ground, arced and ignited the vegetation.

"Won't be a minute," says Tony.

He gets out to unlock it and the kelpie immediately jumps down to join him. From this distance The Castle looks as permanent as a mountain or a boulder, and all of a sudden I don't want to go any nearer and see the damage so instead I watch the dog waiting obediently near Tony. Its whole body, from ears to tail, almost quivers with excitement. With a gesture from Tony, it takes off like a rocket.

"Rabbits," explains Tony, getting back in. "Rowdy goes crazy for them. He misses the farm."

"What farm?" I ask.

Tony clears his throat before answering. "He belonged to the Newburys. They sold up after Alice was killed and couldn't take Rowdy with them. It was the very least I could do but when I went to pick him up, Mrs. Newbury couldn't even look me in the face."

Jaw clenched, he starts the truck down the gravel.

"Surely, they didn't think her death was your fault?" I ask.

He shrugs. "When something that terrible happens, people need someone to blame. They need to believe that it happened for a reason. Being under police investigation didn't help."

"That's awful."

The look of bleakness on his face suggests that the description is barely adequate, but then he shakes it away. "There's something I need to ask you," he says, keeping his eyes fixed on the road ahead. "Mum told me that you're working for Colcart."

The Castle comes closer and closer.

I hesitate, trying to pick my words carefully. "I'm on leave at the moment but yes I work for them."

"Is that why you came back to Kinsale?"

"At the start. That isn't why I'm here now."

We turn from the track onto the circular drive that takes us right to the stairs leading up to the enormous front doors. From this angle The Castle looks worn down. A layer of grime has been added to the façade and there is no formal garden now to soften the stone.

"Our lawyers say that Colcart might try and blame me for the fires, try to resurrect the investigation. Is that what you'll do?" asks Tony.

I think of ways to justify my job and the tactics that even a few weeks ago I might have been prepared to use but all of my excuses have disappeared.

The obligations that I have to my client suddenly don't seem important. Maybe it is time to stop thinking like a lawyer.

"No," I tell him. "Not if I am running the case because our expert report says that the fire was started by the electricity wires."

Tony looks at me, his gray eyes pewter. "Should you have told me that?"

"Probably not," I say, "but it's true."

We get out of the car. It is so quiet that the sound of the doors closing echoes back at us. Without waiting for me, Tony walks off along a path running along the side of the house. As I follow him, I can see darker patches on the external walls, windows that have been broken. Shreds of tape, which once blocked people from entering, flap in the breeze. The smell of smoke seems to get stronger, or is that just my imagination playing with me?

Tony stops at the back of the house. The more modern addition, added a century after the original, has been reduced to a skeletal black lace, with the sky poking through the skeleton that's been left. A creeping carpet of green has begun to rim the edges, beginning the long process of reclaiming the building. It's terrible.

"This is the worst part," he says. "The outbuildings were destroyed as well but we knocked those down. No one was sure what to do with The Castle and then Mum went and sold it anyway."

"I only ever came out here for that function," I say. "It was so beautiful. I thought you were so lucky to own it."

"That was a good night," Tony answers. "I remember how you stood up to my father when he refused to pay you."

"I was a terrible waitress."

"Took guts. I never heard anyone talk to Dad like that before. Not even Mum and she's the bravest person I know."

"You've got through the last two years. That's pretty brave."

He tries to laugh, but there's a mirthless quality to it. "If I was brave, I'd tell people what really happened that day."

The words swirl in the air like dust.

"You told me about that expert report, I guess I should give you something in return."

I hold my breath and for a long time he doesn't speak but then, "Everyone knew that day was going to be bad and it was important to be organized so I was out here all that morning. You know, hoses ready, cleaning out gutters on the outbuildings, trimming the surrounds, lashing things down. I was about to head back into town and was down near the front gate." He points back the way we came. "There was this noise loud enough to be heard over the wind and that was already howling. It was like whip crack but louder and then a buzzing, enormous and metallic somehow."

His hand pinches and then flicks back of its own accord as he tries to give a shape to the sound.

"I ran toward it. The wire was arcing along the fence line and the fire had already started in the dry grass. I should have stomped it out with my boots but I couldn't move. Just stood there watching it. Every fire truck in the district was on standby, but this was minor, I could deal with it. It wasn't like I felt panic, more like I was numb. And as I'm there doing nothing, the fire is getting bigger and bigger and I keep standing there until I'm practically getting roasted from the heat. I couldn't quite believe it was happening."

He rubs a thumb along his face and covers his chin with his hand.

"It grew into a wall of smoke. Only when I was struggling to breathe did I run back to shelter in the house. Didn't even drive, left the car there, panicking I guess. Even when I got back inside I didn't phone it in, the thought didn't even cross my mind. All I wanted to do was hide. It was left to fire watchers who eventually saw the smoke. I thought I was going to die that day but other people did instead. The whole town almost went up and it was because I did nothing."

I turn away from Tony and try to assess what he is telling me. Fifty meters away there is fresh police tape near a mound of dirt, marking out the recent dig, but my mind doesn't stretch to thoughts of the bones and Grace's necklace. Instead, I can't stop myself from trying to dice his story into nice legal paragraphs that could sink a class action.

"Why are you telling me this?" I ask, looking back at him again.

Tony's shoulders slump, like he's weighed down by his confession.

"There's no one else I can tell. I can't tell Mum. She's not scared of anything. If I told the police, maybe they would charge me with endangering people's lives because people might not have died if they had more warning, like Alice Newbury. She got caught in her car only a couple of kilometers from here. A few minutes earlier she might have made it to town. I think about that most days."

There are tears in his words.

"Are the Newburys right to blame me? Am I guilty?"

"I'm not a judge," I say.

"But you're a lawyer," he answers. "What would Colcart say if they knew?"

I could use what he told me. In the right hands, this sort of testimony would be ammunition. It might not win the day but it would certainly muddy the waters.

"What happened that day was terrible," I say. "But if you were my client, I'd tell you that you are not legally responsible. You don't control the weather. You didn't cause the wires to break. You could have been electrocuted if you went near the live wire on the ground. You were a witness to something terrible but that doesn't make you responsible for it. There was no legal obligation for you to do anything."

"What about morally?" he asks.

That's a harder question but Tony has suffered enough already.

"You were a bystander caught up in a terrible event. It wasn't your fault that the powerlines hadn't been checked in years. You've been unlucky, that's all."

There's a sigh from him, a mixture of regret but perhaps also the beginnings of relief, that this burden doesn't fall directly on him.

We walk the perimeter of the house, silently tracing the path of destruction, until Tony is satisfied that his job is done. Rowdy appears, panting and rabbitless, and we head back to the car. The trip back to the motel is quiet, conversation kept to safe topics as the weather and Janey's upcoming election as the setting sun gives the world a fiery glow.

It isn't until Tony is standing on the steps of Cabin 2 that he brings it up again.

"You said I was a bystander and that's exactly how I feel," he says. "It's not just about the fire, it's bigger than that. I'm watching my life pass by and in my head I keep thinking grab it, do something, but instead I stand there. It's like that night we were at the beach."

We have circled back again to that night so right now we are both adults and sixteen at the same time.

He reaches out to take my hand in his and I know he wants to choose the other path offered to him that night. That we might kiss, skinny-dip, have sex and somehow rewrite the last twenty years.

It's too late.

I pull my hand back gently.

"Is it because of Donal?" he asks. "I know you and him . . ."

I shake my head even though he is probably right. "It's been a pretty eventful day. Thanks for everything but I'm pretty tired."

If he's disappointed, he hides it well.

"Sure," he says. "Maybe dinner sometime."

Standing at the doorway, insects buzz around the outside light as he heads off.

When I close the door, I make sure to lock it.

24

Aaron sits on a chair in the foyer looking out at the city as I wait for the receptionist to get off the phone. He is dressed in his version of formal, tracksuit pants covering up the tattoos and a collared football shirt so synthetic you could get electric shocks just looking at him. I'm wearing my best tailored blazer, nipped at the waist, with a matching pencil skirt. We could be a criminal lawyer and her client off to court.

The receptionist fiddles with my business card, murmuring something into her headset and then looks up at me again.

"And you say you have an appointment with Dr. Adler?"

"My assistant rang last week." I try to sound confident enough for both of us.

"And this was organized through the police?"

"It was the police who gave me Dr. Adler's name." It's technically correct.

More whisperings into the phone, which I do my best to decipher. My law firm is being mentioned nervously. Law firms have that effect on people.

"I'm afraid there's no record of it," she says, part apologetically and part wanting to make it clear that this isn't her fault. "If you're here about a deceased family member who is currently being examined, you can talk to one of our liaison officers."

I don't want to be liaised with, which implies sympathetic cups of tea and someone junior fobbing us off. Instead, my forehead crinkles as I pretend this is all very vexing.

"My client has driven up from Kinsale this morning especially for this meeting. Could you see if Dr. Adler is available now? We won't take up much of her time."

She makes a face but has another discreet discussion with the faceless person on the other end. I'm certain that it is Dr. Adler herself. That's objective number one achieved, establishing that she is in the building. Finishing her conversation, the receptionist turns back to me, shaking her head, more forcefully this time. She's obviously been given an earful.

"I'm afraid that isn't possible. Unless we are notified directly by the police or the Heritage Department, it isn't appropriate that Dr. Adler speaks to you."

"The Heritage Department?" I ask, momentarily confused. The receptionist's mouth thins in response. Before she asks security to escort us out, I put up my hands to placate her.

"We'll go back to the police and get it sorted," I say. "Could you tell me the nearest place to grab coffee?"

"So what do we do now?" Aaron asks, after we sit down at a table in a nearby café. He doesn't really look at me, preferring a space that's about two feet to my left. It was an uncomfortable drive to the city this morning.

"We're just going to have to wait until she comes out." I pass him the photographs of her that I've printed from her LinkedIn profile. "We can take turns if you like."

"No," he says. "We'll do it together or not at all."

Aaron stares at the entrance to the Forensic Medicine Institute, a revolving carousel of glass, as I check my phone messages, more out of habit rather than expecting anything of importance. There's one from my personal assistant asking if I have seen the legal section in today's paper. Twisting in my chair, I notice the newspapers all lined up in a row on the counter.

"I'll be back in a minute." Aaron nods his head but his gaze doesn't move from the entrance.

There's a large picture of Colcart's in-house counsel on the second page of the Legal Affairs supplement. He's looking impressive on a Chesterfield armchair, one hand resting on the arm of it and the other on his leg but you get the feeling that the photographer doesn't like him. There's a double chin and a smile of infinite smugness. It's a half-page profile about his glowing career. The fourth paragraph in particular catches my eye, as it outlines the current class action.

"We intend to vigorously defend this claim," says the quote. The piece itself reads like his PR wrote it, which is probably the case since most of the journalists took buyouts last year. On the face of it, this propaganda is intended to wrong-foot the plaintiffs' lawyers, letting them know Colcart won't settle and that they are prepared to run up the costs to win, but there is also a coded message for me. This is a declaration of war. I either join the battle or get the hell out of the way.

Disheartened, I head back to where Aaron is sitting. Thankfully, he doesn't talk to me and we sit there, drinking endless coffee and waiting. The day is overcast and we have to tell the time by the clock not the sun. The mid-morning break passes. Occasionally an employee comes out for a sneaky smoke but it isn't until lunchtime that a woman, dressed casually in jeans and a T-shirt with a schoolgirl ponytail, strides out, a lanyard swinging from her neck. It's Aaron who notices her first.

"There she is," he says in a low voice.

Dr. Adler is younger than I expected, more cheerful, too. There is a jauntiness to her.

"Let me do the talking," I say under my breath to Aaron. He hangs back, a little reluctantly, as I walk toward her.

"Dr. Adler." I hold out my hand. "What a coincidence."

She has the sun-weathered complexion of someone who has spent a lot of time outside. There is a puzzled smile and then, "Nilla, please. I'm sorry, you are?"

"Eliza Carmody," I say. "We were just having lunch when we saw you." I gesture toward Aaron. "We thought we were meeting with you today."

Aaron stands there silently.

"Is this about that mix-up earlier?" she asks.

"We could all have a coffee now. My shout." I'm doing my best busy lawyer impression in a bid to railroad her. "Only take a few minutes. Seeing as Mr. Hedland has traveled all this way."

But Nilla is made of stronger stuff than that. Her smile becomes wary. "This is about the bones found in Kinsale?"

"I understand that you wrote the report."

There is a slight hesitation before she replies. "Can I ask what your interest in this matter is?"

"There's evidence that you may not be aware of that would assist with the identification," I tell her. "We believe those bones may belong to a relative of Mr. Hedland."

Aaron nods his head. She studies Aaron and then addresses him directly.

"If you have any evidence, you should give it to the police. TV shows have the scientists fighting crime and solving cases, but the truth is a little more prosaic. My job is to provide independent advice in relation to questions that the police have about bones. Nothing more than that."

She is making an apologetic face and I can see we are heading for a bureaucratic brush-off.

"So," she continues, "it really is up to them what they want to make publicly available. I'm afraid I can't help." Already she is starting to edge away from us.

"But what if they don't release the information?" Instinctively I grab her arm to stop her going. "What if the police are covering up what went on?"

Aaron gives me a shocked look and Nilla's face becomes closed, like she's pulling the shutters down.

"I can't be of any more help," she says, and detaches herself from my grip.

"We didn't have an appointment," says Aaron.

"I'm sorry?" Nilla turns toward him, confused.

"There was no mix-up. The truth is we just wanted to talk to you to make sure."

"Make sure of what?" Her voice is sharp now, the words angular.

"That the police were right and those bones aren't my sister's."

Aaron says this as simple fact. He's not attempting to fool or bully her into cooperating as I've been doing. He reaches into his pocket and pulls out the photo and hands it to her. "My sister Grace was sixteen when she disappeared. Her necklace was found near where the bones were discovered. When we heard that they were of a young woman, we thought . . ." He can't quite bring himself to finish the sentence but it has the desired effect. Dr. Adler purses her lips and then checks her watch.

"I'm very sorry to hear about your sister," she says. There is compassion in her face. "While I can't say anything to you about those bones specifically, perhaps I can explain the process involved, which might indirectly answer some of your questions. If you agree to respect those limitations," a quick glance in my direction, "then that might work."

"We will," he says, not looking at me. Both of them would be happy if I disappeared off the face of the earth.

"Let's find somewhere quieter," Nilla says. She leads us along the river that cuts the city in two, past buskers, flocks of tourists and the cafés and bars heaving with customers. We order coffee at a shop the size of a postage stamp and then perch on some outside cube seats that feel about as comfortable as overturned milk crates and probably cost ten times more. Nilla starts talking as we wait for our drinks to arrive.

"I want you to know that whenever bones come into my care, I never forget that this person was once alive and that people loved them. They are always treated respectfully. Every investigation dictates its own processes but I'll try to outline roughly how I work. When we find bones, the first question is: are they human? The police have already said this publicly, so

I can confirm that the Kinsale bones are. The second question the police want me to answer is, are they of forensic significance. Basically that means: are they less than a hundred years old. If they are, then the coroner must investigate."

"How can you tell their age?" asks Aaron.

The waitress comes over with our coffees and we sit there in silence until she has gone again.

"At times it can be hard to find out, especially if only a single bone is found, say, washed up on a beach, but that's not the case here. Again, it has already been released that what was discovered was a full skeleton." She looks at Aaron as if trying to assess how blunt she can be.

"In my job, that's the equivalent of finding gold. We can tell a lot from the bones themselves, from their teeth, for example, and also the context in which they were found."

"Grace had two fillings," Aaron volunteers, as if that's a detail he's already thought about.

Nilla looks sympathetically at him. "When did Grace go missing?"

Aaron is quick to offer the date, as though it is tattooed on his mind.

She is choosing her words carefully. "When we find bones that are over a hundred years old, and therefore not of forensic significance, we will notify other organizations that may be interested, such as the Heritage Department and relevant Aboriginal organizations."

"Oh," I say, suddenly deflated. "Are you saying these bones are over a hundred years old?"

Nilla makes the sort of face that says yes without actually saying anything.

Aaron takes a long slow breath. He almost crumples into someone smaller as he puts his face in his hands. He takes a moment before speaking.

"So it is just a coincidence that the necklace of a young teenage girl who disappeared was found near the bones of another teenage girl?"

"Sorry, I can't help you there," Nilla says.

"Wasn't there evidence on site of other buried bodies?" I ask. "Shouldn't you dig some more?"

Aaron stands as wel

"Even if it is a grav

means that her famil

her." It is clear that

"I understand,"

Every family I me

information as I

"That's good

talking to me."

"I hope you

If it was a c

the Mustang

I pull up

mother wa

He clic

"My

out wha

it wasn

He

"S

Tha

tol

M

b

Don't c

He slams the door o

She folds her arms a
set out.

"As I said from th
know, no mass buria
an unlikely possibi'

"What about si
about all these b<
ground for youn

"This site is
"Those bones i
gest to you th
she is startin
are too lazy

"But wil
Nilla sh
digging v
historiar
Techno
landsc
distu<
mon

"
des

t'

25

I lie in bed thinking dark thoughts, waiting for sunrise. Aaron's words are on a loop in my head, and I keep seeing the way he lumbered across the road and up the footpath. How the door had opened before he even got to the porch. Mrs. Hedland standing there looking ancient and frail. I've messed this up so badly, maybe I should just leave town and go back to the city, but that is overridden with thoughts of Grace.

What happened to her? Where did she go?

Before dawn, my phone shudders on the table next to my head. It's a text message from Gus.

Their baby has been born by emergency caesarian at Kinsale Community Hospital. Amy is seriously ill.

I sit in the emergency waiting room so scared I cannot cry. Gus comes and goes, pale, wordless, but eventually he sits down next to me. He's shell-shocked.

"She's asleep," he says. For a moment I think he means Amy but then I realize he is talking about the baby. In all the rushing I had forgotten.

"It's a girl?" I ask.

Gus nods.

I know I should say congratulations or ask how the baby is, the weight, the size, the name, something but the words break in my mouth because I only care about her mother.

"Amy knew there were risks," he tells me.

"Since when did Amy take risks?" I ask. "She's supposed to be the sensible one."

"I tried talking her out of it but she wouldn't listen," Gus says. "I told her that I couldn't bring up a baby without her and she told me that Eliza was brought up by her dad and she turned out great."

My face becomes sticky with tears and I cry into his shoulder.

We sit for what seems like forever. Relatives arrive, Amy's parents, Gus's siblings. I move a little farther away, making room for their questions and attempts to comfort Gus. The women go off in search of the baby, the men sit there silent, grim-faced. Other patients turn up in various states of disrepair, two car accidents and a suspected heart attack but I am indifferent. My sole focus is Amy.

A few hours in, I check my phone and see that Tristan, Amy's cousin, has left a message. Walking outside, dawn breaking but the air still smelling of night, I return his call. The information he's received has been scant and it's not medical enough. He has questions I can't answer and makes me promise to ask his uncle, Dr. Liu, to ring him so he can work out exactly what is going on. Gavin has also rung but I don't even bother to listen to his message.

When I go back inside, Gus has gone and Dr. Liu has disappeared as well.

"They just finished operating," says one of Gus's brothers. I sit and think about all the people I love. There were more of them when I was sixteen. That was the summer I spent infatuated with Tony Bayless. That was the summer I lost Grace. My father will be gone soon and any attachment to Tess comes heavily qualified. My whole life, the easiest person to love has been Amy. What will it be like if I lose her as well?

I stare at the faces of the nurses going to and fro, trying to glean information. I've spent enough time around medical professionals to know what they look like when it goes bad but they seem normal and I feel a sliver of hope. When Gus comes back into the room, his father-in-law by his side, his face radiates relief. He tells us that she's stabilized and that we can all go home and he'll keep us updated. I feel like kissing everyone I see but instead I head down the hill to walk along the ocean.

I stay a long time by the water saying thank you, thank you, thank you, to whoever, whatever, decided Amy and her daughter would be OK. It feels like a bargain has been struck and something bigger than me has kept their end of it. I trace the steps I took with Donal until I find myself at the end of the rocks. Around the point is Cromwell's Beach. I haven't been back there since that night, never wanted to, but standing here it suddenly seems the right time and I clamber across, not stopping until I splash through the water to the sand on the other side.

Above me is a flock of seabirds, black darts catching invisible waves of air, but the only footprints on the shore are mine. Silty waves churn up the sand and the rip lingers in the whitewater. This is not a beach to go swimming at night or day. If Luke hadn't swum out when he did, perhaps I would have been the one who disappeared.

There is a red and yellow sign stuck in the ground at the edge of the lot. It warns of strong currents, unexpected waves and unpredictable tides but not of teenage stupidity or treacherous friends, which can be just as dangerous. Memories flicker past quickly as though caught in a current. Thoughts of Grace are pushed toward me again and again.

By the time I head back to town, I know what my side of the bargain is.

When I open the door of the nearest café, I catch a glimpse of tanned lanky legs in workman shorts with muddy boots attached, under a nearby table. It's Kinsale's local treasure hunter, Dave Deasey, giver of broken necklaces and bare-faced liar to the police. To my surprise, he actually gestures for me to join him.

"Odd Eyes . . . I mean Eliza," he says, "take a seat. You look like you could do with a coffee."

I order my coffee from the girl behind the counter and walk over to his table but I don't sit down.

"I just want to say at the start, it should never have happened. A teenage prank that got out of hand. No harm done and send me the bill for any cleaning."

My eyes close momentarily because my brain has no capacity to cope with Crazy Dave and his ideas.

"She's only sixteen," he goes on. "We all did dumb things when we were sixteen, right."

Too slowly the cogs start turning. "This isn't about . . ." I begin, and at the same time Dave, realizing I don't understand, starts backtracking. "Is that the time?" He pushes away from the table, leaving his breakfast half-eaten, but I have had enough and grab his fork.

"Try to leave and I will ram this into you."

He looks at the fork and then back at me. "Jesus," he says. "You need to relax."

He sits back down and I take a seat as well.

"Are you saying you know how my room got trashed?"

"It was my daughter, Kayla. She had some idea in her head that if you left town, Gavin would stop hassling me about that necklace. She's a good girl." He watches me with anxious eyes. "No harm done, not really."

Another parent finding excuses. I think of Paul Keenan's mother, and Luke Tyrell's. Was my father ever reduced to this? Will Amy be?

"How did Kayla know where I was staying?" I ask.

"Everyone knows where you are," he says. "You're driving Mick's Mustang. It stands out."

My coffee arrives. Dave holds out a hand for his fork and I return it. He starts spearing bacon with it.

"Grace Hedland was only sixteen when she disappeared," I say.

Dave becomes very conscientious about chewing his food.

"Same age as Kayla."

"So what?" Dave says. "Those bones weren't Grace's."

Obviously the story has gone round the town.

"But the necklace you found is hers. Those bones might not be Grace but they belonged to someone like her, a young teenage girl. We don't even know her name. What if that's Grace in eighty years' time? What if she is found after we are dead and no one ever knows what happened to her? How is that going to change if we ignore evidence or lie about it? The world is pretty different from a hundred years ago and yet teenage girls still disappear."

"It's not the same now," Dave says. "I've got Kayla this app where I can find her whenever I want. Track her down. Make sure she's OK."

"Great, so you'll know where her body is."

Dave gives me the sort of look that would crack stone. It was a cheap, emotional shot but I don't care. "Grace's mum thought she was safe with her friends."

Dave's mouth sags enough to let me know that's hit home.

"I saw her that night," he says. "She was at the party."

"Grace?"

"It was supposed to just be fun but it got a bit out of hand. I mean, you'd have heard about that." He looks around and then lowers his voice. "We were just stupid, not thinking. Too drunk to step in to stop stuff. Now I have a daughter it's all different, you know. I see those women walking around town, women like . . . well you know, and I want to say sorry, but it's all too late."

"Did something happen to Grace there?" My voice is urgent.

"No, not Grace. Not that I saw. She wasn't drinking for starters. Maybe that's why she left. She could see it wasn't a good place for a girl by herself to hang around."

"When was the last time you saw her?"

"Wouldn't know the time or anything. She was with Tony Bayless though. He might know. Anyway, we all good about Kayla?" he asks. "I can bring her around to apologize if you want."

"No," I say. "What you are going to do is ring up Gavin and tell him where you found that necklace. If you want to do something to make up for the past, do that."

Very slowly he nods. "All right."

It isn't until the next day that I visit Amy and her daughter in hospital. When I get to her room, Stella Gibson, the intern from the *Coastal Times*, is taking a picture of the baby for the newspaper's Hatch, Match & Dispatch column. Her hair is now a silvery-purple. Amy has refused point blank to get in the photo. The way she looks, I can't blame her. It's like a truck has mowed her down.

"It's my last day on the paper," Stella tells me. "I've quit."

"Is this about the bones?" I ask. "I'm sorry I got it wrong."

"It's not that," she says. "Newspapers are dying anyway. I'm pitching stories to Buzzfeed and HuffPo about the top ten reasons not to visit this dump."

This seems a bit harsh, even for "Bonestown." As she finishes up quickly with a few more half-hearted clicks of the camera I head over to hug Amy. She looks shattered but happy, hooked up to machines and a drip. She makes me hold her baby. As I pick her up like she is made of glass, Amy makes a sudden grimace of pain.

"Do I need to get a doctor?" I ask.

"I am one, remember," she says.

"But everything's good, isn't it? For both of you?"

"She's perfect and I'm surviving." Amy gives her daughter a big tired hormonal smile full of love and endorphins.

"Does she have a name yet?"

Amy shakes her head. "We're still deciding, but not Grace."

I look at the squashed little face, the thick mop of the blackest hair and the tiny chipolata fingers clenched into a fist that has worked its way out of the tightly wrapped blanket. The baby who is not Grace opens her mouth and looks blearily up at me but her eyelids are too weighed down and she sinks back into sleep. For a long time in the room the only sound, other than the occasional beep from a machine, is her breath. The sighs are so soft I hold my own breath to hear them. Just when you think there's a rhythm, it stops, pauses, and then starts again. It's very different to my father's breath now, the constant wheezing rattle from a pair of worn-out bellows. His is the sound of days being counted down.

"I've been thinking about what you said in the car," says Amy eventually. "There were so many questions we never asked. Why did we just accept it when they told us she ran away? We knew her better than anyone. We trusted the adults to fix it."

"We're adults now," I say.

"Isn't it too late?" she asks.

"There's something wrong with the original police investigation. Dad would never have missed Jim Keaveney lying about the train and then he was secretly paying money to Aaron Hedland."

"Maybe he felt sorry for him?"

"Or he felt guilty because he messed up."

The words hang there in the space between us.

"Mistakes get made, compromises are forced on us," says Amy. "No one wants to be judged by their worst day. Fundamentally, your father was a good man who tried to do what was right. Have faith in him."

"I need to know what happened."

Amy moves, looking like she's about to argue but then gasps, swearing under her breath. "Who thought something so small could do so much damage? I don't think I'll ever be the same again."

I wince and her baby stirs in my arms and gives a plaintive mewl. Amy glances at the clock. "Time for another feed," she says.

There is a comedy of errors as she attempts to latch the baby to her. A tiny mouth opens but misses its target. Finally, there is success of sorts. It's a surprisingly noisy affair with the sound of suckling and gulping. Both Amy and the baby are concentrating intently on each other and it isn't until hiccups are finished that she speaks again.

"All right."

"What?" I ask.

"All right, you should keep trying to find out what happened.'

"Are you giving me your blessing?"

"Would it stop you if I didn't?"

I shake my head. "But it would be nice."

"Then, yes," Amy says. "But stay safe. You owe it to your goddaughter."

"Goddaughter? But I don't believe in God."

"That's optional," she says. "All you've got to do is love her."

And just like that there's another one added to the list, but before I can get too sappy about it, my goddaughter brings up her own weight in milk all over herself and her mother.

As I walk out of the hospital entrance, an ambulance comes racing up the street. I stand there watching as the EMTs open up the back. It's Ryan, the clinical nurse from Emerald Coast Homes, who gets out, followed by a stretcher. There is a body strapped to it. I'm too far away to make out the face but as they turn it around I see my father's hair poking out the top.

My feet react quicker than my brain and I'm running before I realize, yelling at them to stop so I can see Dad but they ignore me. Ryan hears and looks around. By the time I am at the entrance, his arms outstretched, gathering me up before I run straight past.

"It isn't Mick," he says, holding me back. "It isn't Mick."

I push against him, shouting out "wait, wait," even though they've gone. Ryan repeats himself, gripping me tightly with both arms.

"It's Jim," he says. "It's not your father. It's Jim."

The ground lurches and Ryan holds me steady.

"Sit down. You've had a bit of a shock." He guides me to a nearby bench. "You stay here," he says. "I'll get you some water."

By the time he returns I'm less hysterical and more embarrassed. He passes me a plastic bottle to drink from.

"Sorry it took so long. There was paperwork to get him admitted."

"It's me who should be sorry," I say. "I'm OK now, just I was sure . . ."

"I know," he says.

"I thought I was ready for Dad to die but I'm really not. There are things I need to get resolved before he goes."

"I'd get them done soon," Ryan says. "I mean it could be weeks but it might not be."

"What happened to Jim?"

Ryan's mouth hardens. "Laurelle found him lying in the maintenance shed."

"A heart attack?"

"He had copped a nasty knock to the head."

"An accident?"

"I don't know," he says, his face worried.

"Was he attacked?"

"I'm not sure. Today has been chaos with Janey electioneering around the place again and we were short staffed as usual, what with the police coming for Cadee."

"Cadee? She's been arrested?"

If the police have arrested Cadee, maybe they are closer to tracking down Luke.

Ryan tells me he doesn't know.

My mind is whirling. "Could Jim have been attacked?"

Ryan's face tells me that he thinks it's possible. "I don't think he got that wound by falling. It could have killed him—it still might."

"Have you told the police?"

"What if I'm wrong?" he says. "Might be a fuss over nothing and my boss wouldn't like it."

"You need to tell them," I say. Jim knew something about Grace's disappearance. Perhaps that's why he was attacked.

Ryan doesn't seem convinced.

"Thanks for everything. I'm OK now." I stand up.

"Are you sure?" he says. "Maybe you should take it easy for a bit." I tell him I will but it's a complete lie because that could have so easily been Dad in the ambulance today and I need to work out what happened to Grace before he dies.

26

Tess opens the door when I knock. A scarf covers her hair, two sweaty plaits poking out from under it. There's paint on her shirt and she stinks of turpentine.

"You're still in town," she says.

"That's right," I reply. "What are you painting?"

"My old room," she answers. "You gave me the idea, actually."

"Can I come in?"

She says nothing but moves to the side and lets me pass. The house has changed again since I was here. Photos have disappeared off the wall, clutter has been removed and furniture is missing. As I am delving further into the past, my sister is doing the opposite. She's taking an eraser to our childhood, rubbing it out.

"Do you want to see it?" Tess asks.

Tess's room has been a permanent bruise, the ultimate reminder that she was more treasured than me.

"All right," I say.

She walks past the living room, down the hall and opens the door. Her bedroom has been completely emptied of all the furniture and drop cloths are on the floor. The place that I have felt such a grievance about has been transformed into a medium-sized square with a couple of newly painted white walls. As I stare at it, the shard of frozen resentment that I've carried with me for so long dissolves. This room is not important. It has taken me all this time to realize, but suddenly I am free of it.

"I should have done this years ago," she says with real venom in her voice. "I hated this room. It was like Dad never accepted that I grew up."

"What are you talking about?" I say.

"He thought I needed it."

"What about my room? What about me?" There's still a trace of the forgotten sister's whine as though it's an accent that I can't completely shake.

"He knew you were fine." There's a half-smile from her, the suggestion of sun from behind the clouds, and for one moment I think that we can come out into our own personal demilitarized zone and have a proper conversation.

"Why did he think you needed it?" I ask.

Her smile flatlines. I've tripped the wire. "What are you doing here, Eliza?" she says, and we go back to being virtual strangers who are genetically handcuffed to each other.

"I need to see Gavin."

She shakes her head.

"His car is in the driveway. I know he's here."

"He's busy."

"Then I'll wait."

She stands there and I expect her to order me to leave but instead she shrugs. "Stay in the kitchen," she says, and slams the door on her old room as if she's closing it in my face.

I am sitting at the kitchen table when she returns.

"He's on the phone."

"That's OK."

Tess is on edge now, jumpy and sharp, as if she's exposed too much. For the first time in forever I feel something like sorrow for her. Perhaps being the favored beautiful child wasn't quite the blessing that I imagined. It certainly hasn't made her happy.

"I'm staying out at Ocean Breeze," I say. "Bridie Walker runs it these days."

Tess clangs around in the cupboard, pretending she can't hear.

"She's still a laugh, Bridie. Remember about the cherries?" It's an outstretched hand, an old shared memory of childhood, an appeal in sisterly shorthand to try and get her talking.

Her head pokes out and looks at me. There is a curve to her mouth at the memory of an old misdemeanor.

"We blamed it all on you," she says. "An entire box of cherries splattered across the garage wall."

"Of course Dad believed you," I say.

"No, he didn't," Tess answers. "It was just easier that way. You were too small to get into real trouble and he couldn't get mad at Bridie, she was a visitor. His whole job was dealing with people who had done the wrong thing. He couldn't face doing the same thing at home. Better to ignore it."

This is more insight from Tess than I have had in years. Perhaps painting that room has freed something in her, too.

"Gavin will be off the phone now," she says. "You should go in."

I stand up. "Is everything OK? You seem . . ."

"What?" she asks.

"I don't know, different."

"I'm fine," she says, and gives me one of her unreadable blank blue looks as though I've left the room already.

When I push the door of my old bedroom open, Gavin is sitting at my father's desk, the room stuffed full of relics that I recognize, safe from Tess's purge.

When he sees me a defeated look crosses his face.

"What's this? The Mick Carmody Museum?" I ask.

"More of a temporary refuge," he replies. "Take a seat, if you can find one." He motions his large hand toward a chair. I move a bundle of files off it and sit down as he pulls open a drawer.

"Want a drink?" and he takes out a half-empty bottle of whiskey.

"Is that Dad's as well?"

"You accusing me of theft now?" He wants to get angry but his heart isn't in it.

"Thought you might have inherited it along with the job."

"That and the rest of the mess." He splashes the whiskey into a chipped police golf day mug and hands it to me. A considerably larger tipple goes into the tarnished pewter tankard that's already next to him on the desk.

"You only had to call me," Gavin says. "Didn't require a visit but I guess you've heard the news."

I'm not really sure what he's talking about but working on the principle that you never admit to ignorance, I make a sort of "hmm" sound.

"So," he begins, "Cadee's identified the body. It's definitely Luke."

The shock hits me between the eyes.

"Luke Tyrell," I say slowly. "Luke is dead."

"His body was found in an old burnt-out shed along the Bridle Track, a shotgun next to it. Probably self-inflicted."

Gavin pushes back his chair until he almost hits the wall behind him, then stares up at the ceiling. There's a long pause. I'm not quite sure how I feel about this. A mixture of sadness and frustration but undeniably relief. Donal and his mother won't be put through a trial. I am no longer the prosecution's main witness. But when I think of Luke as a boy and Cadee now, those feelings soften.

"I find it hard to believe he killed himself," I say. "He didn't strike me as the type."

"And you're the expert, of course," Gavin says. "On the strength of crossing his path twice in twenty years. He was public enemy number one for any publicity-seeking politician walking past a microphone, was looking at considerable jail time and his former partner, farm and livelihood had been destroyed. I think that's enough to sink anyone."

"I did grow up with him," I say.

"People change," Gavin replies, draining his tankard.

"What was it that he and Paul were involved in?"

"Guess it doesn't matter now," he says. "Months of work and a potential informant just put a bullet in his head."

"Was it drugs?"

"Drugs?" Gavin looks at me quizzically. "No. It was eggs."

For a moment I think I've misheard. I'd expected something along the lines of ice, speed, coke or heroin. "Is that some new kind of street slang?"

"What do you think the price of a red-tailed black cockatoo is on the illegal market?"

I pluck a figure from the air. "A thousand bucks."

"A hundred thousand dollars alive," Gavin says. "Maybe more after the fires. Eggs get stolen during nesting season, taken out of the country to be hand-raised and then sold. As lucrative as drugs but not as risky. Until recently, if you were caught, which was unlikely, chances were you'd get a slap on the wrist from a magistrate. That's if we bothered to prosecute at all. Now there are proper penalties in place, big fines, jail time, an understanding that the same routes for this kind of smuggling could be used for drugs and guns as well."

"And that's what Paul Keenan was involved in?" I ask.

Gavin nods.

"When I first came to the district years ago, this area was notorious for wildlife smuggling, thanks to a combination of little police interest and an abundance of native cockatoos, galahs and lorikeets. Your dad and Alan weren't concerned so I tried investigating it myself but all of a sudden the operation shut down. Naively, I thought it might have been me starting to make enquiries but I doubt that now. Something went badly wrong with the operation and it stopped. Fast forward to last year when Paul Keenan comes to town, hears the old stories and starts up the racket again. He needs local knowledge about possible nesting sites and finds a financially desperate Luke Tyrell."

This fits perfectly with what Luke told me. That he had information about an operation. How they had argued about a delivery and ended up in a fight.

"What information did you want from Luke?" I ask. "Paul was already dead."

Gavin stretches out in the chair.

"Both of them were just the front end. Paul wouldn't have a clue how to smuggle birds into Asia. I've got my own suspicions but I need evidence."

"That's a very good reason to kill Luke then," I say. "For a start, Jim Keaveney must have been involved."

I can see Jim standing in the aviary at the nursing home, his large hand wrapped around the finch's neck, talking about Asia and the Middle East.

Gavin doesn't deny it.

"Did you know Jim has just been rushed to hospital?" I say. "Maybe someone is shutting down the syndicate. First Luke and now Jim."

I can see he's going to lecture me again about not getting involved in police investigations, but then his shoulders square and his face takes on the mask of professionalism that says the shift is never really over. He grabs his phone and walks around the desk, moving past me.

"That's valuable information." I put out a hand to stop him. "I want payment."

"What?" Gavin's distracted, his mind already elsewhere, working out what to do first, who to ring.

"Consider it a trade," I say.

"You need to play the game better, Eliza. You've already told me what you know."

I ignore him, even though he's right. "Grace," I say. "There's something you aren't telling me. Some problem with the original investigation. Dad messed up? What?"

He pulls his arm away from me, stumbling slightly. He's had more whiskey than I realized.

"Kayla Deasey wrecked your room, angry that you got her father in trouble. Nothing to do with Grace's disappearance. It's all in your head."

"No." I stand up, blocking his path. "There's that necklace still. Dave will confirm what I told you. That he found it at The Castle. And now there's Jim, possibly the last person to see Grace alive, who lied about her catching the train. I'm not going to stop until I find out what happened. I need to know. I think Dad needs to know."

Rather than getting angry at me, his eyes swell with pity as though I'm just not seeing the obvious.

Something clicks in my mind.

"Dad already knows?" I ask in a dry dead whisper.

The expression on Gavin's face tells me that I am right. His eyes flicker to the doorway and I'm aware that someone is standing there just beyond my peripheral vision. For one moment I think it is Dad. We are in a room filled with his belongings and we're talking about his case, the one Pat said he was obsessed with, the family he gave money to. His daughter's best friend.

I turn very slowly, edging my head around as if one false move will make him disappear but it isn't my father at all.

It is Tess.

"It was me," she says. "I killed Grace."

27

New Year's Eve 1996

Mick

Sergeant Mick Carmody stood at the top of the embankment and looked down at the people on the beach waiting for the sun to set. He could recognize just about every face. Tourists had seen the forecast of rain for the entire week, the landslides and blocked roads and decided to stay in the city until summer finally turned up.

The other coastal police stations had been told to take care of highway traffic, which was bypassing Kinsale anyway, so it would just be the three of them on shift. Mick hoped for a quiet night because there wasn't much chance of outside help.

"This bonfire's a waste of time and money," Senior Constable Alan Sharp said. Sharpy was a drive-by cop, all lights, sirens, guns and bad guys. Paperwork and community relations didn't figure at all and Mick had given up trying to get him to do it.

Mick's radio crackled.

"The Boy Wonder radioing in on the dot." Sharpy smirked.

"It's his first New Year's," said Mick. "Give him a break."

"Ten bucks says it's his last." Sharpy had hated Gavin from the start. Mick guessed it was because he instinctively knew that, long term, a more experienced Gavin would leapfrog over him. On paper Gavin looked great. In real life, the new probationary constable was proving to be a headache. Mick had been finding jobs for him to do all day, farm visits, returning property, checking in on emergency services and road closures, anything to wear down his enthusiasm to manageable levels. Even so, hours later, the excitement was still in his voice so Mick told him to meet them at Main Beach.

"If he's coming, I'll head off," said Sharpy. "Do a patrol of the town."

"All right," said Mick. He suspected that Sharpy had some woman he was keen to catch up with. Lately he'd been ending phone calls quickly when Mick walked into the room and volunteering for more night shifts and patrols than usual. If Mick had to guess, it suspected it might be the new nurse in town who had laid a complaint about an ex-boyfriend hassling her a few weeks back. Still, it wasn't any of his business as long as it didn't affect Sharpy's work.

As Sharpy walked away, Mick went back to searching through the crowds. He found Eliza conspiring with her friends. She felt his gaze boring into the back of her skull and turned around, her head momentarily drooping when she realized it was him but recovered almost instantly and looked brazenly blank in the other direction. He gave a big parents-are-so-embarrassing wave as the other two girls' guilty faces followed suit. Eliza had something planned for tonight, he could tell. Even as a young child she had been an adventurer, scarpering off at a moment's notice to get up to mischief. Mick always wondered if it was because Helen had died when she was so young, if Eliza had realized too early that life was short and needed to be seized, or maybe it was the accident with her eye that made her look at the world in a different way. He looked at the girls, trying to decipher what they were up to when his view was blocked by Janey Bayless making her way toward him. She walked with a pendulum momentum to her hips that was best appreciated from behind.

"Eliza pretending she doesn't know you?" she asked. Janey never missed a thing.

And Mick suddenly remembered a different Eliza, a smaller version who would cling to his legs like a stick insect, begging to be taken everywhere with him. What he would give for her to be like that again.

"Turns my hair gray, that one," he said.

"Bright as a button, she is," laughed Janey. "Her mother's genes."

Mick looked at Janey. Not many people talked about Helen to him these days.

"Helen's been gone a long time now," said Janey. "It must be lonely. You should get out more. Might find someone who can help with the girls as well."

There was always a hidden agenda with Janey but she played her cards well. Mick had to give her that.

"Two women in the house is about all I can handle," he said. "We'll muddle through."

"Of course," she said. "Sure, I was a tearaway myself at the same age. The hidings I got from my dad."

From what he had heard, Janey's father never needed much of an excuse to use his fists.

"I'd like to know what they're up to," he said, nodding in the direction of Eliza and her friends.

"I can tell you that," Janey answered. "Boys tell their mums everything."

Mick, who had regular dealings with a significant cross-section of Kinsale's teenage population, had his doubts.

"They're going around the rocks to meet a few fellas at Crummies. My Tony included."

"Who?" he asked, suspicious now.

"That young Gus, Luke Tyrell as well. I've told Tony to keep an eye on the girls, make sure they get home. Could be worse. They're all good lads."

Mick nodded. Still, he would get Gavin to take a detour along the bush track later on, just to check.

The smell of gas drifted over to them. Jim Keaveney was dousing the wood.

"Crowd's disappointing," she sighed. "Stupid council, could have made it more of a carnival with rides and sideshows. Get the families in. No vision, this lot."

"You should stand next election," said Mick.

Janey laughed. She had a throaty, sexy, groin-tingling kind of laugh that was designed to have the customers lining up to put money in her till. "And give Wes a heart attack." She patted Mick on his chest, holding her hand there for a beat too long before removing it. "You know, a bad summer's trading would finish off quite a few businesses."

"The pub all right?" asked Mick.

"You have to be pretty hopeless to make a loss on a pub," said Janey. "The Castle's a different story but Wes is too busy showing the world that a working-class boy can end up king."

"I heard there might be a buyer," said Mick.

Janey gave him an appraising look. "Where'd you hear that?"

"A policeman never divulges his sources."

"You're a dark horse, Mick Carmody. Wes doesn't even know anything about it yet, so you keep quiet. I need to wave a wad of cash in front of his face to try and convince him."

"I promise," said Mick.

"Thanks. Always had a soft spot for a man in uniform."

Janey was flirting with him but Mick didn't let it go to his head. It was practically a professional requirement in her line of work.

"Besides," she went on, "if you can't trust the police, who can you trust?" Mick almost laughed in reply.

"Better get moving. Lovely light at sunset for taking photos," she said. "And Wes needs me back at the pub."

"Take a nice one of Eliza and her mates, and check if they're planning to go anywhere else after the beach."

"A police informant now, am I?" Janey answered. "You'll need to buy me a drink sometime to keep me sweet." She was dialing the flirting up a notch now and Mick felt almost relieved when Janey turned and began walking away. He watched her ass swinging saucily in her short summer dress. Flicking her head around, she caught him doing it. A sly cat-like stare and then a wink and she was on her way again, carving a path through the crowd.

Gavin was already standing out the front of The Royal when Mick got there just before 3 A.M.

"How's it been?" Mick asked.

"Talked a few out of driving who shouldn't," said Gavin. "Otherwise all quiet."

"Did you drive down to Crummies?"

"No one there, Boss," Gavin said. "Even put out their campfire properly. Very responsible." He pushed open the door to the pub.

Wes, squat and sweaty, was behind the bar. Sighting the two policemen, he quickly called out last drinks to a jovial crowd.

"All good?" asked Mick.

"Nothing we can't handle," said Wes.

Mick looked around for Janey but he couldn't see her.

"Your wife about?" he asked.

Wes was pouring a beer at the other end of the bar. "Headed out to pick up Tony," he said. "Molly coddles that boy."

Mick trusted Janey enough to make sure Eliza made it home as well. He began walking through the crowd. There were backslaps, handshakes and "Happy New Year's" and an equal number of backs turned and cold stares, which was the policeman's lot in a country town. Everyone had an opinion. As people finished up their drinks, he made his way back to the bar.

Wes held up a beer and gestured it toward him. Mick shook his head.

"Numbers down. You missing a few?" he asked Wes.

Wes made a great show of shrugging his shoulders.

"Don't see anyone from the club?" Mick said. Outside of the pub, the football club was the other social hub in town. "Went past the clubhouse earlier, all locked up. Where's the party this year?"

Wes's face was expressionless as he grabbed a cloth and began wiping down the bar. It didn't matter how many young men wrapped their cars around trees, how many fenceposts had wilted bouquets sticky-taped to them, people's attitudes didn't change. Mick had tried talking to Wes weeks ago, in the hope he would put a stop to it or at least arrange for someone sober to drive the lot of them home. Wes had nodded his head and said he'd see what he could do but still the undercurrent was "boys will be boys." Mick was determined to take Wes to the next crash and see if that generated a bit more action.

Stepping outside into the street, Mick could smell the sea. It was one of those nights when the salt wrapped itself around the town. Kinsale was slowly partying itself to sleep. Next to the patrol car stood a disappointed Gavin, looking as though he'd expected a night with a bit more punch to it.

"Heard from Sharpy?" Mick asked.

"He said he'd meet you back at the station," said Gavin. "Anything else you want me to do, Boss?"

Mick shook his head. He half-thought about sending him out on the road to see if he could find wherever the footballers' piss-up was, but what was the point? This late in the night, a lone cop, especially one as inexperienced as Gavin, might just make matters worse.

"Stay here for a bit longer until they clear out."

Mick walked back to the police station. The place was empty expect for Sharpy, who had his feet up on the desk nursing a beer.

"More in the fridge," Sharpy said and when Mick frowned at the beer, Sharpy justified himself by saying, "Quietest New Year's Eve on record, I reckon."

"Turns out I don't like quiet," said Mick. "Makes me think we've missed something. The Royal was missing a few of the recalcitrants."

"Did a drive-by of the usual spots. Park. Oval. Clubhouse," said Sharpy. "No one there."

Mick grunted in surprise at Sharpy's dedication to the job. Feeling slightly guilty at presuming the worst of him, he looked at his watch.

"You can head home," he said to Sharpy. "Give Karen a hand with the night feed."

Sharpy shook his head. "Spoke to her earlier. Looks like the baby has gastro so I'm in no rush."

The nurse must have turned him down as well, thought Mick.

"Maybe I should let Gavin head off," he said. "Seeing he's the first one back on shift." Gavin would spend most of tomorrow tracking down all the missing pets that had been spooked by the fireworks that had been going off at irregular intervals all night.

Sharpy snorted at this. "It's not like Boy Wonder's got anyone warming his bed. You go, Boss."

It wasn't like Mick had anyone warming his bed either. Still, he would head home and check that Eliza had got back in one piece. Tess was at Bridie's so he had to remember to pick her up tomorrow morning.

"Call me if there are any problems," he said.

"What could go wrong?" asked Sharpy, and then laughed like a drain before getting another beer from the fridge.

The first thing he saw when he walked through the door was a shrunken Tess huddled up on the armchair with the look on her face. He knew the look. All cops did. He'd seen it on girls younger than ten and women who were grandmothers. The occasional boy as well. It was when their eyes grow wide with what has been done to them while their mouths disappear into nothing because words can't really describe it.

He stood there waiting for Tess to start talking, to tell him he was wrong but instead there was a terrible silence as if she wanted him to take charge. He crouched down in front of her, balancing on his toes and already he could feel himself starting to assess her like a cop, because right now it hurt too much to be her father. She was wrapped in her fluffy dressing gown, which she only wore when she was sick. He could tell from the slicked back hair that she had showered, which would have washed away evidence but there was still a chance there was something under her fingernails and perhaps on her clothes. How badly was she hurt? Which doctor could he get to come out and look at her? Photos must be taken. Should he pick Tess up and put her in the squad car and drive like a madman through the back roads to find a way out of town and to a station that would have female officers to take her through the examination?

He had all those questions in his head but the one he asked was "Who did it?" and even though he didn't mean it to, it sounded like an interrogation. At the same time he reached out to hold her, to let her know that she was safe now, that he would get whoever was responsible but the movement frightened her and she flinched, her face changing. He recognized that look, too. It said she blamed him, that he was supposed to protect her and now this had happened. Mick stood up, feeling as if he wanted to tear the place apart. He backed away from her and then Tess spoke in a small voice.

"I hit something in the Mustang, Dad."

"What did you hit, love?" he asked, more gently this time because right now he couldn't care less about a car.

"I don't know," and she began to cry, an ugly cry of humiliation and despair.

"I'll call Dr. Liu," he told her. Liu would be methodical but kind. He had a daughter and would understand. "You need to be checked out."

Tess shook her head, crying so hard her whole body shook and he knew he was losing control of the situation.

"You have to tell me who did it."

The name Tess told him was one he could have guessed himself if he had been thinking straight, someone he would have warned other parents to keep their daughters away from but had never thought to tell his own because they were far too young for any of that. He could see the letters of it forming in front of his eyes and he mentally drew a black line through them. Standing up, he pulled out his keys from his pocket.

"Where are you going?" Tess grabbed at his hand, her fingers digging in so hard he almost expected blood to appear. She dragged him back down until their faces were level.

"I'm going to . . ." and he almost said something dangerous but stopped himself in time, "arrest him." Arresting bad guys was what he did.

"No," she was pleading now. "Don't leave me alone. Don't leave me alone."

She said it over and over until Mick got one of the sleeping pills he sometimes took during the day when he was on night shift and tucked her into bed. He stayed beside her, holding her hand until she fell asleep. What if she didn't remember in the morning? She could wake up and he'd tell her it was a nightmare and she was just the same as she had always been. That nothing had changed at all.

Looking at her face, moon-pale in the half-dark, he could remember the jubilation he had felt when he held her as a baby for the first time, amazed that something so delicate and small could be related to him. "You've got a beauty on your hands, Mick," the nurse had said. "All the boys will be after her," and he had laughed because he knew he'd never let any of them get close. Whenever he looked at Tess he saw her mother, the girl he fell in love with when she was the age his daughter was now. If Helen was here she'd know what to do, how to make Tess all right again.

Mick sat at the kitchen table, thoughts galloping in his head but not getting anywhere. Cops talked about this on the slow shifts, in whispers and broken sentences. The "what if" conversations where it was your daughter or your wife. He had never given an answer when asked but had listened to the others. The response was always biblical, an eye for an eye. No one ever said they'd lay charges. They had all seen what defense lawyers did. He assessed Tess's case. She had been drinking, he had smelt it on her breath. She was at a party. All his friends would have been there and none of hers. But most of all he knew how the courts treated girls like Tess and what juries will ignore for young men who play football well.

He thought about how he hadn't protected his daughter until the hot stink of shame came from every pore. It wasn't until the sun started coming up that he even bothered looking at the car in the garage. Kneeling next to the car, his fingers traced the damage done, running along the ugly marks and newly made hollows. He found a smear of blood and wondered what Tess had struck, but not for long. Instead, Mick stored every nick and groove in his mind, resolving to inflict much worse on Travis Young. He knew what fists could do but had never really understood the anger required to punch someone until your own hands were raw and bloody. Now he could imagine battering Travis Young's skull until the bones splintered, getting his head between his hands and squeezing until it cracked.

He shut his eyes as his world turned blood-red and when he opened them again, it was Eliza's face that he saw, standing above him, her mouth round with surprise. He had forgotten all about her. She was supposed to have been home hours ago. In an instant he realized that she knew nothing of what had happened, that she still lived in a world where the worst thing that could happen was getting grounded by your father for getting home after curfew. Suddenly he was furious at her, livid that he had wasted his time keeping tabs on her earlier in the night, when Tess was the one in trouble.

"Out, Eliza." He needed to get her away from him and the rage that was threatening to explode.

"But what happened?" she asked, and moved toward the car, putting out a hand to touch the damage.

"Out," he said, and he could hear his voice straining not to say more. "Out now."

28

That's not funny," I say to Tess.

She leans against the doorway, her face unreadable.

"Please, Tess," Gavin says. "Don't do this."

She doesn't look at him.

"There was no evidence," he says. The words are like falling pebbles, stones about to start an avalanche.

"Eliza's a lawyer. She can make up her own mind," says Tess.

In a rush Gavin gathers her up, gripping her tightly.

"I'm telling you not to do it," he demands.

"It isn't up to you," she answers.

"Are you happy now?" Gavin turns to me, red-faced. "You need to leave."

Before I can argue, Tess says, "This is Eliza's home. She doesn't need anyone's permission to be here."

I expect him to start shouting but his resolve breaks.

"Don't expect me to pick up the pieces this time," he says and then walks out, leaving Tess and I staring at one another. A moment later the front door slams.

I sit down knowing that if I remain standing, I will be tempted to follow his example and run away from what Tess wants to tell me.

"Not in here," she answers. "Let's go outside."

We sit on the concrete steps leading into the backyard, the cold from the ground seeping through my jeans. Out here is unrecognizable as well. The grass has been mown, garden beds turned over and mulched. The lemon tree has been savagely clipped back. Unlike in his study, I can't feel my father out here. There is just the two of us.

Tess sits completely still next to me. She doesn't turn her face in my direction.

"My first mistake," she tells me, "was taking the Mustang," and she begins her story at the beach, letting me see all the ways that night could have been so different, how many choices she was given and how she kept picking the wrong ones again and again until she found herself in a situation where no choice was offered to her. The words are factual and dry. There is no asking for sympathy or railing against the unfairness of it. She doesn't even use the word rape. When she tells me how people watched and did nothing, I think of what Dave told me. Was this what he meant? My own sister and he couldn't even say her name. Maybe he thought I already knew. And then I think about sitting in a car watching Luke Tyrell terrorize that woman, being stunned, wanting to do something but not knowing what, and as a result doing nothing helpful at all.

There was no green hat to save Tess.

She pauses as if temporarily all her words have been used up.

"I've sat on his bench," I say, horrified at myself. "Sat there and looked out at the view."

"That's OK," she replies. "I've gone there myself sometimes. It helps me think. Funny what you find useful can be so different to what other people think will help. Dad thought by keeping my room the same we could pretend that I was still the same. Gavin thought if we left town it would get better and when it didn't, decided we should come back and face it directly."

"But why wasn't Travis charged?"

Tess's mouth twists sharp like barbed wire. "Dad came up with a different solution. A more direct one."

I scramble to put together everything I know about Travis Young.

"There was a car accident. Wasn't he drunk driving?" But Mary's version of events is already echoing in my head.

"That's what was put in the official police report."

'What are you saying?"

"Gavin would tell you there's no evidence that Dad killed him," she says.

I want to grab her and shake the truth out but I try to keep calm.

"Are you saying Dad did it?"

She doesn't answer me directly. "He woke me up in the middle of the night, sat me down at the table and told me Travis was dead. And I felt something close to triumph, that he had felt pain, that he wouldn't hurt another girl. But then I realized that Dad was wearing the same clothes as the day before and knew he hadn't gone to bed at all."

"That's not enough," I begin, but Tess keeps talking.

"I asked him and he couldn't look me in the eye and deny it. He thought killing Travis would make me better. In the following days there were more details. Dad had been first on the scene. He just happened to be driving up that road and radioed it in, but by the time the ambulance arrived it was too late."

None of this is concrete proof, I tell myself. Dad could have been so horrified by her accusation that he didn't answer. The rest could be a coincidence.

"He thought Travis would disappear and we'd never have to think about him again. Instead he was everywhere. There were memorial football matches, perpetual trophies in his name, his picture in shop windows with candles and flowers. We attended his funeral because what would people think if we didn't. I had to stand there and watch the entire town say what a wonderful person he was and know it was my fault he was dead."

"No. It wasn't your fault." In all this mess, I am sure of that. Tess wasn't responsible for whatever had happened.

"You think I'm completely blameless?" she asks. "I knew that sex was part of the deal. Wore my prettiest dress, best knickers, packed condoms. I'd heard the stories about him, seen the way he treated other girls, analyzed the whispers, tried to fill in the blanks. I'd been warned and yet was arrogant to think that he would treat me differently. That he would hold my hand first, tell me I was beautiful. How pathetic to set the bar that low, to want so very little and in the end not even get that."

"It's sexual assault," I tell her. "Even if he'd lit candles and bought you chocolates. He got what he deserved, Tess."

"Then maybe I got what I deserved as well," says Tess.

"No." I shake my head.

"What, only people you dislike get what they deserve?"

"Is this why you don't visit Dad?" I ask.

She angles her head, looking at me for the first time.

"I told him that night I'd never forgive him for what he did. That he was a terrible father and I hated him. That I was damaged and he was damaged but you weren't and he needed to keep it that way. That's why you were sent to boarding school."

"That's the reason I was sent away?"

"You always thought it was a punishment but I was trying to protect you. I had ruined everything. I didn't want you to get caught up in it."

"Oh, Tess."

"It was years before I regretted what I said to Dad that night but I could never find the words to tell him. Then he had his accident."

"It's not too late," I say. "We could go to the nursing home together."

She shakes her head. "I tried once, drove down there but then I saw Travis's grandmother out the front and knew I couldn't go in. The problem is, if I stop thinking Dad isn't the one to blame for Travis's death, then the only one left is me and I can't cope with that on my conscience. Not two people's deaths."

I put my head in my hands.

"Do you remember," she says, "when you accused me of hitting the kangaroo, what I said?"

My throat is constricting so the words come out in a thin whisper. "That you never hit a kangaroo in your life."

"You were so sure of yourself that I almost told you then, that it was Grace I hit coming back from the party."

The force of this nearly knocks me over. I have been driving around in the car that killed Grace.

I curl into a small ball, my arms wrapped tight around my knees. Tess reaches out to touch me but I pull away from her. When I do lift my head, all I can see is the sixteen-year-old version of myself creeping up the driveway all those years ago.

It was so early in the morning that the sun was a flat line on the horizon. My mission was to try and get into the house without any awkward questions being asked. Tess's scuffed sandals were in my hand, one strap broken and I knew she'd be furious with me. Almost at the back door, I noticed the light was on in the garage and the side door open. Someone hadn't locked up properly. I stuck my head through the doorway and there was my father, kneeling down next to his damaged car. Suddenly, the picture disappears and I'm back in the present.

"Tell me what happened," I say to my sister.

"I was too busy looking in the rearview mirror checking if anyone was following me," Tess says. The words come fast, falling out of her mouth as if she has stored them in there all this time just waiting for the vow of silence to end. "No headlights on, probably still drunk, going too fast. There was a thump from the front of the car, an enormous jolt as the wheels went over, knocking me and the car sideways. It was something big but I didn't see anything clearly, a flash of movement beforehand perhaps."

I can't take it all in. It is too big, too nightmarish, so I try to focus on the small details.

"What time was it?"

"A quarter to two."

"How can you be so precise?"

I'm trying to resist the urge to challenge her, to dispute every word, to pick holes in her story.

"I watched the clock the whole way home, telling myself all I had to do was drive for fifteen minutes and I would be safe."

"What road was it?"

"Ophir Road."

"And you were driving away from the party back into town?"

She nods.

"Did you stop?" I breathe hard, trying to fill up my lungs before she plunges me under.

"I wouldn't have stopped for anything. No one came to help me. I wasn't going to help anyone else. By the time I got home I knew it was the wrong thing. I told Dad about it but he just dismissed it, so I tried to do the same, to push it away because I was the victim here."

Each word she says knocks shards off the flinty exterior she has created for herself over the years, splinters in the smooth façade exposing the damage underneath.

"When did you realize it was Grace?" The thought makes me sick to the bone. Did Grace die straight away or did Tess leave her to bleed to death on the side of the road?

"Dad thought I'd hit a kangaroo. He told me that I was lucky it wasn't a wombat. Because he didn't want me focusing on it, he got the Mustang repaired straight away. I think he was trying to show me that anything can be fixed. He took it to the city rather than wait for his usual repairer to come back from holidays, wanting to hide it so people didn't bother me with questions. Don't you remember? He yelled at you at breakfast a few days later when you brought it up."

The event had completely fallen out of my head.

"It wasn't until the next week that Alan Sharp told him about Grace, how she hadn't been seen since New Year's Eve and Dad asked me if I had seen her that night. Straight away I said she had been at the party and had asked me for a lift and then talked about walking home and that's when I realized."

"How can you be sure?" It hovers between a question and an accusation.

"She had wanted to leave and the quickest way was along that road. When I told Dad, he immediately took over the case."

"He wanted to cover it up?"

"No, he wanted to prove me wrong. The Mustang had already been mended so instead we drove up and down Ophir Road to help me remember where the accident occurred, but it didn't look the same in the daylight and Dad refused to take me at night because he was already worried about my mental health. Instead, he chased up every possible lead, annoyed people up and down the coast for potential sightings of her because just one would mean that I didn't hit her. But there were never any. She had disappeared."

"But if there was no body, how can you be sure?"

"There was no dead kangaroo either."

"What about Jim's statement?" I ask. "He said he took her to the train."

"Dad wanted to believe that but he knew the trains weren't running. Still he investigated it just in case she had left town some other way. Went up to the city to see if she made it there but found nothing. In the end, he thought it was Jim making mischief, especially seeing he included you in his statement. Dad figured Jim was deliberately tying up police resources with this investigation as payback for Gavin annoying him."

Tess's story is like a labyrinth that confuses me at every turn.

"In the end, he knew I was right," said Tess. "That's why he got Aaron that job. He was trying to make up for what I'd done."

"No, you're wrong," I say. "You must be. About Dad, about Grace, about everything."

She's tear-stained and I didn't even notice that she'd started crying. I know I should feel empathy or at least pity, but I can't. All I can be is angry, because if I stay angry, then I don't have to deal with any of this.

"What are you expecting me to do, Tess?" I grab her face with my hand and turn it so she is forced to look directly at me.

"You wanted to know who killed Grace," she says. "And now you do."

"What if I go down to the police station and report you?"

"I tried to do that once," she says. "Went down when Dad wasn't on duty and got Gavin to take my statement. But Dad told him what happened with Travis and how I was so mixed up that he shouldn't believe me, that really I hit a big Eastern grey kangaroo. So Gavin told me he couldn't accept my statement. He could see how close to the edge I was and started dropping round to check up on me. He was kind."

I can't stay here a second longer. Turning away, I leave her sitting on the back step and walk out of the house to the car. I stand next to the Mustang, not sure I can even get back in it again, but steeling myself, I unlock it and get behind the steering wheel. The past clambers in beside me.

What I want more than anything is to be able to talk to Dad, ask him what he really thinks happened. Tess was dismissive about him needing evidence but he was right. Where was Grace's body? Tess has given me her version of events but there are only fragments of answers here, part-guesses filling in the blanks. One eyewitness report isn't enough. She has told me a story. Just because she thinks that it's true doesn't necessarily make it so.

I'm not a police officer but I can treat this as if I'm writing a memo with logically ordered paragraphs, cases cited, clarifying footnotes. This is someone else's knot that has been presented for me to untie. Fishing out paper and a pen from my bag, I sit in the front seat of the car and begin to write, setting out all the facts but my brain is dull. I keep trying to make it fit all together but it's like crazy paving with massive holes in between.

Because the one question I come back to again and again is the one that started everything off.

Tess says Grace was walking back into town along Ophir Road, but The Castle is in the opposite direction so I still don't understand how her necklace ended up there.

29

I ask the woman drying glasses behind the bar where Tony is. She tells me to try his room on the second floor. I take the stairs two at a time and then slam my hand repeatedly on the door. Eventually, Tony opens it, his eyes sleepy and unfocused as he stands there only wearing a pair of boxers. He stretches, combs his fingers through his hair, and tries to wake up.

"Sorry, didn't realize you were sleeping," I say, turning my gaze to the floor.

"Day off," he says. "Got up early to go surfing. Everything OK?"

"Can I talk to you?"

A yawn. "Give me five minutes. I'll get some clothes on."

When he opens the door again he's dressed in an old T-shirt and board shorts.

"You want a coffee?" he asks.

"Anything stronger?"

His smile shows even, white teeth. "I own a pub, should have something tucked away somewhere." Then he looks closer at me. "Everything all right?"

The adrenaline that I had felt rushing over in the car is disappearing, my urgency replaced by despair. The reality of what Tess told me is slowly sinking in, dissolving my defenses.

"Not really."

"The restaurant isn't open yet," he says. "Let's head down there."

The room is in shadow with all the lights switched off. Tony winds his way through tables covered in white cloths and leads me to the first wooden nook against the wall.

"Grab a seat," he says. "I'll get the drinks."

Muted triangles of sun illuminate the dust swirling in the air.

"I can turn on the lights if you like," he calls from somewhere in the gloom.

"It's good," I say, and it is, perfect for talking about the ghosts of the past. "We won't be interrupted?"

"Shouldn't be," he says. "Mum's been a maniac the last few days, I've barely seen her. Thank god the election's tomorrow."

Tony comes over carrying a bottle and two glasses. Now that I am here, I'm reluctant to start asking him questions in case the answers confirm what Tess told me.

"I sat in this booth for my twelfth birthday dinner," I say. "It hasn't changed at all."

"They remind me of confessionals." Tony raps a knuckle on the wooden partition behind him. "Same wood as the church. I told you all my secrets last time. Must be your turn for confession."

"I need to talk to you about the night Grace disappeared."

A complicated expression ripples across his face, like a wave that doesn't break.

"Two people told me that Grace was at the paddock party," I say. "Do you know how she got there?"

He pauses, looking at me as though wondering how I will react. "She went with me," he says. "I was driving there from the beach and she was walking along the track. I told her to go back to you lot, but she didn't listen."

"Was she wearing a necklace?"

His face frowns thoughtfully. "Yeah," he says. "Maybe. At least I think so. A gold one perhaps."

"Then what happened?" I asked.

"We drove to The Castle and then through the back paddocks to the party."

"You could have driven along Ophir Road straight to the party."

He pauses before answering and I am almost counting the seconds. "We were running late and I still detoured that way. I guess I was showing off to her."

"Did you get out at The Castle?" I ask.

"Is this important?"

"Yes," I say. "Please. Did you get out at The Castle?"

His head is shaking "no" but then he stops. "Actually we did. Not for long, a couple of minutes. Then we got back in the car."

"Was she wearing the necklace then?"

He half-laughs. "I haven't a clue."

"So it could have fallen off at The Castle?"

"It's possible, I guess. She didn't mention it. What's this about, Eliza?"

But I ignore that because right now I'm only interested in his answers, not his questions.

"What happened when you got to the party?"

"She ditched me as soon as she could," he says.

"Did she tell you what she was going to do next?"

"No. I saw her talking to your sister."

"What time was that?"

"Pretty soon after we got there. Half past one or so."

The missing sections are slotting into place. The gaps are narrowing. It fits what Tess remembers about the party. If she's right about that then it's more likely she's right about what happened next.

"What is this about, Eliza?" he asks again. "Grace left, pure and simple. She caught a train to the city."

I'm trying not to get upset but part of me wants to blurt out what Tess told me. It is too big a burden to keep to myself but instead I shake my head. "It's not true. Jim made that story up. There was no train."

"Jim?" says Tony. "What's he got to do with it?"

At that moment the lights flicker on.

"Thought I heard voices," Janey says. "Look at the two of you sitting in the dark on such a lovely day. What can you be talking about?" There's an arch smile in her voice like she's caught two canoodling teenagers.

"Nothing important." I quickly pull my hand away from Tony. "Just chatting."

"You got everything sorted, Mum?" asks Tony, but his eyes are fixed on me.

"Loose ends are all tied up," she says. "Just when you think it's organized, there's always something that pops up unexpectedly."

"Best of luck for tomorrow," I say, grabbing my bag.

"Thanks, love," Janey smiles. "When are you heading back home to the city?"

"Soon," I tell her. "Anyway, I have to go see Dad now."

"Say hello to Mick for us."

Tony frowns at us both and says nothing.

The nursing home is quiet. Mary isn't sitting on the bench outside, for which I am grateful. I take Dad out to the empty garden and watch the birds. Flashy jewels of color, they seem happy enough chirping and clattering in their cage. I think of the psychology of a man who loves their bright feathers and sweet songs so much that he must lock them up. The sort of man who makes false statements about a missing girl to the police. But it might be too late for Jim to explain his actions now. Maybe it doesn't even matter because I have been given the answer. The problem is I don't want it to be true.

My eyes turn away from the birds and watch my father instead. His skin is the color of rain. I had thought Dad was waiting for me to find out who killed Grace when he knew all along. According to Ryan, hearing is one of the last senses to disappear so I choose my words carefully and speak them clearly.

"Tess told me what happened to Grace."

For one awful moment I am so angry at him, at all of them, at myself, that my words start and finish with a clenched hiss and I sit there shaking, my breath catching in furious little puffs.

I steel myself to try again.

"I didn't want to believe her. She said at the start you didn't believe her either."

I wait for a reaction from him, a twitch of the head, pressure on my fingers. Anything.

"But in the end you thought she was right."

And then I whisper, "I think she is right."

There, I've said it.

"Tess told me something else," I go on, and this is even harder to say aloud. I look around to make sure that no one can hear us.

"She told me you killed Travis Young because of what he did to her." The words are poured into my father's ear.

My father's breath gurgles in his chest as the birds sing. I want to walk over to that cage, unlock the door and let them all escape. I want the same for my father. He has done terrible things to protect his daughters but I can't condemn him for that. Dad thought I was better off without him and loved me enough to let me go. It's time for me to let him go.

I try to think about what will give him comfort now.

"I forgive you." I pause and then, "I want you to know that Tess forgives you," I lie. "She told me to tell you that."

His eyelids half open and my heart skips a beat. I squeeze his hand gently but his fingers are like ice so I tuck the blanket around him and wait. His eyes soon shut of their own accord. I wheel him carefully back to his room, tell him I love him and then kiss him gently on the forehead. His skin feels hot under my lips. It's me that is getting cold.

That night I sit in my bungalow at Ocean Breeze Motel. I'm leaving in the morning. There is nothing more I can do here. The 11 P.M. news comes on the radio and I almost miss the report about Luke Tyrell's death. A nearby car engine roars at the wrong time, headlights flash around the room and I hear only a sentence.

The police are investigating.

That doesn't comfort me as much as it once did.

I think about ringing Tess to tell her that if she wants to see Dad alive, she should go soon, but I have no words to talk about the rest of what has happened. Her story chases itself around my head. I try to flatten it out in my mind so I can find the weaknesses but it stubbornly refuses to fall apart. Aaron said he never wanted me to contact them again. Am I so much of a coward that I will cling to that as an excuse not to tell them? What do I tell Amy? If I choose silence than Grace's friends and family will never know how their daughter died. The words I said to Dave come back to haunt me. What do I owe a young woman's bones, dead over a hundred years ago, and a baby girl only days old?

I sit at the window but don't turn on the light. Resting my head on the sill, my eyes adjust, the lines of the screen dissolve and I watch the world. Another car comes closer, quieter and slower than the last one. No headlights this time—someone is being more thoughtful of the sleeping inhabitants. As the car slides past, the moon catches the face of the driver. It's Alan Sharp. He takes the track up to Jim's place.

My phone buzzes and jumps like a nervous cat. In the quiet, I do as well. I grab it, expecting the nursing home but it's Tony.

"You're awake," he says.

"Alan Sharp just drove past, heading up to Jim Keaveney's," I tell him. "Have you heard how he is?" but Tony isn't interested.

"This afternoon you said something about Jim and Grace. What were you talking about?"

"He told the police about driving her into town and Grace catching a train."

"But he wasn't there," says Tony.

"What?"

"It was Mum who drove Grace into town, not Jim. I asked her to."

My heart almost stops.

"Everything I said this afternoon was right but I saw Grace again that night. She left me at the party and I went and drank with some mates. Then it started turning pretty nasty."

He hesitates and I wonder if he was one of the boys who stood and watched what happened to Tess. For one black moment I almost hate Tony Bayless.

"I knew I shouldn't drive so I decided to walk back and sleep at The Castle. I was halfway there when Grace caught up with me. I phoned Mum and she came out. Told me to go back to sleep and that she'd take Grace into town."

As I'm listening to this, I switch on my light and hunt through my bag for the piece of scribbled-on paper.

"What time?" I ask.

"It must have been around 2 A.M. when I called. I remembered I thought about waiting until after the pub shut at three but Grace made me phone straight away."

"What time did they drive back into town?"

Never ask a witness a question you don't know the answer to. I close my eyes. This could still all go wrong. That Grace got out of the car and said she'd walk into town. On the same road that Tess came speeding along. That Tess was later than she thought.

"I was asleep by then, but it has to have been after four."

Tears spill onto a handwritten number that I have circled. Tess swore she was home before 2 A.M.

"Are you crying, Eliza?" Tony's confusion crackles through the phone. "Is everything all right?"

"Are you sure about the times? Are you sure?" There's so much I don't understand but all I can think about is that if Grace was still alive at 4 A.M. then Tess couldn't have killed her.

"Check Mum's police statement if you need to know exact times."

"She went to Dad?"

"No, Alan Sharp. When I heard Grace was missing, Mum and I made a statement to him straight away. Mum always blamed herself for not taking Grace home but Grace wouldn't even tell her where she lived. She kept saying she wanted to be dropped at the train station. There was nothing Mum could do really."

"Did Dad ever come to talk to you?" I ask.

"No."

"Look, I've got to go," I say. "Thanks for ringing."

"It's no big deal. This is ancient history, right?"

Not to me it isn't. "Bye, Tony, I've got to talk to Alan," I say, and disconnect.

Straight away my phone begins to buzz. It's Tony again but I'm not interested. Alan hasn't come back down the track yet and I need to talk to him, to find out if my sister is innocent, to tell my Dad before he dies. Pulling on my sneakers and a jumper over my pajamas, I head out the door. Behind me, my phone rings again.

Outside is colder than I expected, lighter as well. The moon is almost full, chalky-white, with stars spilling out across the sky. I'm running up the hill along the track, listening for a car coming back along it. In the dark, the distance seems farther and the bush wilder. Alan might still be reluctant to talk about it, but once he hears what Tess has been through these years, what Dad feared, he'll have to understand there are bigger issues at play. All I need is for him to confirm the times.

A breeze rustles the leaves, but I can hear a humming noise as well. The bullet-riddled NO TRESPASSERS sign comes into view. The sound gets louder. It's a generator. I move quickly past the line of dead foxes and keep running over the ridge. There is a small dark tumbledown house with a great big shed, all lit up, next to it. Two cars are parked outside the open shed door. One is Alan's and there is another beside it. As I move closer to the shed I can hear someone talking over the noise of the generator.

Picking my way through the broken shadows, I peer carefully in through the door. Alan is only ten feet away, standing with his back to me. There's a concrete floor, a table and chairs in the corner and an old filing cabinet next to them with a kettle on top. Warehouse shelves run from floor to ceiling. They are crammed full with bottles, tins, rusted equipment, cardboard boxes and other bits and pieces. A couple of hay bales are in front of large wire cages which are stacked in front of a rack of serious firearms, way beyond the standard shotguns farmers use. This is a serious arsenal. I step closer, stumble and bump into the door, which makes a loud metal clang against the wall.

Alan turns in an instant.

"Eliza," he says. "What are you doing here?"

"You drove past my window."

"Thought I better make sure Jim's shed was properly locked up," he says. "He died in the hospital tonight."

Whatever information Jim had about Grace is gone forever.

"Did they work out what killed him?"

"Bad fall," says Alan. "Jim had been getting unsteady on his feet."

Jim had looked pretty healthy to me last time I'd seen him.

I walk farther into the shed. "Anyone here with you?"

"Just me talking to myself," he says. "Bad habits develop when you live alone."

I go over to the guns. Black, large and dangerous.

"Quite the hoarder," says Alan. "Most of this stuff has been here since he closed the shop." He points at the cages.

"Gavin needs to be told about those guns," I say. "They should be locked up."

Alan doesn't reply and it occurs to me that perhaps Alan is actually looting the place.

He nods. "Yeah, it's not safe to have those lying around. I was just finishing up. You want a lift back to the motel?"

"Thanks," I say. "I need to talk to you about something urgent."

"What's that?"

"Grace Hedland's disappearance. Apparently, Janey made a statement to you."

There's the flicker of a frown.

"You still asking questions about that?"

"It's important."

He makes a resigned face. "OK, wait outside while I turn off the generator."

Standing next to the car, the rumbling noise finally stops and with it all the lights go out.

"Alan," I call.

There's no answer.

"Alan, are you there?"

There's a movement behind me and as I half turn toward it, my head explodes with pain, my legs buckle and I feel myself falling and then nothing.

30

New Year's Eve 1996

Janey

Jim Keaveney had commandeered the microphone and was taking requests. Janey kept a beer waiting for him to wet his whistle in between numbers. There was a momentary lull as "Auld Lang Syne" ended to a smattering of applause. Jim stopped to recharge and that's when Wes heard the ringing.

"Phone," he called out to his wife, jerking this thumb toward it. He'd been behind the bar all night, unwilling to move too far from the till.

"Yes sir, no sir, three bags full sir," Janey muttered in Wes's direction, as she placed a stack of dirty glasses on the table and headed through the doors and out into the hall.

It was Tony.

"Hang on, love," she said. "Bit noisy in here. Give us a sec." She unraveled the extension cord from behind the coat stand and pulled it along until she came to the cupboard, opened the door and popped inside, pulling it almost shut behind her. She'd been asking Wes for a proper office for years.

"Say that again."

She could tell he was upset. Had plenty to drink as well, she guessed. He kept stopping and starting but she heard the words "The Castle" and there was a girl's voice in the background, prompting him with details.

"Who's that with you?" she asked.

It was one of the girls who'd been with Eliza Carmody earlier on the beach, the tall one, if she remembered rightly.

"No one else?"

A negative reply and then a question.

"No," she said. "There's no need to bother them. I'm on my way. You two sit tight and don't touch anything."

She waited until her son promised before hanging up the phone.

"I'm heading out," she said to Wes. "Tony needs to be picked up."

"I'll be single-handed here," he complained. "I've already sent the others home." He was perched up on his bar stool like it was a throne. "Tony can make his own way."

But tonight Janey wasn't going to defer to him.

"You'll survive," said Janey. "Get them to pour their own drinks if you have to. Just make sure they pay for them. No more freebies."

Wes gave her a disgruntled look as she grabbed the car keys from the hook.

Heading out the back door, Janey called out cheery hellos to those sitting in the beer garden looking a little worse for wear. Some were keen to chat, but Janey was well practiced in extricating herself quickly from drunken rambling conversations. With her bag over her shoulder, she unlocked the car.

"Mrs. Bayless," came a voice.

Janey jumped.

It was that new constable, looming out of the darkness. So thin, he was like the bony outline of a person still waiting to be filled in.

"Gavin," she said. "Whatever are you doing lurking in the bushes?"

"The boss sent me down here to keep an eye on the pub. To make sure the party doesn't get out of hand."

He was one of those tall men who adopt a wide-legged stance when talking to a short person. It always made Janey feel like directing a good kick to the balls.

"Is that right?" She made a mental note to give Mick Carmody a piece of her mind next time she saw him. "Why don't you pop inside? Have a beer on the house. New Year's Eve and all."

She didn't expect him to agree. It was just a little test to see how he would react.

"Thank you but no," he said. Even the pompous way he spoke annoyed her. "I'm fine out here. Keeping busy."

"I'll be sure to let Mick know your commitment to the job." She walked around the car and unlocked the driver's door.

"Are you going somewhere?" asked Gavin. "The boss didn't want anyone driving who might have had a bit to drink."

This was going too far. Janey smiled her most dangerous smile.

"Lemonade all night, Constable." She crossed her heart and moved forward so there was only a breath between the two of them. "I never drink when I'm working, just like you. Promise. You can smell me if you like."

It was the little schoolgirl voice that always wrong-footed them, the sweet sound of it coming from a body that looked far more experienced. Men were predictable and sure enough, Gavin looked uncomfortable and straightened up, backing off a little.

"That's all right," he said. "I'm sure we can trust you to be sensible."

If only I could say the same, thought Janey, as she adjusted the rearview mirror so she could see Gavin in it.

Two worried faces were outside in the dark waiting for her as she pulled up in front of The Castle. Just kids, thought Janey. This was going to be easily sorted.

"You poor things," she said, getting out of the car. "You've had a bit of an adventure." It both acknowledged and reduced what they had found at the same time.

She reached up and hugged her son and then turned to the girl.

"Grace, isn't it?" she said. "I took your picture earlier."

The girl nodded, her arms tightly folded. Janey decided against hugging her. Grace didn't look the type.

"Where are your friends?" Janey asked.

"We left them hours ago," said Tony. "Back at the beach."

Still the girl said nothing.

"Well, you'd better show me what you've found then," said Janey. "Lead the way, Tony."

He swung a flashlight up and clicked it on.

"It's in the furthest outbuilding. Right around the back. We thought we saw lights near it earlier when we were driving to the party."

What's this "we"? thought Janey, and gave Grace another look.

They walked in single file, Tony at the front, Janey at the rear, Grace safely sandwiched between them. The breeze carried the faint but unmistakable sounds of the paddock party. Wes hadn't told her about it but she should have guessed he'd been busy playing the big man again.

"So, Anthony Wesley Bayless," she said, her voice laced with regret, "you went to the paddock party."

There was instant contrition. "Sorry, Mum," he said. "I know—" but she interrupted him. "How about you, Grace? Your mum know that you were going to that party?"

A hesitation before a reluctant, "No."

"Well, I guess we can talk about that later."

It was a threat, lightly issued.

Tony stopped once they got to the low-slung building. Janey tried to remember what it had been built for originally—a small stable, perhaps? Tony handed the flashlight over to his mother, who shone it at the door.

"And it was unlocked?" she said.

"Yes," said Grace. "We were walking back from the party. I saw a fox crawling under the door. It was attacking something inside."

"It was still around when we went in," Tony said. "I had to get the shotgun from the house to scare it off."

"Where's the gun now?" asked Janey.

"Back at the house," Tony answered.

"Good boy," said Janey. "We don't want any stupid accidents. Now, you two stay here," and she pushed the door.

Tony did what he was told. He wasn't in any hurry to go back inside but Grace darted straight past her and began pulling covers off the cages. Instantly the noise began, a godawful shrieking as birds beat their wings against the metal, feathers and shit gathering in the bottom of mesh wire boxes barely bigger than the birds. The stink of ammonia filled the air.

"It's just a bunch of galahs," said Janey.

Grace pointed at a cage. "That's a glossy black cockatoo. They're rare." She moved toward the back of the shed. "Here's a Major Mitchell."

"Stay next to me," ordered Janey. "Wouldn't do to touch anything."

She shone the light around the room. In the glare of the light, the bird tried to hide its face under its wing. It almost looked like it was ashamed of itself, Janey thought. Not your fault, she felt like saying, you poor little bugger.

It was clear Grace had taken a thorough look around. Janey doubted that Tony had set foot in here once he had seen what was inside. He'd never liked birds and had been a bit scared of them as a kid. Janey shone the flashlight here and there, trying to work out if anything had been disturbed but it didn't seem to been.

"Well, I've seen enough," she said to Grace.

"Wait," said Grace. "There's something more." She tried to grab the flashlight but Janey held hard and wouldn't give it up, so Grace pushed it onto the floor next to one of the cages. Janey crouched down to look at it more closely. It was an old hanky. She was certain she recognized it.

"There's blood on it," said Grace. "Lots of it. We need to call the police."

Tony was waiting for them outside, his bleached anxious face caught in the spotlight. "What do you reckon, Mum? Those lights earlier, someone must have been dumping the birds."

Janey said nothing but watched Grace out of the corner of her eye, waiting to see which way she would jump.

"It's wildlife smuggling," Grace said, her voice emphatic. "It's got to be."

"I'm sure Jim could help us," said Janey. "I can try him in the morning. See what we should do about it."

"No one who loved birds could leave them like that," said Grace. "There's no room. We should open the cages and let them free."

"I don't know," said Janey. "Some might be injured. We don't want to make that fox's job any easier."

"We need to ring the police," said Grace again.

"You two would have to be prepared for some questions, including what you've been up to tonight. Underage drinking and the rest of it."

The petrified look on Tony's face almost made her laugh.

"The police won't be worried about us, not when they see what's inside there," said Grace. "There's blood. Someone could be really hurt."

"It's the middle of the night," said Janey.

Grace bit her bottom lip. She's little more than a child, thought Janey. Still there was plenty of pluck in her, not like poor Tony.

"Eliza's dad is a policeman," said Grace. "I'll ring their house. He won't mind."

"We don't need to get Mick out of bed," Janey said. "Not when he's already put in a full shift. Tell you what, I'll drive you home and then go by his house when it gets light. No sense in you two getting involved. I'll say I was out here, saw the fox, did some investigating and found the birds."

Tony's head nodded so emphatically he looked like a wind-up toy, but Grace didn't budge.

"No," she said. "We're all involved. It's the right thing to do."

Janey took a deep breath. Her feet hurt and she'd been banking on seeing her bed before sunrise. This was getting ridiculous.

"Very well," she said, trying to control her crossness. "Let's go back to the house and I'll ring the station."

She waited until Grace had gone ahead with the flashlight and then grabbed Tony's arm. He had been keeping his head down, reluctant to get involved.

"Talk some sense into your friend," she whispered to him. "We don't want the police out here. What if those developers heard? It could jeopardize their offer."

Obligingly, he jogged ahead and caught up to Grace. She listened to their conversation. Tony tried but Grace wasn't budging. Janey wondered if this was what having a daughter would be like, a defiant mix of friend and foe. She thought she would enjoy the challenge but not at 3 A.M. If this ended up in a police investigation it would be a disaster.

They were walking in the shadows of The Castle now. It was just a big mausoleum, thought Janey, a place where you sent good money to die. If Wes hadn't bought it she'd have never had to worry about their finances and taken risks, but someone had to keep them afloat.

"You two head into the kitchen and put on the kettle, Tony," said Janey. "Make us a nice cup of tea while I phone."

It was an old rotary dial phone that they kept at The Castle, not like the push-button one they had at the pub. When they were doing the renovations, Wes wanted the best of everything, but Janey had put her foot down. Until the place started making some money, it would make do with whatever bits and pieces she could find.

She didn't call triple zero because that would give her an operator who would redirect her to the twenty-four hour station farther up the coast full of people she didn't know. Instead, she dialed local, putting her finger in each circle, pulling it up and then letting it click back down, audible enough for those in the kitchen to hear.

It was answered on the third ring.

"Good," she said when she heard the voice. "I need you to come out to The Castle. It's a police matter."

When she came back into the kitchen, Tony had his arms on the table, his head resting on them, half-asleep. Grace was sitting across from him, her face unreadable. She would have got Tony to drive home but he was too drunk to do that safely, so she shook him instead.

"Not asleep," he said, eyes still closed. "Just resting."

"Go upstairs," she told him. "The camping beds are still up in the front bedrooms. Sleep it off and we'll talk about it in the morning."

"What about the police?" Grace asked. "We heard you talking to them."

"They're coming out for a look. Told me you didn't have to wait around. They'll get in contact if they need more information. Said I could take you home."

"But if you're not here and Tony's asleep, how will they know which shed?" argued Grace. "No, I'm heading back down to the birds and waiting for them there."

Janey had just about had enough. She glared at the girl. "Well, you go do that then," and she didn't say another word until Grace had left the room. Tony stood there helplessly and Janey felt tempted to box his ears in frustration.

"I'm really sorry," he said. "But maybe it was lucky I went to the party, otherwise we wouldn't know about those birds."

Janey's blood ran hot but outwardly she stayed calm. "This is a serious business best left to the police," she said. "You're not to talk about it to anyone. If those buyers get wind of it, we are sunk. The pub, everything. Do you understand?"

There were more big nods of his man-child head.

"Mum, you'll make sure Grace gets home?"

"Of course I will, love."

"Just she got mad with Eliza Carmody over a boy and I think she's still upset. Talked about catching a train to the city."

"Is that so?" said Janey. "Sounds like it has been quite a night."

She found Grace on her hands and knees searching around the grass in front of the shed.

"What are you doing?" Janey asked.

"My necklace," Grace said. "I've lost my necklace." She looked at the shotgun in Janey's hands. "Why have you got that?"

"In case that pesky fox comes back," said Janey, sitting next to her, placing the gun down carefully.

She tried to talk to the girl, but all she got was one-word answers. It was clear that Grace was hostile, but of what it was hard to tell. Maybe this was standard teenage girl behavior. All Janey knew was that if she'd acted like that, she'd have been given a good clattering smack from her father. So instead, she stared up at The Castle. Tony would be asleep now, she was sure of that. One thing the pub had taught him was to sleep even if there was a hurricane outside.

This whole place gave her the creeps. Wes loved all that history but if left her cold. Only the living mattered. I'd pay them to knock it down, she thought, but instead they can pay me, build a golf course and bring rich tourists to the town and to the pub.

It was over half an hour before the truck came slowly up the track toward them. Janey waved the light in his direction.

"That's not a police car," said Grace.

"About time," Janey answered, ignoring her. "You wait here and I'll have a quick word."

A dark outline got out of the cab. A shadow in the headlights. She hadn't expected the girl to obey, but Grace stayed sitting on the ground.

"You didn't rush," Janey said, steering him toward the back of the car. There was alcohol on his breath, which wasn't encouraging.

"Who's the girl?" he asked.

"A law-abiding citizen, waiting for the police to take her statement, to tell what she's found."

"And what's that?"

Janey shrugged. "You ask her."

He grunted, taking a baton-like flashlight from the tray. Switching it on, the spotlight caught the outline of something lying in the truck, half covered by a tarp. It had the curve of a hip, a long line of leg.

"Jesus," said Janey, stepping backward. "What have you got there?"

"Came out the Ophir Road way and found this," he said. "Must have been hit by a car. A big roo too. Taking it home for my dogs."

"Made quite a mess," said Janey.

"Hose it out and it will be just like new."

Janey thought for a bit and decided that could be quite useful.

Grace scrambled to her feet as they walked toward her. Janey could see her face visibly relax as she took in the police uniform.

"Grace, love," Janey said, walking around her until she was standing behind the girl, "you know Constable Alan Sharp. Tell him what you saw." She put a hand on the girl's shoulder.

The words tumbled out in a rush. "It wasn't just birds," Grace said. "They're sitting on boxes. I moved a cage and looked inside one. It was full of guns and bags of pills."

"Sounds serious," said Sharpy. "Who else knows about it?" He turned and caught Janey's eye.

Janey shook her head.

"I didn't tell anyone," Grace explained, "not even Tony. I wanted the police to know first."

Janey sighed, and as the girl kept talking and Sharpy nodded his head, she knelt down and picked up the shotgun.

31

Before I see anything, before I hear anything, I feel the painful bite of tight twists of metal against my skin and throbbing in my head. When I open my eyes, everything is sideways, but it turns out only I am.

I'm lying on the floor, chicken wire under me, and my head feels like pulp. I lift a hand to it and feel the hot stickiness of blood. It's still wet which means I haven't been unconscious long.

There's a figure standing there, a little blurry, but I recognize her. Janey Bayless is watching me.

Pushing myself to sitting, I realize I'm in a cage. It is one of the large aviaries but the truth is cages only look big when you are on the outside. Hooking my fingers through the mesh, I pull myself up in increments, legs shaking.

"Alan Sharp," I tell her urgently. "Where is he?"

The lights flicker and then everything goes dark and for a moment I think I've passed out again.

Janey's voice cuts through the night. "That generator's buggered."

Around me there is the sound of scuffling and swearing. A flashlight switches on and then another.

"I'll get it working," says a male voice. It's Alan's.

A circle of light comes toward me, shining directly into my eyes. I let go of the wire to cover my face and lose my balance, falling again to cower on the floor.

Janey lowers the light, her features made blunt by the darkness, her nose a strong curved beak, her fingers talons. She is a bird of prey, ready to attack. "You always were a bit different, Eliza, with your funny eyes and big mouth. You stood out. I liked you. I still do but now you're in my way. You should have gone back to the city when I told you. In a funny way you remind me of Grace Hedland. Smart but not quite smart enough."

The generator starts and the lights come back on. Alan returns and stands beside Janey.

I stare at them, horrified. Alan refuses to look at me.

"Not much gas left," he grunts. "It won't last long."

"There's a full jerry can over here," she says, walking toward the wall. She picks it up and I can hear the glug of sloshing feul. "Jim, so practical in many respects and then useless in others." When she turns around there is a pistol in her hand. "It's your fault he's dead, you know, Eliza. Asking questions, getting him panicked that you knew something. Luke as well, now that I think of it. Tried to blackmail me once he put your information together with old stories he'd heard from Jim."

"Why did Jim say Grace caught a train?"

Janey shook her head. "That was a mistake. He was supposed to throw your father off the scent. Tell him the girl had run away. Mick never bought the train story and for a while there I thought it was all going to fall apart. But here we are, still surviving."

She nods to Alan, who pulls open the cage door.

"Come out slowly," says Janey. "No heroics."

I crawl on my hands and knees, numb with fear.

"Deal with her, Alan," says Janey. "Make her dreams come true. Chuck her down the same mine shaft you put her friend in."

Alan shakes his head. "I took care of Tyrell for you. Not Mick's daughter."

Janey tucks the pistol into the back of her waistband, her face like granite. "Give me your shotgun then."

"No," I croak. "Please, Alan, you can't. For Dad's sake."

At long last he raises his eyes and looks at my face and then blinks, breaks the connection and passes the shotgun to Janey.

"No!" I scream, but she wastes no time in grabbing it. "Weak prick," she mutters, raising the gun. Whimpering, I put out my hands and shut my eyes.

There's an earsplitting bang and then another.

I slowly open one eye to see Alan Sharp lying on the floor. Panic floods my system and I scramble to him. There's a hole in his chest, blood gushing out. Instinctively, I put my hands over it to stem the flow. His eyes roll back in his head and his breath is a wet whistling red and then stops.

"You've killed him!" I yell at Janey.

"And now it's your turn, you smartass nosy lawyer. You betrayed this town and everyone in it."

Janey moves beside me, diminished somehow, much paler but maybe that's because all I can see is blood. The smell of death switches all my senses to fight mode. My odds have just improved dramatically. She's smaller and older. I need to get the shotgun off her first.

"How did Paul fit into this?"

A knife blade of a smile flickers across her face. "Paul loved to worm people's secrets out of them. Jim was putty in his hands, bragging to him about how much money we all made with the birds all those years ago. Paul said why not start it up again to get the town back on track, after a healthy cut for him. It wasn't a bad idea. You lawyers don't come cheap. Still, there'd be enough to get a settlement for everyone and finance the campaign to run for mayor. Set everything up nicely for the town and me. And then that pathetic excuse Tyrell had to go and wreck everything."

Her face contorts in a moment of fury, a split second loss of focus and I spring, grabbing her hands, trying to wrench the gun away. I kick at her legs, she overbalances and we fall backward, the shotgun between us.

Bang.

There's a horse kick to the chest but I don't let go. Janey's grip lessens and I yank the gun away from her and throw it across the floor. Pushing down on her with all my weight, I look for something to hit her with, to knock her out like they did to me. Every contact leaves a trace, so I grab a fistful of her hair and pull hard. If police forensics ever analyze this place, I want to give them something to find. She screams with fury and pushes me away with one hand, twisting the other behind her back.

She comes up with her pistol just as the generator gives up again, plunging the shed into darkness.

Throwing myself to one side, I actually see the flash from the muzzle, feel the shot rushing past my head. In an instant I'm running, seeing nothing, hands outstretched. I'm trying to find the door but I smack straight into metal. It's the shelving. I've come the wrong way. I swallow my cry of pain and grasp the shelf tightly, using it as a guide, trying to make as little noise as possible.

I trip, then fall and kick something over. There's the smash of glass.

Another shot in my direction.

Cowering, I start to crawl. Something sharp cuts my leg.

"I'm going to find the flashlight," calls Janey, "and then I'm going to kill you."

I stand up and run away from the direction of her voice, going deeper into the shed. First hide, then think. Everywhere is dark but I can't count on it staying like that.

Standing still, I hear her moving. I could creep up behind and throttle her or find something to smack her skull in but I can't do it. I just want to find somewhere safe.

She swears as there's a loud clang. It sounds like the jerry can. Janey laughs. "Now that's an idea," she calls, and I hear liquid pouring out, and then more.

"You know, for years I fantasized about burning The Castle down for the insurance. That bushfire was the answer to my prayers. Finally, I could get rid of it. And that's what I'll do here. Burn it all down and you with it."

I hear the match lighting.

"I like the irony of Eliza Carmody being caught up in a fire in the bush," she says, and with that she ignites the gas. There's a whoosh as a line of flames leaps up. Janey is a black form behind it. The fire dies down for a moment and I stand there, thinking I should run toward it and try to stamp it out but Janey could be waiting there with a gun. In that moment of hesitation the fire has already found the hay bales. There's probably a myriad of flammable substances in here. For all I know this place could become a fireball in an instant.

The light from the flickering flames are enough to work out where I am. I move toward the back, trying to find an exit. Running frantically, my hands outstretched, my fingers catch on a handle. I grab at it desperately but it's locked. Slamming my hands on it, I feel around for a bolt but find nothing. I'm locked in and now the flames are too intense to run through.

I pull my jumper over my nose and mouth. The fire blazes so hot that it evaporates my tears. All is smoky now, an acrid haze. The world blurs black with edges of red and gold. Staggering back to the farthest corner next to the back door, I curl up on the floor trying to breathe the air from outside.

I know what's coming next.

Already metal is beginning to warm and parts of the shed are starting to glow. The roar of the fire drowns out everything else because it is alive now, more alive than I am, growing in strength as I pitifully shrink. It won't be too much longer now; breathing has become almost impossible. I pray the smoke gets me before the fire does, that I'll be unconscious as all around me blisters and burns.

Falling.

Exploding.

The world is red.

My eyes start to shut.

Through closing eyelids I glimpse a dark shape coming toward me.

It must be my father.

He holds out his hand.

We're here at the end together.

32

Voices rush toward me as I struggle to pry my eyes open. Faces close to mine start talking. Words like "sedation" and "ventilator" float in the air. I try to turn my head but it's impossible. There are flashing lights, people asking if I can hear them, excruciating pain cutting through before I fall back into darkness again.

The next time I wake there are two policemen beside my bed. I only know one of them. Gavin bends over me.

"You're at Southern Cross Hospital."

I try to nod but my head won't move.

"I need to ask you some questions," says the policeman who is not Gavin. He is older with a serious expression. His questions are answered in a voice I don't recognize, but the burning in my throat tells me it is mine. I watch Gavin's face when I talk about Janey and Grace. He stands up abruptly and disappears from my field of vision and doesn't come back until the other cop thanks me and leaves.

"A stranger," I whisper to Gavin.

"There's been enough family involvement in this mess already," he says.

"How long?" My breath is heavy with smoke.

"You've been out for three days," he says. "They had to intubate you. Janey's under arrest for Jim's murder. With your evidence we can charge her with Alan's."

"And Grace?" I say.

He nods and then, "Eliza." He moves to hold my hand but hesitates because it is covered in bandages. "Mick died."

It takes a long time for my mouth to work. "Alone?" I rasp.

Gavin shakes his head. "Tess and I were both there."

The tears come, but they are all Gavin's. I've dried up inside. Ash runs through my veins.

"I'm not involved in the investigation," says Gavin, "but I'll look in every mine shaft in the state to find Grace if I have to."

My eyes close all by themselves.

Tony Bayless stands by the window, lost in his own thoughts. According to Gavin it was Tony that ran into the shed to save me. I owe him my life. I watch him for a while. He has bandages on his right hand but otherwise looks unchanged, until he turns around and I see his face.

"Awake at last." He sits down next to the bed. Gavin told me he had been admitted to the hospital with burns and smoke inhalation but only had to stay a couple of days.

"I've visited a few times," he says, "but you've always been asleep. How are you?"

The natural response is to say fine but I am far from it. Peel back my skin and it feels all you would see is black.

"I'm alive," I say. "Thanks to you."

His mouth twists. "I brought you something." He lifts it up to show me. It's a copy of the picture Aaron Hedland has kept in his wallet for twenty years. The three of us on the beach. The one Janey Bayless took of us the same night she killed Grace.

"Did you put that in the Hedland's mailbox?" I ask.

He nods. "I felt guilty."

"Did you know?"

"I thought she ran away," he says. "I've been trying to convince myself I'd have done something if I knew what had happened."

He wants me to say of course he would have but I can't. It's hard to do the right thing when your parent has killed someone.

"I should have asked more questions," he says. "If not about Grace, about all the other stuff. Seen what was right in front of me. But I ignored it. I'm not brave like you."

"You ran into a burning building and pulled me out," I say, but already my eyelids are flickering.

"You're tired," he says. "I just wanted to say goodbye."

"Back to Kinsale?"

Tony shakes his head. "Not after this. Maybe never again."

He bends over and kisses me on the cheek and then walks out of the room.

Slowly, I begin to put myself together. As my medication levels drop, the world comes back into increasing focus. The swelling starts to disappear. Some of the dressings come off, but not all of them. The red rawness underneath will harden into scars that I will have for life.

My lungs and arterial blood gases are checked. The medics worry about infection or pneumonia and talk of electrolytes and sugar levels. A psych team comes in and does an assessment. It's bad but under the circumstances "perfectly normal," according to the kind doctor.

Every medical person who comes into my room tells me I'm lucky, all except one. Tristan pops by every day on Amy's orders. I've come to appreciate his complete lack of bedside manner and how he never gives me an ounce of sympathy.

I slip into the routine of the hospital. The awful meals that arrive at regular intervals, the changing of the ward staff, the organized chaos of day shift, the fleeting ghosts of night shift, the little acts of kindness and dedication from the nurses. In this ordered world I spend time thinking, methodically making connections where there hadn't been any, trying to put all the pieces together and work out what will happen next.

People visit. Work sends flowers. When Amy visits she brings her baby and the green hat to cheer me up and it works. Tess was right when she said it was hard to predict what helps.

Two weeks later it is my last day in hospital and I'm sitting on my bed with my bag packed beside me. Tristan pokes his head around the door.

"Haven't you gone yet?" he says.

"Waiting to be discharged."

"Amy's been trying to call you. Ring her back so she stops texting me. I've got a job to do you know."

"Will do," I say.

"Hopefully we'll never need to see each other again," he says. "But if you have to come back, try and make it a bit more run of the mill, like a burst appendix or your tonsils."

After he leaves, I unzip my handbag with stiff bandaged hands and slowly unlock my phone. There are a million messages from Amy, peppered with exclamation marks. Various media reports are attached and I scroll through them, enjoying the headlines, but my phone rings before I can read them all.

"How did you do it?" asks Amy.

"What do you mean?" I say. "I've been stuck in the hospital."

"You don't fool me," she says. "Your confidential expert report is all over the news."

I feel like smiling for the first time in ages.

"Apparently, Colcart's in-house counsel got impatient when I was on leave and sent out the latest round of court documents to all parties himself and accidentally attached the old expert report instead of his rubbish new one."

"You're kidding."

"My firm realized his mistake, of course, claimed privilege and got them returned, but perhaps one of the other parties made a copy and then picked the perfect moment to leak it."

"To Stella Gibson? That's quite a coincidence," says Amy.

"Kinsale's answer to Lois Lane? She's the natural pick."

I hear Amy laughing on the other end of the phone. "You've done the right thing, Eliza. I'm proud of you."

"I have no idea what you are talking about."

"Yeah, right. What do you think will happen to the case now?"

"Colcart will have to settle. They've got no choice now everyone's seen their own expert report."

I can almost hear Amy grinning through the phone. Eventually she says, "So when are you leaving?"

"Gavin should be here any moment," I tell her.

"Take it easy," she says.

"Give Sophie a kiss from me," I reply, and hang up.

A young doctor comes by and ticks all the boxes, which means I can go. "Is someone picking you up?" she asks.

"He must be waiting outside," I say.

"I'll organize a wheelchair."

I am wheeled through the hospital with my bag on my lap and the hat on my head so I don't accidentally squash it. The Mustang is in the two-minute parking bay but instead of Gavin, Tess gets out.

"You?" I say.

"Gavin got caught up with work."

Tess has been a regular presence by my hospital bed, but this is the first time we've been alone together. She takes my bags, giving the hat a sideways glance, but says nothing. I sit down slowly. The dressing on my back pulls at my skin and I carefully straighten myself in the seat.

"So you drive the Mustang now?" I say.

She nods. "Didn't want the battery to get flat on you. Where do you want to go?" she asks.

I don't want to go back to my apartment. It was never really home, just some kind of placeholder that became permanent without me even realizing.

"Kinsale."

Tess looks surprised but then nods.

She takes it easy but even so the drive is difficult. We stop regularly to give me a break, so I can gingerly move around and take my painkillers. I try to drowse. On the outskirts of Kinsale, Tess's phone rings and I manage to answer it for her. Gavin says to pull over because he needs to tell us something. His voice crackles in and out but the message is clear. They've found bones on the property next to Alan Sharp's.

An entirely different pain starts to radiate out from my chest.

Grief.

"Dr. Adler will be on site in the morning," he says. "We'll know for sure tomorrow."

It's got priority now.

"Have you told Grace's family?" I try to say, but I can't because it's too hard to breathe. Somehow Gavin guesses and answers yes.

We sit there for a long time. I think Tess is waiting for me to say something but I can't. This isn't Grace, it's just her bones. No one can bring Grace back. Amy was right. The truth of what happened has freed my sister but all it has done to Grace's family is replace a benign lie with a horrible truth. Is that better?

We drive on in silence because we're still not used to talking to each other, or perhaps there are some subjects so big that words are not enough.

Tess pulls up in front of the house.

"Here we are," she says.

I unclip my seatbelt.

"I never got a chance to say . . ." Tess begins, "and you nearly died . . . you don't know what it's like not having that as a burden anymore." She starts to cry.

"It's OK," I say.

"But you're not."

"I will be again. Both of us are going to be OK."

I wish I could say more to her, tell her I can see a glimmer of things being better between us, that one day our relationship will be fixed, but I'm too tired right now.

It's like I've got to the finish line and there is nothing left.

33

We had Dad's funeral. The town turned out for it like they always do. Gavin spoke on behalf of the family. Tess and I sat next to each other in the front row. Scores of police lined the streets as the hearse went past. The female detective from the Luke Tyrell case tried to shake my bandaged hand and spoke comforting words to Tess. The wake was at the footy club because The Royal has been closed. Rumors are it will be sold but no one knows for sure. Dave came along to the drinks. He brought his daughter and made her apologize. I told her not to worry, in my new husky voice. Being a teenager in Kinsale isn't easy. Aaron Hedland sat at the back of the church during the service. That was kind of him, I thought. Aaron didn't try to talk to me or come along afterward. His mother is unwell again. The funeral for Grace was family only, which upset Amy, but I don't blame them.

Tess and Gavin expected me to leave Kinsale once it was done but I'm not ready. I want to choose when I leave this time. My lungs feel like an ashtray but the bandages come off and I am getting stronger, walking further along the beach every day. Breathing in air can still feel like swallowing stones, but occasionally I try to run a few steps, to punish myself physically so there's a normal explanation for my wheezing.

I don't talk as much.

One cold morning, Amy, with Sophie strapped to her, marsupial-like, walks along Main Beach with me.

"Are you still getting flashbacks?" she asks.

"Less often."

"What's it been? Five weeks?"

"About that."

"If they keep coming, tell me," she says. "We can help you."

"Are you making sure that I'm not falling apart?"

"Yes," she said. "That's what doctors do. Friends, too."

"I thought I saw Dad the other day. Sitting next to me when I was driving the Mustang. Is that normal?"

"Nothing much about grief is normal but it is common. Did he say anything?"

"That I need to hurry up and order the window seals."

Amy smiles as she reaches into the pocket of her jeans and checks her phone. A quick glance and then she puts it away. "I've seen Grace," she says. "Never saw her all those years I thought she was alive, but now we know she's dead, I see her."

"Where?"

"Sometimes in the distance, like she's walking up ahead and any moment now she'll turn back to wait for me."

"Is she happy?" I ask. "Does she look OK?"

Amy takes a while before answering. "She's home. I think that's the best we can hope for."

It is.

Amy checks her phone a couple more times.

"Everything good?" I ask, when she pulls it out yet again.

"This one will wake up soon and want feeding," she says. "You going to stay here a bit?"

"Yeah."

I watch her trudge up the beach and then walk down to the wet sand to listen to the thrum of the ocean. I don't yell at the sea anymore, my throat is too sore but I've cried a few times. Not today, though. At the water's edge I breathe in the salt, exhale the smoke and remember Dad and Grace. I watch the deep swell moving parallel to the beach, the way the waves break a translucent green and the yellow-tinged froth and bubbles close to shore. Seagulls hang-glide on air currents above the water, unperturbed by the world around them. I envy them. Amy keeps telling me to take one day at a time so I only think ahead as far as this afternoon. I'll visit Mary and see if she wants to go for a drive with me.

Clambering up the wooden stairs to the parking lot, brushing my feet clean, I see a man bent over, peering into the Mustang.

"Can I help you?" I ask his back.

"I think I left something of mine behind, a while ago." He straightens up and points to the green hat sitting on the front seat.

It is Donal.

His grin falters. "Jesus, Eliza. What did they do to you?" He puts out his arms but then stops. "Can I?" he asks, and I wrap my arms around him instead. It hurts but it's good pain. He lifts a hand and tenderly cups my face.

"How did you know?" I ask.

"Tony," he says. "He told me."

"Everything?"

Donal nods. "Paul, Janey, the whole mad lot. And the bits he didn't know, Amy and your sister filled me in."

"Tess?" I say.

He laughs. "You know, she isn't as bad as you made out," he says, and then he becomes serious. "I had to see you."

I reach out and slip my scarred hand into his.

His fingers clasp mine.

Here it begins.

ACKNOWLEDGMENTS

This book about a policeman's daughter started from a conversation with Melissa Owen, who is one. Liz McQueen was also incredibly helpful as was Kelly Wan and Retired Victorian Police Assistant Commissioner Sandra Nicholson, who spoke to me about their own service. Melissa Lowe and John Gallagher patiently answered continuous medical questions and changed the course of the novel for the better. Thanks to Leanne Hunter-Knight for fortuitously buying an old Mustang and Colleen Miller who thought if I was going to mention wine, it should be her Merlot (delicious!). Sophie Osborn and Paul Wenk advised on legal matters. My brother-in-law, Jonathan McAleese, gave me a firefighter's view of fires big and small and my mother-in-law, Glenys Harris, cast her eagle eye over every draft. My discussion with Dr. Soren Blau was so fascinating that I had to include a forensic anthropologist as a character. All mistakes and twisted truths, deliberate or otherwise, are down to me.

I owe much to my writing pals. Ruth Cooper for being a constant virtual companion during the process, Carolyn Tetaz who I still pretend lives around the corner, Anna George for all our book and writing discussions, and Tom Bromley for your expertise.

ACKNOWLEDGMENTS

Thanks to my agent, Clare Forster, and the team at Curtis Brown, and also Catherine Drayton at Inkwell Management. To all at Simon & Schuster Australia, especially my editor, Roberta Ivers, who made this a better book, Dan Ruffino, Fiona Henderson, Vanessa Lanaway and all in sales and marketing, for their expertise, hard work and constant support. Not forgetting Anna O'Grady who does all this plus gives the best book recommendations. In the United States, working with Bowen Dunnan and Claiborne Hancock at Pegasus Books has been wonderful.

And thanks lastly to Kerry Ruiz for the support and wise words and to Richard, Aidan, Genevieve and Evangeline with all my love (again and always).